"I was rais~~ed~~ ~~to take care~~ of myself, Sloan," Brianne said. **"I can put a bullet in the center of an ace of spades at a hundred paces."**

"But can you put a bullet in a man's heart?"

"If I have to."

"I don't believe you," he said.

Swiftly she moved to where her gear was piled and grabbed her rifle. Pointing it straight at his heart, she asked, "Do you want me to prove it?"

He smiled. "You wouldn't even get that rifle cocked, redhead."

She believed him. She tossed the rifle down. "Get out, Sloan."

"When I'm good and ready."

Brianne exploded. "I don't understand you!"

He didn't understand himself either. And he didn't understand her. She was standing within arm's reach of him, her hair streaming in wild glory down her back, her skin giving off a sweetly seducing fragrance. Only a thin sash held her robe closed. He reached for her.

She didn't come to him easily. She pushed against him, fighting with all her might. But his strength was the greater, and so was his need. . . .

And watch for the concluding trilogy
to the series coming in fall 1988

THE DELANEYS, THE UNTAMED YEARS

Copper Fire

Fayrene Preston

BANTAM BOOKS

TORONTO • NEW YORK • LONDON • SYDNEY • AUCKLAND

COPPER FIRE
A Bantam Book / May 1988

ISBN 0-553-21897-2

Published simultaneously in the United States and Canada

Bantam Books are published by Bantam Books, a division of
Bantam Doubleday Dell Publishing Group, Inc. Its trademark,
consisting of the words "Bantam Books" and the portrayal of a
rooster, is Registered in U.S. Patent and Trademark Office and in
other countries. Marca Registrada. Bantam Books, 666 Fifth
Avenue, New York, New York 10103.

PRINTED IN THE UNITED STATES OF AMERICA

O   0 9 8 7 6 5 4 3 2

Copper Fire

Prologue

West Texas
1858

Heat radiated off the hard-baked ground, penetrating Sloan's skin like the needles of a cactus. The mesquite tree just a few feet above his head provided meager shade, yet he was immensely grateful for even that scant protection.

Sloan glanced down at his brother, David, cradled in his arms. David's fair skin had been burnt an ugly red. And his leg—Sloan could hardly look at his brother's upper thigh—was mottled and swollen to three times its normal size.

David had to be in terrible pain, but at fourteen years old, three years younger than Sloan, he was proving to be quite a man, uttering not a sound.

The muscles in Sloan's arms were cramping from the hours of holding David, but he didn't dare move. David needed all the rest he could get. And he couldn't let himself think about what a desperate situation they were in; that was a weakening thought and he needed to find the strength to get them both home.

He gazed out over the desolate landscape of West Texas. The vastness of it intensified his feelings of loneliness. Oh, God, he was so alone! If only he knew where they were! He had tried to keep them walking due east, but he was very much afraid they had been traveling in circles for the last two days.

Again Sloan glanced at his brother, sleeping in his arms, so frail, so near death. Ominously, a buzzard had begun to circle overhead. Sloan held David closer, wishing he knew more, wishing he weren't just a green farmboy from East Texas.

David stirred in Sloan's arms, moaning. Tenderly, Sloan tried to soothe him, cupping the burnt flesh of his cheek with his hand.

Had it been just this morning that they had come upon the rocks shaped like a turtle? David had let out a shout of joy. "The water can't be far now!"

A stone that had penetrated the sole of his boot had held Sloan up at the base of the rise, but David hadn't been able to wait. He disappeared over the rise. As Sloan sat down to take off his boot, he heard him yell, "It's here. The water hole is here, but it's dry! That son of a bitch led us to a dry water hole! Wait a minute, I'm going to try to dig down and see if I can find water." Sloan was putting his boot back on just as he heard "Jesus Christ!" and then a cry of pain and terror.

Sloan jumped to his feet and raced over the rise in time to see his brother, writhing on the ground, holding his leg, and the biggest, longest rattler he had ever seen slither off into a large outcropping of rocks.

Sloan had never known such fear. With no knife, he had nothing sharp with which to cut into his brother's leg so that he could suck out the venom. His helplessness had turned to a desperate anger. He had ripped open David's jeans at the seam and tied his belt tight above the wound. His prayer was that it would slow the deadly effects of the snake's venom long enough for him to get help for David.

Damn Wes McCord's black soul to hell!

"Sloan." His name trembled from his brother's lips.

"I'm here."

"Are . . . we going to make it?"

"Of course we are. Just hang on. Tonight, when it's cooler, we'll move out. Tomorrow, for sure, we'll find a town and water, and it'll be clear and clean."

"My leg. There's no way I can put any weight on it. I can't make it."

"Yes, you can. I'm going to carry you."

David's eyes fluttered open for a brief moment, revealing an awful pain. "You go . . . leave me."

"You know Dad would skin me alive if I left you out here," he said, a forced smile punctuating his words. "Don't you dare give up, David! Promise me. We're going to get out of this. Don't give up."

Again David looked at his brother. "I won't. Honest."

David lapsed into silence, his breathing labored, and Sloan slipped into a light sleep.

"Momma . . . I'm sorry . . . I didn't mean to break your teapot."

His brother's words jolted him from sleep. "David, wake up."

"I won't do it again . . . Momma . . . it was so pretty . . . I'm sorry . . . Momma."

When he realized that David was delirious, Sloan was filled with despair. David was raving about the

time when he had been six years old and he had
accidentally broken his mother's favorite teapot. It
was something she had treasured, one of the few
things she had managed to bring with her from her
home in the East.

What Sloan wouldn't give to see her just one more
time. Their beautiful mother, whom David favored so
strongly with his blond hair and blue eyes, had died
shortly after the accident with the teapot. Of course
there was no connection between her death and the
broken teapot, but deep down David hadn't been able
to separate the two events.

A tear spilled from Sloan's eye and trickled down
his dirt-stained face. Sweet, shy David, whose love for
everyone was always reflected in his ready smile.
Sloan couldn't lose him too. "David, oh, David."

Eventually, Sloan again dozed off. When next he
woke, the sun was low in the sky. The horizon
shimmered with feverish waves, distorting the landscape into weird shapes. Sloan squinted against the
intense brightness. Was that . . . could that possibly
be . . . a rider? His heartbeat accelerated. He shook
his brother.

"David, wake up, there's someone coming! David!"
David's eyes remained closed. Sloan's hand went to
his face and found it strangely cool. His fingers
searched for David's pulse point on the neck and
found it frighteningly still. No!

"Noooo!" The scream tore from Sloan's throat,
pushing into the searing air, filling it with his grief.
His scream continued, layering the land with his rage
and his sorrow.

1

New York City
1873

Having neither the inclination nor the patience to use the glass within easy reach, Sloan Lassiter swigged from the bottle of whiskey. He plunked it back down on the cluttered surface of his mahogany desk that sat in the center of the opulently furnished room. The flame in the lamp next to him flickered weakly as if tired of trying to illuminate the large room all by itself. Heavy dark blue velvet curtains drawn across the tall windows in the large room were a shroud against the night. Deep shadows crept up to the dim pool of light in which he sat.

From habit, not interest, Sloan kept slogging through the papers in front of him. And drinking. Lately, drinking had become not so much a habit as a necessity to get him through the long days and endless nights that had come to make up his life.

At age thirty-two, he was head of an empire that had a shipping line as its base. No one would argue that he was a phenomenal success. Sloan's lips twisted into an unkind smile. As a matter of fact, very few would argue with him about anything at all. A score of men would crawl to him if he commanded;

even more women would go on their knees for him if he asked them to.

All that he knew, he had taught himself. All that he was, he had purposely become. He was a self-made man who had learned to be as deadly with a gun as he was with his investments.

So where was the happiness? Where was the peace?

Damn! He needed to shake himself out of this depressed state and get back to his business. He drew another set of papers to him, careful to keep his attention from the document he had received today that lay at the edge of the desk. He didn't need to read again the missive from the Pinkerton Agency. The words were burned into his mind, because finally, after fifteen years, Sloan knew where Wesley McCord was.

Once more he reached for the bottle and swilled down more whiskey. He wanted to get good and drunk. Right now he didn't want to remember the hell that he and David had gone through. He didn't want to remember how he hated Wesley McCord, hated him with a sickness that had eaten into him for far too long. He wanted only the blessed blackness, the cool, airy nothingness that too much drink would bring him.

Cally Lassiter smiled as she saw the sliver of light coming from Sloan's study. The door was ajar and she carefully opened it wider so she could slip into the shadowed room.

Leaning back against the wall, she watched her half brother. She wished she could believe that he had stayed up to see she arrived home safely, but she knew he didn't care about her. As far as she knew, there was no one Sloan cared about. And because he didn't, her mind constantly whirled with schemes that would make him sit up and take notice of her.

Cally toyed with a long black curl of her hair as she observed Sloan. Even still and quiet, his head bent over a pile of papers, he excited her as no other man could. His indifference to her had made her quake with wild excitement a thousand times during this last year or two. She knew what a virile man he was and how sought after he was by a host of women in New York.

Besides the power he wielded, there was his extraordinary appearance. He was a broad-shouldered, slim-hipped man who moved with astonishing grace. Deep creases vertically dissected his bronzed cheeks. But those lines had not been carved there by frequent smiles. Rather, they'd come from time, weather, and, most intriguing of all to Cally, hard living.

With his brown hair and deep moods, he was a dark man both in color and in character. Except for his eyes. They were gold—not yellow, not amber, but pure gold. And then there was his body. To Cally's mind, his body was a perfect mixture of smooth planes and muscled bulges. She loved the way he wore clothes, as if he didn't know he had them on. But other people noticed. They noticed everything he did, especially the women.

Cally had long envied the women with whom he slept. Her favorite pastime was to imagine what it would be like for him to make love to her. Because by nature he was such a ruthless man and physically he was so strong, he was bound to treat his women rough. At least she hoped so.

She wanted him. And she had made it obvious to him any number of times that he could have her by a mere lift of a finger. But always he had rebuffed her.

Her gaze went to the nearly empty whiskey bottle, and she smiled. Drunk. He would have no defense against her.

As she watched, his head nodded, then dropped to the desktop. As usual, he was oblivious to her. Tonight it was because of alcohol, but normally he deliberately ignored her, just as he ignored her mother and his father. She could understand his indifference to her parents. Emily, her long-suffering mother, was very close to being a saint and, as a result, she was a complete bore. Her father was a bitter old man who hadn't left his room since the three of them had moved in with Sloan. His health had been broken when his darling David hadn't come back all those years ago.

But why should Sloan ignore her?

At eighteen, with her black hair and violet eyes, she was beautiful. Everyone said so.

Her hand slipped from her curl to the top of her breast, and she began to lightly caress herself through the ruby-colored silk of her dress. The dress had been designed to be worn off the shoulder, but her mother had insisted on the stupidly decorous neckline.

She moved her shoulders with an unconscious gesture of dismissal. It didn't matter. The modest design of her dresses hadn't proved a hindrance. Most men found the way her breasts mounded lusciously against the bodices of her dresses enticement enough. And most men found no difficulty in getting under her skirts. Only Sloan resisted.

With her gaze still firmly fixed on Sloan, Cally dipped a finger beneath the neckline of her dress to stroke a tight nipple. Take tonight, for instance. Her breasts were still throbbing from the caresses Peter had given them in the Alexanders' garden during their party. She hadn't allowed him to go any further, of course. It wasn't time yet. He couldn't be allowed to think that she was easy. Besides, she didn't really want him.

She wanted Sloan, and tonight she was going to have him.

Pushing away from the wall, she crossed the room. She laid her hands on his shoulders and shook him. "Sloan, Sloan, wake up!"

"What?" He raised his head, trying to see who was shaking him, but he couldn't seem to get his eyes to focus.

"Sloan, I can't get my dress unhooked. Would you do it for me please?"

He heard a sweet, breathy voice very close to his ear. He smelled the scent of a heavy perfume, musky and erotic. "What?"

"My dress, Sloan. Unhook it."

The room seemed darker than it had been just a short while before, and it was spinning strangely. Blindly, his hands went out, but instead of encountering hooks, they found skin—smooth, satiny, female skin.

"Ohhh, that feels so good."

She was right, he thought. There was nothing like the bare flesh of a woman to divert a man's mind from his troubles. He let his hands rub across her back and felt her shiver. Then the feminine weight of the woman lowered onto his lap, and he noticed that his head was hurting.

"Here, rub here."

He could hear a gentle voice crooning, giving him directions, and he did its bidding. His hands slid around the warm, soft form until they closed on two large breasts. It was habit for him to shape his hands around the generous globes, because sex had become an unthinking act to him.

He heard the rustle of silk and realized the woman had slipped her dress down to her waist.

"Sloan, oh, Lord, Sloan . . . I want to feel your lips on every part of me just as I've always imagined."

The woman twisted in his arms and he took what was offered. Maybe this was all he needed, his brain dimly told him. A woman. He received a long, hardened nipple into his mouth and began to suck. When he heard the woman's passionate cry, he increased the suction, pulling hard. This was what he needed! Oh, God, yes! His hands worked under her skirt and petticoats and began to loosen her drawers.

He needed this, but . . . why did he feel something was wrong? God, but he wished his head didn't hurt so badly and his mind wasn't so foggy.

"Oh, Sloan, I knew it would be like this. I've wanted you for so long. You won't be sorry. I'll be so good to you. Here, take this breast. Suck. Oh, please, harder!"

He did as she asked, accepting the other breast

gladly, knowing that even if he might be hurting her, she wanted it . . . and he—what did he want? He wanted this woman, of course! Why was he even questioning? He had found that while women couldn't solve a man's problems, for a little while, at least, they could make his problems go away. Lately though, even women hadn't been able to ease his pain. Maybe this one would be different. She certainly seemed willing enough, knowing just how to move against him, knowing just how to touch him.

His teeth nipped her flesh and his fingers dug into the pliant mound. Moans of pleasure filled his ears. Who was this woman? He should know, although he couldn't recall the last woman he had had. It must have been just a few days ago. Who was it? Was it Marie? No, no, it must have been Judith. He tried to remember, but all his feelings seemed to be concentrated in the swollen bulge between his legs. He would take this one savagely, he decided, and maybe, just maybe, in doing so he could find some relief.

Her drawers were undone, and his hand delved between her thighs to the waiting warmth and wetness. Through his daze he could feel her urgency as she twisted, trying to undo his pants and at the same time achieve better contact with his fingers.

But . . . what was it? Something was wrong. He didn't want this woman!

Something crashed to the floor. "What was that?"

"Probably just one of your silly documents," she murmured, her fingers closing about his swollen manhood. "Dear God, Sloan, you're so *big*! I knew you would be. You're going to split me in two, and I'm going to love it. Don't hold back."

Document . . . the document . . . Pinkerton . . . reporting on Wesley McCord—the bastard who had killed his brother! Roughly, he shoved the woman from his lap. Damn McCord! Damn the man straight to hell! For fifteen years he had haunted his dreams. Sloan pressed his hands to the sides of his head and pushed, trying to expel the image of a smiling Wes. Wes always smiled.

"What was that noise, Sloan? Has Cally come in yet?"

Sloan's eyes opened and slowly the image of his stepmother, Emily, swam into focus. "Cally?" He rubbed his forehead. "I don't know."

"Cally Lassiter, what are you doing?"

A disgruntled Cally got up from the floor, thrust her arms into the sleeves of her dress, and pulled up the bodice. "Nothing you need to be concerned about, Mother. Why don't you go back to bed?"

Emily's hand went to the high neck of her dressing gown as in shock she took in the state of undress of both her daughter and Sloan. "Cally! Oh, dear God in heaven, how could you?"

Sloan's mind suddenly became crystal clear as his eyes met the defiant violet eyes of his half sister. "Cally?"

"We were just having a little fun, weren't we, Sloan? Nothing for anyone to get upset about."

Emily stood stiff and straight. "I think you'd better go to bed now, young lady."

Cally defiantly stuck her hands on her hips, her

breasts, swollen from Sloan's attention to them, threatening to spill over the top of her still unhooked dress. "I'll go only if Sloan asks me, and I don't think he wants me to go." She went to him and possessively laid her hand on his shoulder. "Do you, Sloan?"

He pushed her hand away. "Get out of my sight."

"Sloan!"

"Cally, for your own safety, get out . . . of . . . my . . . sight."

Her face took on the expression of a spoiled little girl, obliterating any beauty she might have possessed minutes before. "Oh, all right. For now." She flounced out of the room, slamming the door behind her.

Emily's thin face had gone even paler than normal, appearing milky in the dimness. "I'm sorry, Sloan. I don't know what to say."

He rubbed his eyes with thumb and forefinger, willing away the pain in his head. "Why should you say anything at all? There's nothing for you to be sorry about."

Momentarily her hand fluttered to her throat, then dropped away. "She's my daughter."

"And she's my half sister, God help me."

"Sloan—"

He pushed away from his desk and stood up. "Not now, Emily. I'm not feeling very well. I think it's time for me to retire."

"What are you going to do?"

His eyes held a glint of surprise, but his voice carried a great weariness. "I just told you. I'm going to bed."

"That's not what I mean. What are you going to do about Cally?"

"Cally? Why not a damn thing. Good night, Emily."

A week to the day later, at ten o'clock in the evening, there was a knock on the door of Sloan's study.

Timidly, Emily entered at his bidding and made her way across the room to stand in front of his desk.

Sloan tossed down the paper he was reading and leaned back in his chair. "What can I do for you, Emily? Would you care to sit down?"

He hadn't spoken to her since the night she had found Cally with him. He rarely took meals with the family, so it wasn't as though he had been avoiding her. He supposed he liked Emily as much as he liked anyone. His father had married her when Sloan was eleven, and she had made them a good home. He better than anyone knew what a hard life she had had with his father.

"I'd prefer to stand, if you don't mind."

He inclined his head. "All right."

Emily cleared her throat. She found it so difficult to talk to Sloan. He was such a formidable man, and there was such a darkness in him, although she could remember that it hadn't always been so. "Sloan"— nervously, her hand went to the cameo pinned at the center of her high-necked blouse—"there's something I must say to you."

"If this is about Cally, there's no need. I'm leaving tomorrow, you know."

"I—I know, and that's why I must tell you—"

"I'd really rather you didn't, Emily. After tomorrow I'll be out of your lives."

"That's just it. You shouldn't leave." Emily wrung her hands together. If only she didn't get so tongue-tied around Sloan. If only years ago she hadn't buried this secret so deep inside her that now it was almost impossible to get out. "Sloan . . . Cally is not your sister." She dared a look at him, but he remained impassive, silent, and she had no choice but to continue. "Years ago there was a man. Oh, it didn't last long, but . . ." Her voice threatened to break.

"You don't have to tell me this."

"Yes, I do," she cried with more passion than Sloan had thought her capable. "What Cally has become is all my fault. You see, there was never any doubt in my mind whose child Cally was. Your father didn't . . . well—"

"Emily, please don't put yourself through this."

"I must. All these years I've had such guilt, and that guilt caused me to push Cally away most of her life. She knew something was wrong. She must have. A child senses when they're not loved. Your father and her father are not the same. It—it's only these last few months, since she's been home from school, that I've understood what I've done to her. It's time I faced up to my responsibilities for my daughter. I'm praying it's not too late. But even if it is, you don't have to worry about her. She won't bother you again."

"I'm not worried."

"Oh, Sloan, I simply can't stand the thought that Cally is driving you away. This is *your* home. After the war, when you moved to New York, you didn't have to offer us a place here, but you did. And now if anyone should leave, it should be us."

Sloan stood up and walked around to the front of the desk. Leaning back against it, he crossed his arms over his chest. "Don't distress yourself, Emily. Cally isn't driving me away. I'm leaving because I'm too tired to stay here anymore."

"Tired? But of what?"

"Of life, I think. I've known for a long time that my life is empty and dissipated. Now I know that I'm empty."

"You frighten me when you talk like this. I remember when you were a boy. You were so open to life, so giving."

"I've come a long way from that young boy who left East Texas with his head full of dreams."

"Maybe not so far. Even now you haven't judged me."

"How can I judge you, Emily, when my own sins weigh me down? Look at what almost happened with Cally! My God, what a disgrace—she's my sister in all but blood."

"Maybe you can find that small boy again, the one who laughed so easily."

He snorted in self-disgust. "I don't think there's any of him left. He died a long time ago with his brother."

2

Chango, Colorado Territory

Sloan awoke instantly, not immediately sure why. All senses alert, he reached for his gun and scanned his hotel room. No one was there. But something had awakened him, of that much he was sure. Cocking his head, he listened. There was quiet. Then laughter, light and carefree, with an unusual musical quality.

His gaze slew toward the open window, the direction from which the laughter had come. His second-story room faced the back of the hotel, and the mean-looking gray sky beyond the window told him that although the rain had stopped, it wasn't over.

The laughter came again.

With fluid grace Sloan rolled off the bed and strode to the window. Below him, in the middle of a muddy corral, a young woman with red hair sat bareback astride a stocking-legged sorrel. She was dressed in a white blouse that was open at the neck and tucked into a dark brown riding skirt that skimmed over her boots and ended above her ankles. Her hair was woven into a thick red plait that fell to just above her waist, a bright blue ribbon tied the shining ends.

17

Glittering at her throat was a thin chain of gold. Something tiny and delicate dangled from it.

"Darn it, Patrick, wipe that grin off your face. I'm going to do it!"

"Sure you will," the man she had called Patrick drawled in a tone even Sloan could tell was deliberately provoking. His long body was perched with careless elegance on the top rail of the corral.

"That was a dare, wasn't it?" the young woman asked.

Gun still firmly grasped in his hand, Sloan leaned against the side of the window to watch.

"I know better than to dare you, Brianne."

Brianne. Sloan idly turned the name over in his mind. Interesting name. Irish, he decided. It explained her red hair that even on a cloudy day seemed to blaze like the sun at high noon.

"That *was* a dare," she said, glaring at Patrick. Reaching forward, she patted the horse's neck. "We'll show him, won't we, Dancer?" The horse swished his tail in response, apparently ready to agree with anything his young mistress asked of him. She threw one leg over his back until she was sitting with both legs on one side of the patient horse. Still with a narrowed gaze on the grinning Patrick, she raised a foot, skinned off a boot, and hurled it with unerring accuracy. Just in time, Patrick ducked. A sock followed the path the boot had taken, then the other boot and sock. Patrick managed to dodge all three.

Brianne threw her leg over so that she was sitting astride and urged the horse into a lope over the rain-soaked ground of the corral. "Come on, Dancer." To Patrick she yelled, "You've got my money. Every time I make a circle, you match a dollar of my money with a dollar of your money. If I can make it around fifty times, I get all the money."

"And if you don't, of course, I'll be fifty dollars richer."

"I wouldn't go spending that money just yet, Patrick."

With her hands on the horse's back, she leaned forward, paused to get her weight under her and get into the motion of the horse, then carefully stood.

Sloan could see that Brianne was obviously an excellent rider, and he guessed that, normally, circling a small area, standing on the back of a horse, wouldn't have given her that much of a problem. But because of the rain, the ground was thick and sloshy with mud and it was the mud that challenged her. Her horse was already having trouble with his footing, making a smooth gait impossible.

With her hands out for balance, her face a study in concentration, her bare feet on the horse's rump, Brianne circled the corral.

Patrick was sitting between two upright fence posts. On one he had placed his hat, bottom up, on the other he had a stack of dollar bills, and in his hand, he held more money.

As Brianne passed Patrick, she called out, "That's one dollar!" Without commenting, Patrick took a dollar out of his hand and one from the stack on the fence post and deposited both in his hat.

When she passed again, he did the same thing, and she called out gaily, "This is going to be for a new hat!"

Patrick remained silent, and from Sloan's vantage point it appeared that Patrick's refusal to respond to her feat was irritating Brianne. His theory proved correct when on the next go-around, she began elaborating on what kind of hat she wanted.

"With feathers!"

"And a blue satin ribbon to tie under my chin!"

Dutifully Patrick kept depositing money in his hat.

"And a bird on top!"

"Good idea, Brianne," Patrick said mildly. "I could use some target practice."

Up in the hotel window, Sloan found himself smiling at their game. Their energy and humor were entertaining. In particular, Brianne kept his attention. With time to study her, he had discovered she was an extraordinarily beautiful young woman. She seemed so *alive*, he thought, then wondered why he had chosen that word.

The damp air was pressing her clothes against her, delineating high, full breasts, a narrow waist, and slim hips. Showing beneath her riding skirt were a pair of bare feet with shapely ankles. Then suddenly a single ray of sun pierced through the sullen clouds and turned her hair to fiery copper.

A stirring in his loins took him unawares. He had always been careful to target a more mature type of woman for his attentions. In his experience they were much safer and infinitely more stimulating. But he supposed the brief heat he was feeling for the beautiful young woman below was understandable. After all, it had been several weeks since he had had a woman.

"That's fifteen, isn't it?" Brianne called to Patrick.

"Nope. That's ten."

"That's fifteen and you know it!"

"You never did learn to count."

"Patrick Delaney, you're a liar!" In her indignation, Brianne lost her concentration and had to wildly windmill her arms in order to regain her balance. When she had reestablished her footing, she shook her fist. "Damn you, Patrick. Damn you!"

"Tut, tut, what kind of language is that out of my baby sister's mouth."

"I'm only five and a half minutes younger than you, as you very well know."

Patrick shrugged and tossed two more dollars into his hat as she passed again.

So they were brother and sister, and twins to boot. Interesting, Sloan thought.

As he watched, Brianne came even with Patrick again and held up a finger indicating another idea. "A new dress!"

As before, on each successive pass she added a detail. With a big smile she called out, "A red one!"

"A man would go color blind seeing a red dress on you, Bri."

"Who cares! It'll be silk!"

"With pearls and lace!"

"Like the fancy ladies in Hell's Bluff wear!"

Patrick waited until she had nearly completed the circle again, then spoke in a drawl that was definitely calculated. "As a matter of fact, my fancy ladies don't wear anything at all."

Brianne's gaze went to him in surprise. She started to say something, but just then the horse lost his footing and as a result Brianne lost her balance. To Sloan it appeared that she must have been trained to fall, because she tried to manage her body so that she would land on her feet. In this instance, however, she failed. Instead of feet-first, she landed bottom-first with a *splat*, causing mud to fly all over her clothes, her face, and her hair.

Up in his room, Sloan waited for the anger he was sure would come. But after only a moment Brianne began to laugh with that clear, light, musical laughter that had first awakened him. Patrick's laughter joined hers, and soon both brother and sister were doubled over with unrestrained mirth.

Looking on, Sloan listened and tried to remember the last time he had heard such uninhibited, joyous laughter. Certainly there was never any laughter heard in the house that served as his home in New York City. The effect of David's death had been to peel away his father's will to live until he had become a bitter shell of a man. It hadn't been enough for him that Sloan had been saved by a passing rider and brought back to him alive. His father's indifference had hurt, but it had been the last thing that had ever hurt him.

And as for the brittle, forced laughter of the women

he kept company with— No, he finally concluded, he couldn't remember the last time he had heard joyful laughter.

He turned away from the window and returned to the bed, where he'd been taking a nap. He placed the gun on the bedside table within easy reach, then lay back and remembered.

If nothing else, the incident with Cally had provoked him to action. It had taken him a week of twenty-hour days to put his affairs in order. During that time he had dictated detailed instructions to cover any eventuality, including his own death.

Then he had set out on horseback, heading west with one destination in mind—Chango, this town in the southeastern corner of the territory of Colorado— and with one objective in mind—revenge on Wes McCord.

He could have made the trip easier on himself by taking the train as far as he could. But he had deliberately chosen to ride the entire distance on the big black horse he called Demon. Over the years he had maintained top form by frequenting Gentleman Jim's boxing emporium. Trips to his estate in New Jersey for extended periods of shooting and hunting had honed his skills with all types of guns and had kept him lithe in the saddle. The journey from New York City to Chango had added a new layer of toughness.

He had arrived in Chango late in the night during a driving spring rainstorm. Riding in from the south, past the church and the schoolhouse, his first impression of Chango had been that it was no different from any of a dozen small western towns he had ridden through.

Most of the businesses were located on one wide main street. Boxlike one- and two-story buildings lined the street, most with false fronts. On the east side of the town, behind the businesses, cabins and small houses had been erected. And behind them were rows of tents.

On the west side of the street, square in the middle of town, stood a big three-story building with a sign that read DUKE HOTEL. With a wraparound porch and many cupolas to distinguish it, the building had obviously once been a fine mansion.

On the opposite side of the street from the hotel and about six buildings down stood the office of McCord Enterprises. Because of the Duke Hotel's strategic location, Sloan decided to make it his headquarters. Satisfied that Wes's office would be easy to keep an eye on, he had walked Demon to the livery stable. Then he had rented the room and fallen into a deep sleep. But he had been up and out early, walking the streets of Chango, familiarizing himself with its layout and its people. And most important, asking questions. He had found out only that Wes was out of town, but was expected back any day.

The people of Chango were strangely silent on the subject of Wes McCord, but Sloan had learned patience in the last fifteen years, and he could afford to wait. He was utterly confident that his quest for revenge would soon be satisfied, and then his hell would finally be at an end.

For he had come to Chango to die . . . and to take Wes McCord with him.

Mrs. Potter, the proprietress of the Duke Hotel, had made a point of telling Brianne that the bedroom she would be using for the two nights she and Patrick would be staying in Chango was a special room reserved for ladies. Brianne could understand why. The apple green of the velvet covering the medallion-back sofa matched the apple green of the batiste elaborately swagging the bed. Across the room was a rosewood dressing bureau with mirror, and a matching armoire was set against the wall facing the windows. The fireplace was inset with blue and green cloisonné. A Japanese folding screen stood in a corner.

The room was at the back of the hotel, and as she gazed out the lace-curtained window, she could see the corral where she'd taken that ignominious fall. She smiled. But what fun it had been! And well worth it despite all the mud.

The arguments she had had to engage in to get her grandmother and grandfather to agree to this trip to St. Louis by horseback, alone with Patrick, had also been worth it. She had argued that she would miss too much if even a small part of the trip was by ill-smelling coaches or fast-moving trains. On her first trip east, she had told them, she couldn't abide being enclosed in any form of conveyance. Patrick had backed her up, being of the same mind as she, eager for the opportunity to spend precious time with his twin.

Over the years she and Patrick had shared much, running with carefree abandon over Killara and tumbling into trouble that kept their uncles and grandparents busy. They had been constant companions.

But three years ago, when Patrick had returned from the ancient lost city of Kantalan, he had been wealthy beyond anyone's dream. He had also become guardian of Rising Star's newborn baby, Kevin and their explosive, stormy cousin, Silver Dove, now a schoolgirl of eighteen.

Brianne gave a brief chuckle at the thought of Silver. One of the reasons they were making this trip was that Silver had gotten herself into yet another scrap at school, and as her guardian, Patrick would have to get her out of it.

Patrick had responsibilities that few twenty-one-year-old young men had. He was away from Killara more and more, leaving Brianne feeling restless and bereft. And when he came home, there were still ventures to oversee, new projects to start, old projects to finish.

Brianne was proud of the man Patrick had become, but she resented the preoccupations that seemed to prompt fewer and fewer smiles from her brother. With the idea of helping him, she had started keeping the accounts of his investments and made sure that his correspondence stayed up-to-date. Both were duties that Patrick detested.

Humming a little tune under her breath, Brianne swiveled away from the window and walked to the dresser. This trip had proved to be everything she had hoped, giving the two of them the opportunity to be together, just like old times.

And in a few more weeks they would be in St. Louis. She hoped Elspeth and Dom would be back from the Indian Mounds by the time she and Patrick arrived. It would be so good to see them again, and Silver, too.

She gazed into the mirror and grimaced. Dark brown mud smudged her face, arms, and legs, and splotched her hair. She had tried to sponge off what she could here in the room, as the muddy water in the washbowl attested, but a bath would have to take care of the rest.

Shrugging, she turned to survey the three dresses she had laid out on the bed, trying to decide which she would wear to dinner. At Killara, she had an armoire overflowing with fine dresses, and Malvina had wanted her to pack at least half of them so she would look her best in St. Louis. Patrick had saved his sister, telling their grandmother that they were limited by what their pack horse could carry. Brianne had been happy, caring only that she have her sketchbook and charcoals with her. And she had been able to appease Malvina by convincing her that she would buy twice as many clothes in St. Louis and have them shipped home.

So with the decision of what to wear to dinner tonight facing her, she eyed each dress in turn. There was the sensible brown dress that Malvina had insisted she bring because, her grandmother had said, it would travel well. Then there was the dress of emerald green that Patrick always said made her eyes look like the necklace of Kantalan emeralds he had given her and that she wore to dinner practically every night at home. And last there was the pale rose silk with the square neck that was one of Brianne's favorites. The color appealed to her artist's eye, a color not quite pink, not quite peach, but a combination of both. She would wear the rose, she decided.

Sloan turned the knob of the bath and pushed the door open. As he did, he felt the latch on the other side give, then heard it pop off. With one foot already in the room, surprise made him hesitate for, rising out of the white-porcelain claw-footed tub, water sheeting off her naked body, was the young woman he had watched fall into the mud just an hour before—Brianne.

Confronted by a strange man in her bath, Brianne grabbed for a towel and covered herself as best she could.

"Excuse me, but the bath is occupied," she said, and returned his stare. She saw a tall, powerfully built man with an arrestingly rugged face, wearing dark brown pants and a white shirt, opened so that his throat was exposed. In a holster slung low on his hips rested a gun. Not unusual. Actually, the only threat Brianne felt was that of embarrassment. She waited for him to apologize and leave, but at last realized that time was passing and he was neither saying anything nor making any move to go.

"Excuse me," she repeated. "You'll have to come back another time."

The brief seconds it had taken her to grab the towel had given Sloan a tantalizing glimpse of her lovely young body. His hesitation ended. He entered the room and kicked the door closed behind him, then leaned back against it as a sweet fragrance rose and enveloped him. The scent did not assail, but gently seduced.

Sloan felt a flicker of admiration. Caught in what to most women would be a shocking and defenseless position, she was reacting with cool self-assurance. In fact, her imperious, regal attitude reminded Sloan of a princess rather than the high-spirited hoyden he had seen down in the corral.

"I really did have my heart set on a bath before dinner," he told her. "Perhaps I could join you." A fire burned brightly in the fireplace, heating as it cast a soft golden light. A kerosene lamp supplemented the light from the fire, but to Sloan's mind, all the radiance in the room seemed to have gently surrounded the young woman standing in the tub.

How dare he? Brianne wondered. The man's outrageous suggestion had been made in a voice that was deep and arrogant . . . and somehow stirring. "I paid for a *private* bath!" she said, maintaining her dignity. "It should be obvious to anyone with the lowest intelligence that some mistake has been made."

"Ah, but sometimes, if a person is very, very clever, a mistake can be turned to advantage."

"I assure you that won't be the case." Brianne didn't

have to look down to know that the towel she held up covered her only from her breasts to her upper thighs. Extending her arm, she reached for another towel that was folded and laying on a small marble-topped table. But the towel she was holding slipped, and she was forced to give up her quest.

Sloan pushed away from the door and slowly walked toward her, not stopping until he stood in front of her, so close that, if he chose, he could rip the towel from her grasp.

Her fingers tightened on it, and she jerked her head toward the door. "Get out!"

Plainly, he mused, the lady was used to having her wishes obeyed. Well, so was he.

With slowness deliberately designed to disconcert, he surveyed her. Her hair was wet and lay against her skin in dark red rivulets. Her eyes were a deep green and were glittering at him with a fiery indignation. Her skin was pale peach. On her shoulders and above her towel-covered breasts water beaded as if reluctant to abandon such luscious perches. He ignored an urge to lean down and lick off the drops of water one by one. Continuing his survey, he discovered that her breasts were so ample that they swelled enticingly out either side of the towel.

A series of white scars marked her left forearm. Rather than marring her perfection, the scars made her all the more interesting.

Yes, he decided, the situation definitely offered a myriad of possibilities, and all of them were amusing. It had been a long time since anything had amused him. He reached out and ran a finger down her forearm, and she jerked away.

"I'm only going to tell you one more time," she said, her tone icy. "Get out!"

"What will you do if I don't?" he asked, definitely curious. Fully expecting female hysterics, he was surprised to see her smile at him sweetly.

"Well," she said thoughtfully, "first I'd geld you."

Her answer was totally unexpected, but his only reaction was a slight lift of one dark brow. "And second?"

"Do you really think I'd need to do anything else?"

Almost imperceptibly, the corners of his mouth lifted. "Good point."

He reached for the folded towel from the table, held it out to her, and her fingers closed around it. He had every intention of releasing the towel and he started to, but then some impulse stopped him.

This close to her, he could see things he hadn't noticed before. Her skin had the texture of fine porcelain. Her mouth was closed, but still her lips were soft and moist. And her eyes were as clear and green as a magnificent emerald. Yes, there was the icy aloofness in them that he would have expected, but there was also an angry fire. He wondered if he could turn the anger into passion and in the next moment decided to find out.

Slowly, he lowered his head until his lips were barely touching hers. She tried to pull away, but he released the towel and grasped her shoulders. Holding her to him, he found that her damp skin still

retained the heat from the bath and felt as smooth as
satin.

Increasing the pressure of his mouth on hers, he
parted her lips just enough so that his tongue could
enter the warmth of her mouth. There he discovered a
luxuriant array of tastes, textures, sensations.

Her backside was completely bare, and Sloan was
not a man to deny himself a pleasure so readily
available. Holding this delectable woman in his arms,
feeling himself grow hard, was reminding him how
long it had been since he'd had a woman. He slid his
hands down the silky skin of her spine to cup her
buttocks. They were warm and firm and fit into his
hands with a fullness and an ease that was a provoca-
tion in itself.

Brianne clung to him, knowing that she shouldn't,
knowing that it was wickedly improper. Stunned,
both by his actions and her own reaction, she uttered
a sound that held both anger and confusion. She had
kissed before—light, pleasurable, fun kisses—but no
man had ever kissed her with such a primitive
hunger, using his tongue in a sensuous rhythm of
tasting and licking. And certainly no man had ever
dared be so audacious in touching her.

Brianne had not felt jeopardy until he had laid his
hands on her. But now new feelings, new emotions,
new fire stirred within her, and she knew that *there*
was the jeopardy.

Yet still she clung.

Abruptly Sloan broke away. His breathing came
unevenly, his face showed taut sensuality—but his
eyes were completely unreadable. For a long moment

he gazed down at her. Then, after inclining his head, he murmured, "It's been a pleasure, Brianne." He turned his back on her, walked to the door, opened it, and left.

Brianne stared at the closed door, then slowly sank back into the tub of hot water. She felt odd, as if when the dark stranger had left, he had taken all the breath in her body with him.

Throughout her life Brianne had been surrounded by men—the men of her family, the men who worked on Killara, and the men who had tried since she'd entered her teens to make her fall in love with them. No man had ever overwhelmed her . . . until now.

Recalling how she had responded to the stranger's kisses, she was absolutely appalled.

She rested the back of her neck against the rim of the tub, wild impressions of the man whirling through her mind. Strangely, he reminded her of the land where she had been born. She felt as if his strength was as vast as her beloved Arizona. He and the land shared the same hardness, the same untamed ferocity.

His overall coloring had been as dark brown as the desert at dusk. But then there had been his eyes. Because they were gold, they should have been beautiful. Yet she had seen no beauty as she had looked into them. They were hard and opaque, like a nugget of gold that was incapable of showing emotion.

She had never seen a man who exuded such blatant menace, but she couldn't decide if the menace sprang from a danger that long ago had been bred into his bones or from a sensuality so potent it could have been deadly. Perhaps it was both.

In the heated water of her bath she shivered, then decided it would be prudent not to mention the strangely exciting encounter to her brother. Patrick, for all his teasing, was strongly protective of her. And if he knew a strange man had kissed her and touched her, much less had seen her nude, there was no telling what he would do. Patrick was very, very good with a gun, but she remembered that the stranger had also worn a gun, tied down to his muscular thigh. He was either hunting trouble or expecting it.

Then a thought struck her. The man had called her Brianne! He knew who she was.

But who was he?

3

The hotel dining room was nearly empty as Patrick and Brianne finished their dinner. A brass-based chandelier with etched crystal globes hung from the center of the ceiling, and candles burned in a two branch silver candelabrum on their damask-covered table. An ominous boom of thunder cracked in the sky above the hotel.

"Last night's storm is back with a vengeance," Patrick commented before sipping his coffee.

Although Brianne nodded her agreement, she was paying little attention to Patrick's conversation. The scene in the bathroom flashed in her brain like the bolts of lightning flashing their brilliance through the sheer white curtains at the windows. The heavier crimson drapes had not yet been drawn.

"It was great luck finding this nice hotel when we needed it," Patrick said. "Mr. Potter was telling me that it was once the home of an English duke. For a while this duke fancied he might become a cattle rancher, and he built this enormous house and imported all the furnishings from Europe."

"Really?" Brianne asked, Patrick's words at last

snagging her attention. She glanced around, taking in the embossed wallpaper in a pale pearl-gray, and the oversized walnut sideboard heavily carved with a variety of fruit. "What happened to the duke?"

"He found that the American West wasn't as romantic as he had thought, and he eventually got tired and went home. But in the meantime he had started this town, and when he and his people left, he sold everything for a song. The Potters have been here for about ten years now."

Another boom of thunder followed by a crashing sound made Brianne turn, just in time to see the young boy who worked for the Potters—George, she had heard him called—struggling with a heavy tray piled high with dishes. A shattered plate lay at his feet. Brianne smiled reassuringly at him, but the smile didn't have the effect she intended. The rest of the dinnerware toppled from the tray and crashed loudly on the floor. Mrs. Potter appeared and, delivering a tirade, marched the boy out of the room.

Watching his sister, Patrick grinned. "The men in St. Louis don't have a clue as to what's in store for them. I'm going to enjoy watching the chaos you cause."

Brianne made a face at her brother. "I have no idea what you're talking about."

"Your effect on boys and men, my love. We've all lost count of the number of men who have come to Killara to court you, only to leave with a broken heart."

"Can I help it if I've never found a man to equal the men of our family?" Brianne asked, then remembered the man who had come into the room as she had bathed and surveyed her with cold golden eyes that had somehow held a strange heat. And his lips had been hard, yet they had conveyed such sweet passion.

"Thank you," Patrick said.

"With the exception of you, of course," she hastened to add. Attempting to put aside all thoughts of the golden-eyed man, she studied her brother and felt a surge of love.

His broad shoulders were covered by a soft suede Spanish-cut jacket, and his long legs were clothed in close-fitting dark trousers. She thought he looked wonderfully handsome with his warm, intelligent brown eyes, his strong jaw, and his beautifully shaped mouth. And the slight depression in the center of his chin seemed to drive women wild, or so her girl-friends had told her.

"The family's real concerned about you, Bri. Every-one is afraid you're going to be an old maid. Granda's already turned down a score of marriage proposals on your behalf. You're just too picky."

She fixed him with a stern look. "Nonsense. Granda would be perfectly happy if I never married at all, and you know it."

"Maybe," Patrick conceded. "You're his princess and he's bound to be jealous of any man who wins your heart. But there's Malvina to consider." He shook his head sadly. "Night and day she says rosaries for you."

Brianne scooped up a spoonful of mashed potatoes and aimed it at Patrick. "One more word and you'll be wearing this all over that ugly face of yours."

"Okay, okay, we'll drop the subject of your lamentable spinsterhood . . . for now."

"You're too kind," Brianne muttered.

A comfortable silence fell between them, lasting for a few minutes, until Patrick said, "If this weather lets up by morning, we should be able to leave."

"Then Stormy's been shod?"

Patrick nodded. "The blacksmith did it this afternoon."

"Marvelous. I can hardly wait until we get to St. Louis."

"Eager to make new conquests, are you?"

She sighed as if she bore a heavy burden. "You know very well that I'm eager to see Uncle Dom and Elspeth. It's been too long."

"I agree." He lifted his napkin to his mouth to wipe away a few bread crumbs. "By the way, I met the most unusual young woman today."

"Really?" she asked, immediately interested. Although Patrick rarely spoke to her about his amorous adventures, she picked up things here and there, and knew that he had a lot of women scattered about the country. But with a highly refined sense of self-protection, he made sure none of them were of the kind suitable to bring home to Killara and the family. "Who is she?"

"Her name's Anna Nilsen. She's Swedish and the daughter of the man who owns the local emporium."

"Tell me about her."

"There's nothing much to tell. I was just intrigued, that's all. She's beautiful, but cool. Keeps herself to herself." Knowing the reason behind his sister's questions, a grin creased his face. "I talked with her while I was buying you a gift, but plainly she's not a lady who's the least bit flirtatious. I was really hurt, I don't mind telling you."

Brianne had a quick mind. "Gift?" she asked, even as he got out the last word of his sentence.

With a smile, he bent to his side and brought up a hat box. "Here you are."

Brianne snatched the hat box out of his hands and, without ado, lifted the lid and pushed aside tissue paper. Then she gasped. Nestled snugly in the box was a hat unlike any she had ever seen. At first glance it seemed to match the description of the hat she had made up as she had circled the corral. The hat was in the latest fashion, complete with feathers and a blue satin ribbon to tie under her chin. It even had a bird perched perkily on its crown. But, unfortunately, with the bird, the milliner had gone very much awry.

Gingerly she lifted the hat out of the box so she could get a better look. She supposed the bird was intended to be a dove. It certainly had the beautiful pale coloring of that tame breed, yet somewhere along the line the bird had acquired the predatory eyes of a hawk and the crooked, ugly beak of a vulture. To make matters worse, its wings were spread and its feathers raised, so it looked as if any moment it might swoop down off the hat and attack some helpless creature. All in all, it was the most hideous hat she had ever seen in her life.

She raised her gaze to her brother and saw that his brow was crinkled anxiously. "I hope you like it," he said. "The minute I laid eyes on it, I knew it was just the thing to enhance your many and considerable charms."

Brianne's smile was absolutely adoring. "Patrick, you are completely full of horse manure."

Patrick broke into a deep, hearty laugh. "If Malvina were here, she would wash your mouth out with soap."

"It wouldn't be the first time," she said, and began laughing herself.

Sloan, on his way out of the hotel, stopped in the doorway of the dining room, recognizing instantly the laughter he was hearing as Brianne's. He had felt a stirring of desire when he had first seen her gaily circling the corral this afternoon. Later as she had stood naked and indignant in her bath, desire had returned stronger, although, he did have to admit he hadn't expected the flames that had flared when he had kissed her. Now, hearing the light musical tones of her laughter, desire once again visited him.

Sloan knew that nothing would come of the attraction he felt for her. Even if the lady might be willing, he wasn't. He would allow nothing to draw his attention away from his main purpose for being here. This attraction he felt for Brianne was pleasant but temporary. Still the evening did stretch endlessly ahead of him, and so he let himself be drawn to the laughter.

Brianne glanced up just as a lightning bolt slashed to earth, illuminating the room and the dark, hard features of the man who was suddenly standing beside their table. *Him!*

His tall, lean frame was fitted perfectly in a fashionably cut black suit with a white shirt and perfectly folded cravat. A heavy gold watch and chain gleamed against the fine material of his vest. And he still wore his gun tied to his thigh.

He inclined his head politely. "I'm Sloan Lassiter from New York City," he said. "I'm staying at this hotel for a few days. I hope you'll forgive the intrusion, but I was just passing the dining room when I happened to see you and decided to come in and introduce myself.

Patrick stood and extended his hand. "How do you do. I'm Patrick Delaney, and this is my sister, Brianne."

Sloan shook Patrick's hand, then reached for Brianne's, raised it, and pressed warm lips to her cool skin. "I'm charmed to meet you, although, I must tell you, I feel I already know you."

A dull flush seeped slowly up Brianne's neck, reaching her face and tinging the flawless texture of her skin a darker-than-usual shade of peach. This Sloan Lassiter was definitely a bastard, she decided. She had been raised among hard-living cowboys and vaqueros. They might not have the courtly manners and expensive clothes this man did, but they'd never be so ungentlemanly as to refer to an episode such as this afternoon's. Especially not in front of her brother!

Well, she was perfectly capable of handling a bastard like this one. She jerked her hand out of Sloan's grip, resolving not to give him the satisfaction of seeing her cower. "Really?" she murmured coolly and with a touch of challenge. "I have no idea why you would think that."

He smiled, taking in the high square-necked rose silk dress, with its bustle visible as she sat slightly forward in the straight-back chair. She had twisted her red hair into a very proper chignon at the back of her head. All in all, she looked quite elegant. Yet it seemed that no matter what state he saw her in, clothed or unclothed, he still wanted her. "I feel I know you because I was privileged to witness your remarkable exhibition of riding skill earlier today."

Despite her bluff, a feeling of relief washed over Brianne as she realized he wasn't going to bring up the scene in the bathroom. "In the corral? I didn't see you."

"I watched from the window of my room. It faces the corral."

Patrick laughed. "Someone else saw you fall, Brianne. That's good. Now I have a witness." He turned to Sloan. "Would you like to join us?"

Before Brianne could think of an objection, he pulled out a chair and sat down. "Thank you. A few minutes of company would be nice. Traveling can be very lonely."

Brianne leveled a cool green-eyed look at him. "I can't imagine you getting lonely, Mr. Lassiter. You seem to have a unique way of meeting people." His answer to her was a slow smile, and her reply was an unwanted thrill of heat shooting through her body. Damn the man!

"Fetching bonnet, Miss Delaney."

Mortified as she suddenly remembered the outrageous hat she had plopped on her head in fun, she jerked it off and glared at him.

With a puzzled glance at his sister, Patrick intervened. "My sister and I are on our way to St. Louis to visit relatives. My horse threw a shoe just outside town yesterday afternoon, so we decided to rest up here while we got him shod."

Sloan's calculating gaze went from Patrick to Brianne and back to Patrick. "So you'll be leaving in the morning?"

Patrick nodded. "Weather permitting. You said you were from New York City? What line of business are you in?"

"I'm involved in various enterprises"—he shrugged as if his business were of no account—"shipping, banking, investments."

"That's interesting, and where are you headed?"

Sloan leaned back in his chair. "I think I may stay here for a while. Rest, as you say."

Brianne studied Sloan while he and her brother talked. Even if she hadn't just learned that he was a financier, she still wouldn't have thought him to be the type of man who traveled with no destination and no purpose in mind. His golden eyes periodically scanned back and forth between the two doorways of the dining room, almost as if he were afraid of a knife in the back. Yet every time his gaze came back to her, it held something close to intent, giving her the uncanny impression that *she* was the subject very much on his mind.

Young George brought a pitcher of water to the table and began to refill their glasses. Sloan's attention narrowed on him to such an intense degree that Brianne's curiosity was aroused. She turned to study

George, trying to figure out what had drawn Sloan's interest, but all she could see was a boy of about thirteen or fourteen, too thin, and with fair hair and blue eyes.

Just then George tripped, and water was sent flying all over Sloan.

Mrs. Potter was beside them in an instant, wringing her hands and hovering over Sloan. "Oh, I'm so sorry! That boy is so clumsy! I never should have hired him!"

"It's all right, Mrs. Potter," Sloan said calmly, brushing the moisture from his fine suit coat.

"No, it's not!" She swung around and raised her hand, intending to deliver George a stinging slap.

Brianne's "Don't do that!" died in her throat, because as swift as a striking snake and with as much menace, Sloan was on his feet and had Mrs. Potter's hand imprisoned in his.

"That's not at all necessary," he said, his voice quiet and gentle, his eyes cold and deadly.

"You don't understand," Mrs. Potter sputtered. "He gives me nothing but trouble. He's turning out just like that drunken bum of a father of his. He—"

"Mrs. Potter, I will take it very badly if you do anything to punish this boy . . . or even think of dismissing him. This incident was entirely my fault."

"Your—"

"*My* fault." He released her wrist, dipped his hand into his pocket, brought out a handful of coins, and gave them to the obviously distraught boy. "Don't worry. No one's going to hurt you. Understand?"

Stunned, George nodded.

"Oh . . . well, all right then." Mrs. Potter ran an eye over Sloan's suit and decided the damage wasn't too bad. And Mr. Lassiter was an obviously affluent guest, after all. It was always wise to keep the paying customers happy. "Come along, George."

As if nothing had happened, Sloan turned to Patrick. "I was on my way over to Lucky's Saloon for a game or two of poker. Would you care to join me?"

"Sounds good. Brianne, would you mind?"

It took Brianne a moment to recover. Sloan's defense of George had definitely surprised her. Not that he hadn't been right in protecting the boy. It was just that she hadn't expected him to do such a nice thing.

"No, of course I don't mind." She wrinkled her nose affectionately at her brother. "You do seem to be on a winning streak. Win lots of money and don't worry about me. I'll see you in the morning."

Sloan nodded to Patrick. "Then I'll see you later." To Brianne he said, "It's been most . . . memorable."

Brianne turned her head to watch Sloan as he strolled out of the room. So now she knew his name, she thought, and even where he was from. But she still didn't know why he had kissed her. Or why she had responded.

She held her breath until she was sure he had left the dining room, then let it out in a long, loud sigh.

Patrick gazed at her thoughtfully. "What's up, Bri?"

"I don't like Sloan Lassiter," she said flatly and picked up her glass of water to take a deep drink.

Patrick was well aware of the sparks that had jumped between her and Sloan Lassiter. In fact, he

hadn't seen that many sparks since the time he had
set off firecrackers in Hell's Bluff. It was too bad they
had to leave tomorrow. It might be interesting to see
what developed between his beautiful sister and the
smooth but guarded man named Lassiter.

"Why don't you like him?"

"I'm not sure. He looks like a sophisticated city
man, but there's something wrong there." She
shrugged and absently rubbed her left forearm. "I
don't know. His eyes remind me of something or
someone, but I can't quite put my finger on it."

"Maybe it's that bounty hunter who came looking
for Dom that time. Remember?"

Brianne nodded slowly. "I remember. He was carried off Killara in a pine box."

"That's right. And it's my opinion that Mr. Lassiter
is looking for someone, just like that bounty hunter
was."

The golden flames dancing at the tips of the candles
seemed to beckon with their hypnotic motion. She
tore her gaze away. "All I can say is that there's
something terribly unnerving about Sloan Lassiter.
He appears very polite on the surface, but I'm willing
to bet that if you scratched that civilized skin of his,
you'd find something very dark and dangerous."

"Dark and dangerous, huh?" Patrick studied his
sister for a moment. "Then my advice to you, Brianne,
is don't scratch him."

It had been a while since there had been any
thunder, but Sloan could hear the rain as it beat
against the wood roof of the Lucky Saloon. He

narrowed his eyes against the smoke, noticing that the place was almost full. All night he had been keeping track of the comings and goings in the saloon, studying faces, wondering if any of them worked for Wes.

Lucky, the beefy, gray-haired owner, was wiping down the long bar that dominated one side of the room. The back of Lucky's head was reflected in the tall, wide mirror hanging behind the bar. From where Sloan was sitting, he could see that the mirror boasted several bullet holes with accompanying cracks. An upright piano with a tasseled bench was against another wall, but no one was playing it. In the back, a stairway led to a balcony, off of which several rooms opened.

With effort Sloan returned his gaze to his cards, wishing he were more interested in the game. He had hoped a night playing poker might prove diverting, but so far his mind was refusing to stay focused on any one thing. Abruptly he folded the cards shut and tossed them onto the table. "I'm out."

On his left, Maxwell Tucker, a corpulent man with broken blood vessels covering his pudgy face, did the same, grumbling, "Bad night, bad cards. I don't like it. All this rain. Nothin's going right."

The man on Tucker's left was Isaiah Carter. An older man, he was a rancher who had come into town on business and been forced to stay the night because of the heavy rain. He glanced at Tucker. "No sense blamin' it on the night, son. Cards fall where they like. It's how we play them that matters."

The man sitting on Sloan's right, Lee Reardon,

merely smiled and, after a look at Patrick Delaney, tossed more money into the pot. Sloan had sized up Reardon as a professional gambler from first glance. A handsome man, Reardon had long slender fingers that Sloan knew would be capable of expertly stacking a deck or covertly dealing off the bottom. But Sloan had watched him carefully, and tonight, at least, Reardon was playing a fair game.

Across the table Patrick lay down a full house and cheerfully raked the pile of money toward him. "Sorry, gents, but this one's mine."

"Another glass of whiskey!" Tucker hollered over his shoulder and settled down with a glum look on his face.

While Reardon shuffled, Sloan studied Patrick Delaney. He played with cool expertise, yet without any sign of need or greed to win. Katy, one of the saloon girls and a pretty dishwater-blonde, was draping a pale slender arm around his shoulder. Patrick idly stroked her arm as he scanned the new cards Reardon had dealt him.

Sloan's attention switched to Katy. She was wearing a red taffeta dress trimmed with lace. If the dress had been made of silk and the trim had included pearls, it would have fit the description of the dress Brianne had given to her brother as she had ridden around the corral, her arms outstretched, her bare feet balancing on the rump of her horse.

Sloan was having no trouble keeping track of the conversation and the card game, so he let himself envision Brianne in a red silk dress. Her brother had teased her about wearing red, but Sloan decided that a dark, warm shade of it would do wonderful things for her skin and hair.

Katy's dress was deliberately cut low. From the brief glance Sloan had gotten of Brianne's naked body, he knew her breasts would more than fill the bodice of the dress the saloon girl wore. He glanced down at his right hand and wondered if his hand could completely encompass one of her breasts or would his hand be too small. The craving that thought engendered aroused him.

A girl named Janice had attached herself to Sloan for the evening. She had black hair and was wearing a cheap pink satin dress. He felt her long cool fingers slide through his hair. She had one foot resting on the bottom rung of his chair, and she was leaning into him so that her breast was level with the side of his face. If he turned his head, he would be able to fasten his mouth onto the tip of her breast and entertain himself while the cards were being dealt. Even with the two of them surrounded by a room full of people as they were, Sloan was willing to wager that Janice wouldn't object. He had known plenty of Janice's type. Whether they were saloon girls or the highest members of New York City society, they pleasured men for money—the amounts just differed, that was all.

His mind shifted back to Brianne Delaney, traveling under the protection of her brother, on her way to visit relatives. It was too damned bad the situation was so obviously proper.

Annoyed because he couldn't seem to get the red-headed Brianne out of his mind, he decided to avail himself of Janice. He reached his arm around her, pulled her into a more convenient position against him, and closed his mouth over one of her satin-covered nipples. As he strongly sucked, he heard Janice moan. Ah, yes. Janice would be very good tonight. She would know all the right moves, know all the right things to say.

But slowly the heat he had begun to feel as he had thought of Brianne in Katy's dress began to cool. Bloody sweet hell! he thought, and pushed Janice away. Just the sound of Brianne's laughter this afternoon had created more desire than the feel of this willing woman's breast in his mouth.

"Can I bring you a drink?" Janice asked softly.

"No." He glanced at the uncertain expression on her face and added, "I'm not drinking."

"Can't trust a man who doesn't drink," Tucker grumbled.

"On the other hand," Carter said, "it's my opinion that you can't trust one who drinks too much."

Ignoring the comments of both men, Sloan raked his fingers through his dark hair and decided that he knew where to lay the blame for his lack of interest in Janice. *Wes McCord.* Not knowing exactly when Wes would be back in town was frustrating as hell to him. And a woman or a game of cards wasn't going to alleviate that frustration.

His gaze shifted around the bar and stopped at the three men he had seen arrive a few minutes before. One was taller than the other two and slim with a saturnine expression. The other two were of medium height and stocky. All three stood at the bar, their muddy boots resting on the brass railing, their bodies leaning sideways against the bar as they drank and eyed the action.

"Playin', Lassiter?" Patrick Delaney asked, holding up a freshly shuffled deck of cards.

"Deal," he said, not caring what impression he was making. Janice had sidled back to his side and had placed a hand lightly on his shoulder. With barely a thought he reached up to pat it.

Patrick began distributing the cards to each man around the table with a smooth, quick action of his wrist. "You know, I was always taught the way to win at cards was to concentrate on the game." His drawl was laced with humor.

Sloan picked up his cards one by one as they were dealt to him. "You were taught well."

"Hell, I'll say!" Tucker's words came out in a snort. "Once those cards get in your hand, they just sort of seem to turn the right color and get the right number of spots."

As though to counteract the ugly tone in Tucker's voice, Reardon's tone was deliberately cheerful. "So where were you brought up, Delaney? A riverboat on the Mississippi?"

Out of the corner of his eye Sloan noticed that, oddly, the three newcomers at the bar stiffened when they heard the name Delaney. A whispered flurry of what looked like debate followed, and then the tall man snatched up his raingear and strode out of the bar. The two men that remained kept their gazes rigidly trained on Patrick Delaney.

Patrick was idly playing with Katy's fingertips.
"Nope. A ranch in Arizona."

"Doesn't sound like a gamblin' place to me."

A good-natured grin creased Patrick's face. "I can
tell you've never met any members of my family."

"Wouldn't want to if they play like you do,
Delaney!"

Everyone at the table suddenly went very still.

Katy backed slowly away.

Patrick casually dropped his right hand to his hip,
where his gun reposed in its holster. His brown-eyed
gaze rested quite pleasantly on Tucker. "You're not by
any chance saying that I'm cheating, are you?"

Tucker licked his lips and didn't answer, but Isaiah
Carter attempted a jovial laugh. "Of course he's not.
No one is. I've never sat at a fairer table."

"Are you?" Patrick asked again, his eyes never
leaving Tucker's sweating face.

"You know," Lee Reardon said in a conversational
tone he might have used to discuss the rain outside, "I
really don't think Tucker meant anything out of line.
In fact," he continued slowly, "I'm positive he was
referring to your skill and to your family's skill at
cards."

Completely detached, Sloan knew exactly what
each man at the table was thinking and feeling. He
had learned to read men well, and right now Tucker
was wishing he were somewhere else, while at the
same time trying to figure out how he could back
down without losing face. On the other hand, Isaiah
Carter and Lee Reardon were men who had seen too
many killings on the frontier, and they were at-

tempting to defuse the situation. And as for Patrick Delaney, Sloan had never seen a man more capable of taking care of himself. Patrick needed no help from him, and even if he did, Sloan told himself, he had no time to get involved with other people or their problems.

"I'm waiting for your answer, Tucker," Patrick said.

Tucker's gaze went to each man at the table, then he looked away. "I didn't mean anything by it."

Isaiah Carter let out a sigh of relief and swatted Tucker on the back. "What'd'ya say we go up to the bar and get us a drink? It seems a mighty thirsty night to me."

Without a word Tucker pushed his chair back, stood up, and headed for the bar. Carter followed him.

Reardon pushed his hat back on his head and glanced from Patrick to Sloan. "Anyone for another game?"

Sloan shook his head and rose from the table. "Not me. I think I've had it for tonight."

"I don't think so either," Patrick said, and pulled Katy down in his lap. "I think I'll play another game for the rest of the night. Are you interested, darlin'?"

The girl rubbed her bottom against his groin. "Fine by me. Anything special in mind?"

Patrick whispered in her ear and Katy threw back her head, laughing loudly. "That'll be a new experience for me, but I'm willing to give it a go."

Sloan raked the money he had left in front of him off the table and handed it to Janice. "Maybe another night."

She reached her hand behind his neck and pulled his head down for a long, slow kiss. "Anytime," she whispered. "Anytime."

Sloan nodded to Delaney and Reardon. "Have a pleasant rest of the evening, gentlemen."

4

Brianne awoke early in the big, tall, four-poster. For a minute she lay where she was, her eyes fixed on the far wall. Sloan Lassiter had said that his room faced the back of the hotel, overlooking the corral—just as her room did. Patrick had been given the room on her right. That meant the chances were good that Sloan's room was on the left side of hers, just a wall away. Unbidden, her mind conjured a picture of him, prowling his room in that powerful, elegant way he had of moving. Perhaps he hadn't yet gotten dressed. She imagined that his back would be roped with muscles of strength and flexibility. His chest would be wide and blanketed with fine, dark hair. The hair would continue down his abdomen, where it would narrow and descend in a straight line—*Enough*!

She threw back the bedcovers. Today she would be leaving Chango behind, and with it Mr. Sloan Lassiter.

She washed, then dressed in her riding clothes for their journey. After repacking her two portmanteaus, she went next door to Patrick's room. A knock on the door elicited no response. She knocked harder.

"Good morning, Brianne."

At the sound of Sloan Lassiter's voice, her nerves jumped as if he had burnt her flesh with his words. Still, when she turned, she allowed no sign of her agitation to show on her face. "Good morning, Mr. Lassiter."

He gave her a teeth-baring smile. "Sloan, please. After all, I feel I know you so well."

This was the first time they had been alone since their encounter yesterday afternoon, and she was disturbed. She could remember all too well the way she had sensed danger, yet still she had clung to him. "I know this is going to really start your day off badly, Mr. Lassiter, but the fact is you're going to have to find another lady to practice your mocking ways on. And right away too. My brother and I are leaving directly after breakfast."

He chuckled, a rare occurrence for him. But last night Brianne had been stunningly beautiful in the turquoise gown, every inch a desirable woman. This morning she was dressed in her riding clothes. Her hair was plaited, and her hat was dangling by its cord around her neck and down her back. At her throat a gold cross hung on a delicate gold chain. She looked young, fresh, and so obviously untouched, a less experienced man in the ways of a woman might go crazy just thinking about being her first lover. He reached out and grasped the small cross and began to move it back and forth.

The backs of his fingers grazed the hollow of her throat, heating her skin, her blood, her mind. Was it that simple? Brianne wondered. Was it possible that desire could be so easily raised by a mere touch?

She took a step back, and he was forced to release the cross or break the fragile chain.

"Miss Delaney, the town won't seem the same without you," he said, feeling a vague surprise because it was the truth. "Going down to breakfast?"

"Yes." She gave a last look at Patrick's door. "That must be where my brother is."

With a wave of his hand he gestured that she should precede him. "After you."

His politeness grated on Brianne because she had every reason to know that the courtly manners were a sham. She would have known it even if that scene in the bathroom hadn't occurred.

In the dining room there was no sign of Patrick.

"Would you care to join me for breakfast?" Sloan asked. "I'm sure your brother will be along soon."

She turned to him, wondering why in spite of everything, she wished she could take him up on his invitation. "No, thank you. I'm going to go find Patrick."

As he had done the night before, he raised her hand to his mouth. "Then as I might not see you again, let me say how much I've enjoyed our . . . meeting."

The cool of his lips against the back of her hand scorched oddly, and the innuendo of his words infuriated. As he didn't voluntarily release her hand, she removed it as gracefully as she could manage. "Thank you, Mr. Lassiter."

"I really wish you'd call me Sloan," he said softly.

Brianne called upon every deportment lesson Malvina had ever given her to resist the urge to listen to the enticing softness in his voice. "Have a pleasant day, Mr. Lassiter."

The stable was the logical place for Patrick to be, Brianne decided. As she headed in that direction, she noticed that folks had begun to stir up and down the street. The sun was out, but the ground had a long way to go before it dried. Brianne stayed on the boardwalk, and when she crossed the side streets, she was careful to walk on the planks that had been laid over the mud.

Although small, Chango seemed to be a bustling town, businesses and stores lining its main street. Brianne admired the pots of flowers at the doors of several offices and noted how many of the windows sparkled in the morning sun. She felt a touch of regret that she had to leave the town so soon, and she told herself that it was because she wouldn't have the opportunity to do much sketching in Chango rather than because she was having to leave Sloan Lassiter before she could get to know him.

At the wide door of the stable she stopped and peered in. She could see no sign of Patrick, so she walked down the wide aisle that separated the stalls. An old man with long scraggly hair was mucking out one of the stalls, and appeared to be the only other person there. Her horse, Dancer, was there, as was their pack horse, Sam. But Patrick's horse, Stormy, was nowhere to be seen.

She approached the old man. "Pardon me, but have you seen Mr. Delaney this morning?"

Without looking around, the man spoke as he worked. "Hain't seen nobody."

"Are you sure? He's tall, young, with reddish hair." She paused, but the man made no sign that he was even paying attention to her. "He stabled our horses here yesterday afternoon. His horse, a big palomino, had thrown a shoe." Still the man said nothing. "The horse was shod late yesterday, so it should be here, but I can't find it."

The man shifted the angle of his head slightly and spit. "Then it's gone."

Silently giving her brother a piece of her mind, Brianne walked out of the stable and started back up the street. Patrick wouldn't take an early morning ride, not with a hard day ahead of them, and certainly not without telling her. So he had to be up to something. The question was *what*?

Then another thought hit her. Could someone have stolen Patrick's horse? She almost laughed. If someone had, he had made the worst mistake of his life, because Patrick thought the world of Stormy.

She passed the barber shop and the lawyer's office. As she approached Nilsen's Emporium, she noticed a young woman sweeping off the boardwalk in front of the store. Patrick's Anna, she guessed. He had been right. Anna certainly was beautiful with her blonde hair, ivory skin, and clear blue eyes. She was curious about the type of woman who would attract her brother, and it suddenly occurred to her that Patrick might have gone back to visit Anna last night.

"Good morning. I'm Brianne Delaney."

The young woman stopped sweeping and, with a

polite reserve, smiled, showing two perfect dimples. "I'm Anna Nilsen. Can I help you?"

Anna must not have smiled at Patrick, Brianne thought, amused, or he certainly would have mentioned those dimples. "It's just that my brother, Patrick Delaney, was in your store yesterday, and I was wondering—"

A look of concern replaced Anna's smile. "The hat! Oh, I'm awfully sorry! He said it was for his sister. I tried to talk him out of buying it. I told him there had been a mistake and I planned to send it back, but he seemed to think it was just what you'd want."

"Patrick has a peculiar sense of humor," Brianne explained, thinking how pleasant Anna's slightly accented voice was. "He bought it as a joke."

"Oh, then I suppose that's all right."

"Have you by any chance seen my brother this morning?"

"No. I only just came down to open the store." She glanced toward the second-story windows of the store. "My father and I live upstairs."

"I see. Well, thank you anyway. Good-bye."

"Good-bye," Anna said, and resumed her sweeping.

Back at the hotel Brianne got the owner's wife, Mrs. Potter, to open Patrick's door for her. A sweeping glance told her that his belongings were undisturbed—as was his bed.

Mildly irritated, Brianne made her way back down the stairs and out to the front porch of the hotel. Sloan Lassiter was there, lounging in a chair. She had seen him sitting there when she had entered the hotel minutes before and had nodded. Now, though, she realized that he might have the answers she needed.

"You haven't found your brother?" he asked, knowing that she hadn't. From his vantage point on the hotel's porch, Sloan had seen her go into the stables, come back out, then stop and talk to the woman at the emporium.

"No. You were with him last night, weren't you?"

"Part of the night. We played a few hands of poker."

"Did he happen to mention where he was going when the game ended?"

"Not that I can recall." Sloan deliberately refrained from telling her about Katy, the pretty little saloon girl Patrick had had his hands full of last night. Unless he was very much mistaken, Katy had kept Patrick busy for most of the night. Chances were he was still sleeping in one of the rooms above the saloon.

Brianne frowned, puzzled. "He didn't say anything about this morning?"

"Nothing."

Brianne gazed down, noticing absently that she was worriedly tapping the tip of her boot against the wooden planks of the porch. Abruptly, she raised her head. "I'll just have to go over to the saloon and ask around."

"You can't do that."

Sloan's quiet but authoritative statement surprised Brianne for a moment, because *you can't do that* was something she had heard very rarely in her life. Growing up as she had, with the freedom of Killara, she had never been bothered over much with the restraints of being female.

Of course, there had been the day, right before
Brianne was to turn ten, when Malvina had looked
out a window and seen her frolicking with several of
her uncles, cousins, and Patrick in the water hole,
completely naked and unconcerned. Malvina had
jerked her out fast, and ever since had attempted to
mold Brianne into her idea of a young lady.

Brianne had listened and absorbed everything Malvina had said, then had gone out to learn how to do
what she really wanted to do—ride, shoot, track, and
hunt. Luckily, since she had been the first girl child
born in three generations to a large, loving family,
there had always been someone eager to teach her.
Brianne had had uncles, cousins, and a grandfather,
all of whom had seen no reason why she couldn't do
exactly as she wished.

But reasonably, she knew Sloan was right. No
respectable woman ever entered a saloon. But Patrick
was nowhere to be found, and that, to her mind, took
precedence over whatever code of behavior she
should be following.

"I have to go to the saloon," she said calmly.
"Someone over there might know where Patrick is."

Sloan came to his feet slowly and reluctantly. As
much as he didn't want to become involved in
someone else's problems, he couldn't allow Brianne to
go into the saloon. Besides the fact that it just wasn't
done, there was a chance she would find a naked Katy
draped over an equally naked Patrick. Briefly he
wondered what Brianne's reaction would be to such a
scene. Then, remembering the composed way she had
reacted when he had opened the door to see her rising

from the tub, he decided she wouldn't be that shocked.

Brianne Delaney was an interesting lady, and if circumstances were different— But they weren't. And he wouldn't even allow himself to wish that they were.

"I'll go," he said. "Wait here."

Instinctively, Brianne started to protest, but then thought better of it. He was right. It would be better if he went alone. She just hoped he could find something out.

When Sloan entered the door of Lucky's Saloon, he saw Lucky puffing away on a cigar and wiping down the bar. Several men were there, some already drinking the hard stuff, some just drinking coffee. Katy was at a back table, sitting with Janice and eating breakfast.

Janice's bored face brightened when she saw him approaching, and she stood up. "Sloan! I mean, Mr. Lassiter, I'm so glad you came back. I was afraid you'd already left town."

It barely registered with Sloan that her enthusiasm sounded genuine. "I'll be here for a while." He looked at the other woman. "Katy, did you spend the night with Mr. Delaney?"

His question couldn't have embarrassed her, Sloan thought, yet she suddenly appeared flustered.

"I was with him for a few hours," she said cautiously.

"Did you take him upstairs?"

Straightening in her chair, her eyes defied Sloan to

criticize her. "Yes, and I gave him a real good time too."

"Why are you asking Katy these things?" Janice asked, eager to regain his attention.

He ignored her. "Katy, take me to the room where you two were."

For a moment Sloan thought she was going to argue with him, but she finally got up and began leading him up the stairs. Janice's resentful gaze followed them.

"I don't know what all the uproar is about," Katy said. "I did everything Mr. Delaney said. You never saw a man more tuckered out than he was by the time we got finished."

At the top of the stairs she pushed open a door to a small room. Sloan stepped in and looked around. The room was sparsely furnished with a washstand, two chairs, and a bed. The bed was empty, but the sheets, lying in a tangled heap on the tick mattress, testified to the energetic activity of the night before.

Years of having only himself to rely on had honed Sloan's instincts to a fine edge, and now his instincts were telling him that something was wrong here. He could feel it.

Sloan wheeled on Katy. "When did you last see him?"

The saloon girl took a step back. "Mr. Delaney, you mean?" Her tongue snaked out to lick her upper lip. "Well, after we were, you know . . . uh, through, I left him here. He was sleeping."

"And you haven't seen him since?"

Although Katy planted her hands on her hips in a

defiant gesture, she looked about ready to burst into tears. "I told you I haven't! Leave me alone!"

Sloan's hand shot out, knotted in Katy's hair, and pulled her to him. "If I find out that something's happened to Delaney and you know anything, *anything at all*, you will personally answer to me. Do you understand?"

He was pulling her hair with just enough force to give an indication of the pain he could cause her if he chose, and Katy nodded.

He released her with a push. "Good, now get out."

After she had left, Sloan took a closer look around the room. There were no personal items of any sort. He shook out the sheets and found nothing. It was then that he noticed the rag. A corner of a dirty cloth lay just under the bed. He bent and scooped it up. Holding it to his nose, he took a light sniff. *Ether.*

Brianne had no idea how she knew it, but from the minute she saw Sloan walking down the boardwalk toward her, she was certain something was wrong. She waited, though, and did not run to him as she wanted.

Deciding that there was no easy way to tell her, Sloan chose the direct approach. When he was beside her, he held out the rag. *"Ether."*

She took the rag from him and smelled it, nearly gagging as she did. "I don't understand."

"Your brother spent the night over at Lucky's Saloon. My guess is that sometime during the night someone used this rag soaked with ether to put him out."

"Oh, God! Where is he? Is he still at the saloon? Is he still unconscious?"

Thinking of the times he had heard her joyful laughter made him hesitate. What he had to tell her would put a stop to all her laughter.

"Well? Patrick's all right, isn't he?"

"Brianne—"

Unaware of her actions, her hand closed urgently around his forearm. "He's not dead!"

She released the grip on his arm quickly, but Sloan had still had time to register the panic in her eyes and the stricken look on her face. "I don't know," he said quietly, "but there's no sign of him."

Brianne's hand flew to her mouth. "Oh, dear God, he must have been kidnapped!"

"Kidnapped?" His voice reflected surprise. "Why would anyone do that? I can see why someone might jump him and steal his money, but why would they *take* him? That doesn't make sense."

Reaching for control, Brianne straightened. To the watching Sloan, she appeared like royalty in the way she seemed to pull an invisible mantle of composure and dignity around her.

"Thank you for going to the saloon for me," she said. Then without another word she turned on her booted heel and headed for the sheriff's office.

Sloan started to go after her, to help her, to ask her why she hadn't answered his question, but then he stopped, reminding himself that he was in Chango for a specific reason that had nothing to do with a redheaded, green-eyed enchantress. He dropped into the chair he had previously occupied, tilted it back on two legs, and began to watch the activity on Main Street.

Brianne burst into the sheriff's office and advanced on the man sleeping behind the desk, his feet holding down some papers on its top. "I'm Brianne Delaney and something has happened to my brother! Are you the sheriff?"

Sleepily, the man pushed back the brim of the hat that had been covering his eyes and looked at her. "Nope, I'm the deputy, Norman Bowls."

"Where's the sheriff?" she asked impatiently.

"He ain't here. He's over Donley way, roundin' up a bunch of rustlers. Left me in charge."

"Then *do* something! I think my brother has been kidnapped."

"Kidnapped, you say?" With laggardly movements the deputy brought his legs off the desk and sat up. "Well now, ain't that interestin'. We ain't had a kidnappin' in I can't remember when. Killin's, yes. Lots of killin's. But no kidnappin's. Are you sure?"

Brianne felt like yanking the stupid man up by his shirtfront and yelling at him. Instead, she tossed the rag onto the desk. "This ether-soaked rag was found under the bed where my brother spent the night."

"And where was that?"

"At Lucky's Saloon."

"The saloon, huh?" Norman scratched his beard-covered chin. "I wonder which girl he had. Could have been Janice. Might have been Claire. On the other hand—"

"I don't care if he spent the night with the whole lot

of them!" Brianne said icily. "He's gone, and I want him found! What are you going to do about this?"

"Nothin'."

"What?"

Norman leaned back in the chair. "My brother-in-law, Hubert, he's the sheriff, you know, well, he made me promise I wouldn't get into no trouble whilst he was gone. That means I've got to stay right here." He pointed at his chair, then added morosely, "Hubert says I always get into trouble when he's gone."

"But you've got to find my brother! He could be badly hurt!"

"He could be dead," Deputy Norman Bowls pointed out with somber logic.

"He's *not* dead!"

Noting the way Brianne's firm jaw was set, Norman suddenly became suspicious. "What'd you say your name was again?"

"Brianne Delaney."

"You wouldn't happen to come from over Arizona way, now, would you?"

"Yes, I would."

"Uh-oh."

"Uh-oh? What do you mean uh-oh?"

"I ain't gettin' involved with no Delaneys. They ain't exactly got a reputation for bein' an even-tempered bunch. What if that kid turns up dead? My hide wouldn't be worth a skunk's."

She leaned across the desk until she was eye level with the deputy. "You fool," she said softly, "don't you know my family can level this town in a matter of minutes? And that's exactly what they'll do if my brother does turn up dead and you *haven't* done anything."

"Maybe," he mumbled, "but at least I'll still have my skin."

The bone-chilling look in Brianne's green eyes had the deputy hunching his shoulders and sliding his hat back over his eyes. In the next second the windows rattled and papers flew as she slammed out of the office.

Sloan's hand caught Brianne around the upper arm to stop her as she was about to rush past him into the hotel. "What did you find out?"

"That, for a while at least, there is no law here. The sheriff is out of town, and he left his moronic brother-in-law in charge."

Sloan stood up, still holding Brianne's upper arm. "So what are you going to do? Your brother mentioned his family last night. In Arizona, I believe. You'd better telegraph them."

Brianne rejected his idea with a shake of her head and spoke emphatically. "I'll find him."

"*You?*" His hand tightened on her arm. "You can't go out looking for your brother by yourself."

Brianne was genuinely puzzled. "Why? And now that I think about it, why are you still holding my arm?"

Sloan dropped his hand.

Walking toward Sloan, Janice cursed her luck at finding him talking to that redheaded woman. She had caught a brief glimpse of the same woman yesterday afternoon with Patrick. He had called her

Brianne, and Patrick had been giving her his undivided attention, just as Sloan was now.

Janice paused. Sloan's back was to her, so he hadn't seen her yet. Maybe she'd come around to see him later.

Brianne glanced over Sloan's shoulder, and something in her expression made him turn around to look. "Janice?"

"I—I'm sorry, Mr. Lassiter. I've got a message for you, but I'll come back later when you're not so busy."

"That would be better," he said.

"Wait," Brianne called. "Is the message about Patrick Delaney?"

Janice twisted her hands together, glancing at Brianne. Normally, the women of the town didn't acknowledge Janice or the other girls who worked at Lucky's Saloon, and they would turn away when she walked by. But Brianne was looking at her with an eager, expectant expression that encouraged her.

Janice nodded.

"What's the message?" Sloan asked.

She dug into the pocket of her skirt and brought out a folded piece of paper. "Here. Katy asked me to bring it. She was too scared to give it to you."

Sloan unfolded the paper, and as he read the contents, his expression turned grim. "Brianne, I believe this is for you."

With a sinking feeling in her stomach, Brianne took the crumpled sheet of paper and read.

We want fiften hundreed muny for ur brothr.
Well contac u.

Brianne felt herself begin to shake, and strong hands came out to ease her into a chair.

"Oh, my God, she's going to faint!" Janice cried.

"No . . . no, I'll be fine." She gestured with the sheet of paper she held clutched in her hand. "Seeing positive proof of what I'd feared . . . is . . ."

Sloan was kneeling in front of her, his hand clasping her wrist, his fingers on her pulse. "You will send that telegram now."

"Not yet." She took several deep breaths and willed the weakness she was feeling to be temporary. Knowing she was going to have to act, she attempted to gather herself together, venturing a small laugh. "I'd love to know how they came up with their estimate of Patrick's worth."

She glanced into Sloan's eyes and for a moment was held. Far back in their golden depths there seemed to be a light of concern. Warmth seeped back into her body. She laughed again and was pleased to hear that she sounded stronger. "Patrick's going to be furious when he realizes they've asked such a relatively small amount. She looked up at Janice. "Where did you get this note?"

"From Katy. She's a girl I work with over at Lucky's. She was afraid of Mr. Lassiter, so she sent me. Katy was with Mr. Delaney last night. . . ." Janice's voice trailed off as she realized what she had just said. "Are you Mr. Delaney's wife?" she asked worriedly.

"I'm his sister, and I want you to tell me everything you know."

Behind her, Sloan almost smiled at Brianne's mat-

ter-of-fact acceptance of her brother's spending the
night with a saloon girl. The more he learned of Brianne Delaney, the more he liked, the more he admired, and, dammit-all-to-hell, the more he wanted
her.

Janice nervously scanned the boardwalk around
them, checking to see if there was anyone who might
object to her being there, talking with a lady. As nice
as Brianne seemed, Janice wished it were just her and
Sloan talking together. She could still remember how
he had sucked at her breast the night before with such
wonderful skill. She had actually felt something, and
that was unusual.

Sloan shifted his weight impatiently. "Janice!"

"Oh, well, these men gave the note to Katy after . . . after she and Mr. Delaney . . . well, never
mind." She sent a pleading glance toward Sloan, but
he merely nodded for her to continue. "Anyway, Mr.
Delaney was asleep, and . . . I don't know, I guess
these men went up and got Mr. Delaney and took him
out the back way."

Anxious, Brianne touched Janice's arm. "Did they
hurt him?"

"I—I don't know." She again looked at Sloan. She
wanted to make sure he understood that she had had
nothing to do with the kidnapping. "The first I knew
of any of this was when you came into the saloon this
mornin'. And Katy didn't tell me about the men and
the note till after you had left." As an afterthought,
she added, "They gave Katy some money."

A tug on her arm brought her attention back to

Brianne. "Can you remember what these men looked like?"

Janice licked her lips, recalling how she had retreated into a corner of the saloon last night and waited, hoping Sloan would come back. Maybe tonight he would come to her. She cast a longing glance at him. "No, my mind was sort've on other things. I wasn't payin' much attention to what was goin' on around me."

"Thank you, Janice," Sloan said with a dry intonation to his voice. "Tell Katy I'll be over to talk with her later. She'd better be there."

After Janice had left, Brianne turned toward the door of the hotel.

Sloan stopped her by again grasping her upper arm. "Wait a minute! Where are you going now?"

Brianne looked down at his hand around her arm, the back of his hand lightly brushing her breast. "You're making a habit of this, aren't you?"

"There are more pleasant habits a man can form with a woman like you. Would you care for me to show you?"

In spite of her fear for Patrick, his words caused the blood to pick up speed and race through her veins like a hot wind. But if he had expected her to blush, she thought, he was going to be disappointed. "No, I wouldn't. And to answer your question, I'm going upstairs to get my rifle."

With a quick movement she broke out of his grasp and was in the hotel and up the stairs. Sloan let her go because they were attracting more interest from passersby than was proper for either of them. For appearance' sake, Sloan waited a few minutes, then followed her. The door to her room was slightly ajar, so he stepped in without knocking and closed it quickly behind him.

"You know, Brianne, up to now I've thought that you've handled this whole thing rather well, but if you're thinking of trying to find your brother by yourself, then I've got to question your good sense."

Startled, Brianne glanced up. "You shouldn't be in my room."

He pushed away from the door. "Did you hear me?"

She set down the rifle she'd retrieved from her pack and swiveled away to check the amount of ammunition she had in her saddlebag. "Of course I heard you. The problem is, you're just not saying anything I want to listen to."

"Then what would I have to say to make you listen?" He grasped her arms and slowly turned her around to face him. "Would telling you about the Indians that come up out of nowhere to attack the unsuspecting do it?"

"There's nothing you can tell me about Indians that I don't know," she said solemnly, remembering her parents, Rory and Helene, who had been killed in an Indian raid when she and Patrick had been infants. Rapidly, those painful thoughts were replaced by memories of Silver Dove, her spirited and loving cousin.

His hand came up to stroke her neck. "Then what about the men you'll meet on the trail, the men who wear guns and have no scruples?"

She looked up into his cold golden eyes that showed so little emotion. "That description fits you."

His fingers stilled on her neck. "You're right," he said softly. "You're absolutely right."

With deliberation, he crushed his mouth down on hers. The feelings he was experiencing were startling the hell out of him. He'd been dead inside for so long. Right now, though, he had no intention of taking time to figure out what was happening. Coolly, he moved his mouth over hers, and sensations came flooding back from Brianne to him that were anything but cool. This one woman shouldn't be troubling him like this, inflaming him. Dammit, he thought, pulling her closer, she shouldn't be getting under his skin like a rash he wanted to scratch but couldn't.

She struggled against him, but he thrust his tongue into her mouth, and her responding moan told him that she could be subdued.

If her brother hadn't disappeared, she would have ridden out of this town and out of his life this morning, and he wouldn't have cared. Or so he told himself. He pressed his body into hers, wanting to feel her breasts, stomach, and thighs against him.

Brianne felt the fire begin to seep through the motions of his calculated seduction, and she stopped resisting. How could he do this to her? she asked herself with despair. How could he make her forget everything but the heated need that had started in her stomach and was spreading downward? It seemed so easy for him. Too easy. And that made her angry because she couldn't let him make her forget about Patrick and what she had to do.

"No," she whispered, and pushed against him. "No!" she said, this time stronger, and broke free.

Sloan looked down at her. Her eyes were soft, her lips full and red. If ever he saw a woman moved by passion, it was Brianne. Yet she had pulled out of his embrace.

She wrapped her arms around her body and turned her back to Sloan, giving herself time to steady her breathing. He confused her. There had been his intervention with Mrs. Potter on behalf of George. And down on the boardwalk, when he had knelt before her chair, she had had the brief notion that he actually might be concerned about her. But she knew that had to be impossible. He was obviously too hard-bitten a man to know concern for another person.

So knowing that, how could she explain away those times when he touched her, or held her, or kissed her, or all three, those times when he had an uncommon power to make her feel a wanting, a needing?

The answer was simple. What he felt for her was lust, plain and simple. She came from a lusty family, yet while knowing that blatant sexual longing existed, she had never personally experienced it. This was all so new.

With her back still to Sloan, she shook her head as if to clear it. He was a disturbing man, but she had no time for the upheaval he wrought so effortlessly.

She swiveled back around so that she faced him. "You know what I don't understand, Mr. Lassiter? I don't understand what all this means to you. Why should you care one way or the other whether I go out alone to try to find my brother?"

"I suppose because I've never been able to abide stupidity," he said calmly. "In case its escaped your notice, you're in a strange town, surrounded by strangers."

"One of whom is *you*."

"Honey," he drawled in that mocking way he had that caressed the nerves up and down her spine even as it infuriated her, "strangers don't kiss the way we just kissed."

Ignore him, she ordered herself, and started to bend down to pick up her bedroll, but his next words stopped her.

"You're looking for three men."

"What are you talking about?"

"I noticed them last night. Once they heard the name Delaney, they started paying an awful lot of attention to your brother. One was tall, the other two were about medium height and stocky. Of course, I won't know for sure until I talk with Katy."

"Why didn't you tell me this before?"

"Because I thought you were too smart to go tearing out of here by yourself to look for your brother. But since it seems I was wrong about that, you should at least know what you're going to be up against."

"I'll question her."

"You're letting your concern for you brother override your common sense, Brianne. It looks like you're going to be in Chango for a while. Make things easy on yourself. Don't turn these people against you. At the least I should talk to Katy for you."

"At the least?"

"Listen, redhead, you may think that there's no law

here, but outside this town you'll find out what true
lawlessness means." At his side, his hands clenched
into fists as he felt irritation rising inside him. He had
never known a woman who wouldn't pay attention to
him, and he had never known a woman he more
wanted to take again into his arms. "The West is no
place for a woman alone."

"There you go again, telling me about the West. I
find that very interesting, especially since *I'm* the one
who was born in the West, and *you're* the one who's
from the city. Besides, right now I'm the only chance
my brother has." She tilted her head to one side,
regarding him with a clear-eyed green stare. "Hasn't
there ever been anyone in your life you have loved so
much you would do anything to make sure he was
safe?"

David. Sloan felt as if Brianne had reached inside
him and touched an open wound. The fact that she
had done it unknowingly didn't make the hurt any
less. The anguish brought him by the memory of his
brother's death was private, and it was an anguish he
talked about with no one.

"Good-bye, Brianne, and good luck."

Abruptly, Sloan left, and Brianne was left staring at
a closed door, feeling suddenly and strangely lost. She
had told Patrick that Sloan was a dangerous man, and
now she believed that more than ever. She also
believed that inside him there was something black
and cold, hard and untouchable. The men of her
family had traces of the same characteristics, yet they
also had a quality that seemed to be absent in Sloan—
a soul. It was almost as if Sloan were dead inside.

But if that were the case, she asked herself, troubled, how could he make her feel such fire? And how could she account for the glimpse she had had of pain that had crossed his face at her simple question. True, the stricken look had been so brief she would have missed it if she hadn't been concentrating so hard on him.

Her need to know the answers to these questions could easily border on obsession if she allowed it, but obsession with anything other than finding Patrick was just not possible.

She thought about Sloan Lassiter a minute longer, then pushed a strand of hair back from her face and muttered, "Oh, hell!" She couldn't possibly let Sloan disturb her now. They had shared two kisses, and Lord knew she would certainly never forget them. But she needed to get on with what was really important. Patrick was missing and in danger, and *he* was her primary concern.

5

⚜

Just after sundown Brianne came riding back into town. She reigned in Dancer at the front of the hotel and stepped down. Sloan, who was returning from a walk around the town, saw her, and stopped in the shadows a moment to observe her. It was obvious that she hadn't found Patrick, but then, he hadn't really expected she would. She appeared tired, but, strangely enough, not discouraged.

Young George ran out to meet her. "Can I take care of your horse for you, Miz Delaney?"

She nodded. "Take him to the stable, make sure you rub him down well, and remember to give him plenty of water and oats."

Brianne untied the bedroll and the saddlebag and threw them over her shoulder. Sloan thought the saddlebag looked too heavy for her slim body, but by not so much as a grimace did she indicate it might be.

While she was taking the rifle out of the scabbard, Sloan suddenly appeared at her side. Her heart gave a hard jolt, and as she felt her rib cage absorb the shock, she decided that she really did need to get used to the way he could come upon her so quietly, taking her completely unawares.

He tossed George a couple of coins. "That's for you, George, not for your dad. Understand?"

"Yes, sir. Thank you, Mr. Lassiter!"

Brianne watched George lead Dancer away, then turned to Sloan. "Why did you tell him that?"

"According to Mrs. Potter, his father takes everything the boy makes and uses it to buy liquor."

"Did Mrs. Potter volunteer that information or did you ask?"

One corner of his mouth lifted. "Does it matter?"

"I thought maybe"—Brianne checked herself—"I just wondered why you were concerned about George, that's all."

"Not concerned, curious," he said flatly. "And there's no reason."

"No," she said slowly, "I guess not, but when I find Patrick, I'm going to see what I can do to help George."

"*When* not *if*? Then you found something?"

She began walking. "Unfortunately, no. Last night's rain washed away all signs and tracks. I was afraid it would, but I had to check. And, of course, it didn't help that I got such a late start today."

They stepped beneath the etched ruby glass transom above the front door, and into the lobby of the hotel that had once been the generous foyer of the English duke's mansion. A tall mahogany grandfather clock stood sentinel just inside the doorway. To one side the oak stairway swept upward toward the second and third floors, the wall of the stairway made up of painted panels of different forest creatures.

At a gracious mahogany desk Mrs. Potter raised her head from her perusal of the paper. "Oh, Miss Delaney. I was wondering if you still wanted me to keep Mr. Delaney's room available now that he's disappeared."

Brianne's face showed her shock at the question. "Of course! Don't rent that room! I'll be taking care of the bill until Patrick comes back, and that will be very soon."

Mrs. Potter smoothed down the apron covering her brown bombazine dress. "I'm sure you're right. It's just that, speaking sensibly—"

Unexpectedly, Brianne's laughter peeled out, catching Sloan off guard. Her laughter, he thought, had the strange ability to penetrate a man's skin and enter his bloodstream where it simmered long after the sound of it was gone.

"Mrs. Potter," she said, "no one who knows me would ever accuse me of being sensible." She cast a teasing looking over her shoulder at Sloan. "And I'm sure Mr. Lassiter will back me up on that."

To have a woman flirt with him was a common occurrence for Sloan. He was used to flirtations. He knew how to respond to them. But Brianne wasn't flirting with him. She was treating him as she would any other casual male acquaintance, and the idea rankled the hell out of him.

Mrs. Potter glanced uncertainly from one to the other. "If you say so."

"I do. And I'd also like to buy a bath. I hope the bathroom's free."

Mrs. Potter nodded. She didn't know this beautiful young redheaded woman, and she couldn't comprehend how she could laugh when her brother had just up and disappeared. But she did understand the need for a bath after a day of riding. It would do everyone good to take a bath once a day. It was just a shame that not many people did.

And besides, Miss Delaney, her brother, and Mr. Lassiter were staying in her best rooms. In her view, paying the highest rates without a murmur like these people were doing excused a lot of things. Cowboys and less well-to-do traveling businessmen stayed on the third floor. But even with that more undesirable trade, the hotel was rarely full. Fortunately, that was a condition that would soon end if Mr. McCord's trip to Washington had been successful. The thought cheered her.

"There's not much call for baths at this time of day," Mrs. Potter said. "Most people are eating. I'll send up a clean towel for you when I have George bring up the water."

"Good." Brianne paused at the bottom of the stairs and looked back over the shoulder. "By the way, has the latch been fixed on the bathroom door?"

Mrs. Potter visibly bristled. The question of how the latch had been broken in the first place was a definite mystery. "Mr. Potter fixed it this morning, Miss Delaney. We run a decent, safe establishment here, and we mean to keep it that way. We get no complaints."

Brianne's charming smile took some of the wind out of the lady's sails. "Thank you, Mrs. Potter."

Sloan stared after Brianne as she climbed the stairs, his eyes following the way her hips swayed gracefully beneath the riding skirt. The thickening in his loins that had begun when she had laughed told him to follow her, but with Mrs. Potter's eagle eye on him, he thought better of it and retired to the small parlor, where a tune could be heard coming from the piano.

Fresh and dewy from her bath, Brianne entered her room. The sight of Sloan waiting for her, sitting casually in a chair, his legs crossed, apparently completely at his ease, stopped her in her tracks.

Anticipating her objection, he held up his hand. "I know. I shouldn't be in here, but I am. And if you don't want Mrs. Potter to know you'd better shut the door."

Brianne did as he suggested and tossed the towel and her bathing kit on the bed. "Then since you are as aware of proprieties as I am, you'll leave."

"In a minute," he said, making no effort to move from the chair. He took his time studying the beautiful sight she made in her nightgown and robe. The gown was made of ivory-colored lawn with tiny green flowers scattered over it and ruffles at the nightgown's neck and sleeves. From the neck to the waist, a row of green ribbon bows held the gown closed across her breasts. A gold-colored robe thrown over the gown was a deeper shade than the peach of her skin, and the color, combined with the recent bath, made her skin glow with an alluring luminescence. Her hair fell down her back like a river in flames that blazed even when there was no sun.

"It's a shame you ever have to plait your hair or put it up," he said, his voice a husky whisper.

Hearing that huskiness, Brianne's pulses leapt. "What do you want?"

Hell of a good question, Sloan thought, half angry, but not sure why or at whom. The obvious answer to her question was that he wanted her. But he was a man who had learned not to take things at face value. He had taught himself to probe an opponent, to learn everything he could about a person before he allowed himself to act. He didn't question his view of Brianne as an opponent. Everyone was an opponent to Sloan.

Lying on the floor by the chair was a sketchbook, and, surprised, he reached down to pick it up. "You're an artist?"

Brianne eyed him warily. "Not really." Her family had always told her that she had a real talent. She didn't know whether she did or not. It wouldn't have mattered to her though if she were as talentless as a dead stump. She loved sketching, watching lines take form and shape beneath her pencil point; and she loved to paint, reveling in the colors, the texture, even the smell of oils.

Page by page Sloan studied her drawings—a rock formation, a distant mountain, a flowering tree, an old cowboy. "I have to disagree. You have a real talent. These are sketches made during this trip, aren't they?"

"Yes." Her fingers itched to snatch her sketchbook away from him, instinctively wanting to protect herself from Sloan. The drawings were personal, and it made her feel strangely exposed to have Sloan studying them.

At the last drawing Sloan stopped. On the page was a most remarkable rendering of an Indian woman. Her high-cheekboned face was a model of serenity, but her eyes held unfathomable sadness.

"That's not finished yet," Brianne said hastily. "I started it last night."

"Who is she?"

"My aunt, Rising Star. She died in childbirth three years ago, and ever since, I've wanted to do her portrait. I'll eventually do it in oil."

"Your family is evidently very unusual."

"Because Rising Star was an Apache, you mean?" The tone of her voice told Sloan she was ready to fight if he made so much as one derogatory comment about either her aunt or her family. "That and other things." He closed the sketchbook and laid it aside. "Brianne, I want you to answer the question I asked you this morning. Why kidnapped?"

Thrown off balance, she asked, "I beg your pardon?"

"Why couldn't your brother simply have been robbed? Or even murdered? Why did you so quickly jump to the conclusion that he had been kidnapped?"

Brianne gave careful thought to Sloan's question and how she would answer it. Normally, she would never think of telling anyone anything about her family's business. But she had already told the deputy that she believed Patrick had been kidnapped, and by this time it would be all over town. Plus, it was plain that at least one person, perhaps three people, had known who Patrick was. There would be others. She wove her fingers together and gazed solemnly at Sloan. "My brother is a very wealthy man. The three men in the saloon last night no doubt recognized him or his name."

"Obviously, your family also has a great deal of money."

"Yes."

Sloan sighed, wondering why he wished that Brianne didn't have a penny to her name. "I talked again with Katy and she confirmed that it was the three men I noticed last night who took Delaney. Given the situation, I don't understand why you won't telegraph your family. You're obviously going to need help. Are you afraid of what they'll do to you when they find out your brother's been kidnapped?"

"Do to me?" With her emotions so on edge, the thought of her family hurting her struck her as incredibly funny. Even while knowing the mood swings she was experiencing weren't normal, she let the hilarity replace her fear for Patrick, laughing until tears were rolling down her face. At last, though, gasping with mirth, she caught a glimpse of the dark expression on Sloan's face. Little by little she managed to get herself under control, and, as she did, she tried to decide how best to describe her family to Sloan. As short an explanation as possible would be best, she finally concluded.

"Well, you see, it's like this. The Delaneys are a fierce clan, and if one of us is in trouble, we all come running. Once Granda hears that Patrick has been kidnapped, he'll assemble the Delaney forces. Depending on where my various uncles happen to be and a few other things, the fastest I could get help would be about two weeks. And once they've started, I won't be able to contact them to stop them. Believe me, it's much better all the way around if I give myself a few days. Hopefully, I'll find Patrick, and I won't have to bring the Delaney version of the wrath of God down on this town."

"And of course you think you can find him, don't you?"

All lingering traces of humor left her. She threw back her head, and her red hair shimmered with the movement. "This is my *brother* we're talking about. I'll find him."

Sloan frowned, feeling an irritating mixture of admiration and annoyance. He could snap her delicate wristbone in two with one hand, yet she seemed so strong. Where did that strength come from?

There was a sense of self-possession about Brianne that included no artifice or wiles. Her beauty contained a wildness and an intelligence that no woman he had ever known had come close to having. And there was something in her expression that made him almost believe she could find her brother.

Yet he did remain a disbeliever.

Brianne Delaney seemed an extraordinary woman, *but that couldn't be*. He had tried all the extraordinary women and had been disappointed. All women wanted to cling, and he had to be free.

So instead of taking her into his arms and kissing her as his body told him to do, he rose from the chair and sketched a salute. "Good-bye, Miss Delaney, and best of luck."

Sloan viewed the day's endings from the porch of the Duke Hotel. With the exception of those times when he had taken a stroll around the town or stopped for a bite to eat, he had been sitting there all day. He wasn't a man used to such inactivity, but in this case the inactivity had a purpose.

He hoped that once the townspeople of Chango became accustomed to his presence, they would become less guarded around him and begin dropping bits and pieces of information. To a certain extent, it was already working.

Although reserved and basically cautious, the inhabitants of the town could be pleasant enough if they were convinced you were harmless. No one must suspect his real reason for being in town, at least for now.

First, he had passed the time with some men in Lucky's Saloon. It was there that a portion of his curiosity had been satisfied about Brianne. Casually, he had asked if anyone had ever heard of the Delaney family. The response had been most interesting.

"Hardheaded, hot-tempered bunch," one man offered.

"Brawlers," another man said.

Lucky spoke up. "They settled that land down in Arizona where nobody but Injuns had ever been before. Flat wore the Apaches down until they finally had to decide to live together peacefully."

"They say a couple of them went down to Mexico

and came back with a fortune," someone else said. "Real mysterious, if you ask me."

The first man who had spoken took aim at one of the saloon's brass spittoons. "Not a group of people you'd want to get involved with, and I say we should all find business out of town until this thing blows over with that kid."

Everyone nodded their grim agreement.

Sloan sipped his beer and smiled to himself. The more he learned about the Delaneys, the more he was coming to understand Brianne. A strong-willed, independent family had bred a strong-willed, independent woman. She had grown up running free over land fought for and won by her family—a princess of a Delaney realm. Instead of being put off, he was even more drawn.

But Wes McCord was his reason for being in Chango, and he pressed on. At Nilsen's Emporium, while idly perusing some goods, he had overheard two ladies talking. Activity had been brisk at the bank. Down the street men had loaded up buckboards with building supplies and headed north out of town. Two tough-looking men kept vigil at the office of McCord Enterprises, but there was still no sign of Wes.

And there was something else too. While on his journey around town, he had received the strangest impressions. It was almost as if the people of Chango were protecting Wes, even while being afraid of him. Wes was definitely up to something, and he was going to find out what.

Suddenly alert, Sloan narrowed his eyes against the

gathering dusk. Brianne was riding up the street. And she wasn't alone.

Brianne leaned forward, intending to pat Dancer encouragingly on the neck, but found she couldn't because of the tight grip the woman sitting sidesaddle behind her had on her waist.

"Oh, I'm going to fall!" Henrietta Jones Bartholomew moaned.

"No, you won't," Brianne said soothingly. She had been soothing this woman every few minutes since she had found Henrietta stranded out on the trail. "Just hang on. We're nearly there."

"We're going too fast! Can't you make this beast go slower?"

If Dancer were going any slower, he would be standing still, Brianne mused. But Henrietta's plight did touch her heart. "I promised you I'd get you to the hotel in one piece, and I will. Look, there it is, that three-story building just up the street on the left."

The older woman's grip tightened painfully around Brianne's waist. "I don't know what I'm going to do. I can't depend on you forever. How am I going to live? How am I going to ever get back home? What's to become of me?"

"Henrietta, you're not to worry! I told you I'd take care of everything. You're safe now, and that's what's important."

As Brianne pulled Dancer to a halt in front of the hotel, Sloan rose and walked to the edge of the porch.

"Find any sign of your brother?"

Sloan always seemed to be around, Brianne

thought, trying to disregard the excitement that had shot through her heart as he had risen. Why? she wondered. From what she knew of financiers, they didn't conduct business from the porch of a hotel.

She shook her head. "No." To the woman behind her she said, "You'll have to dismount first."

Henrietta peered at the ground. "It's too far down! Young man," she said, addressing Sloan, "do you think you could find us a ladder?"

With an enigmatic glance at Brianne, Sloan came down from the porch and approached Dancer's left side. "Allow me to help you," he said, holding his arms up.

"Oh, no! I couldn't possibly! Really! Ohhh!"

Sloan set Henrietta's ample form on the ground and turned back for Brianne.

She threw him a dry smile. "Thanks, but I can manage." She swung her leg over and slipped off Dancer. Mr. Lassiter, I'd like you to meet Mrs.—"

"Miss, my dear." She straightened the high starched collar of her blouse. "I will be called by the name I was born with forty-five years ago. I'm Miss Henrietta Jones."

Brianne nodded at her. "Right, Miss Henrietta Jones."

"I refuse to use that man's name!" Henrietta snorted with vehement emphasis and gave a vicious tug to the wren-brown jacket that matched her skirt. "Bartholomew, it was. Horace Bartholomew. The wedding was so rushed, I'm sure it wasn't even legal anyway."

"Henrietta, this is Mr. Sloan Lassiter. He's staying at the hotel."

Henrietta adjusted her hat on her tightly bound mouse-brown hair. "How do you do."

Sloan cast Brianne a look that was full of questions. Ignoring him, she took Henrietta's arm. "This way. We'll get you a room, and after a nice bath and dinner, you'll feel much better."

Henrietta stalled, giving Sloan a suspicious once-over. "Do you live here in the West?" She used the word West as she might have used the word hell.

"No, ma'am. I'm from New York City."

Henrietta visibly relaxed. "A *civilized* man! Thank the Lord. Mr. Lassiter, you cannot imagine the hardships I've endured. I was scarcely off the stage when that man hustled me off to a justice of the peace. Next thing I knew, I was in a hotel room, and it was short of high noon. Well, you can understand how a woman of my sensibilities would have been offended, can't you?"

Brianne had to stifle a great urge to laugh at the obviously puzzled expression on Sloan's hard face. "Miss Jones arrived in California in answer to a mail order bride advertisement. The gentleman in question apparently, uh, rushed her a bit."

"Rushed!" In the fading light of day, Henrietta's face turned red at the memory. She leaned toward Brianne and whispered loudly in her ear. "My dear, *you can't imagine what he wanted me to do*! And in the broad light of day too! The pitcher was the only answer."

"Allow me to help you inside," Sloan said smoothly.

"Thank you; that's very kind, I'm sure. I know I'll feel much more the thing tomorrow."

Brianne closed the door to Henrietta's room and headed toward her own, her gaze thoughtfully focused on the tips of her boots as she reflected on the day that had just passed. She had ridden south, investigating anything that looked promising, going as far as she possibly could. But nothing she had seen had given her any clue as to what might have happened to Patrick or where he could be. If it hadn't been for Henrietta, she would have spent the night on the trail and been able to get an early start in the morning.

"Brianne."

Her head snapped up, and she saw that Sloan was standing beside the door to her room. He was dressed for dinner and looked incredibly attractive.

"Is Miss Jones settled in?"

Brianne swallowed hard and nodded.

Sloan took in the weary set of Brianne's shoulders, and her dust-smudged face. "You *are* going down to dinner, aren't you?"

"I promised Henrietta I would have a tray brought up to her."

"That doesn't answer my question."

"I was thinking of having a tray too." She closed her hand over the doorknob.

"Nonsense. Go in and wash up, but don't bother changing. I'll wait for you."

She turned back to him and gave him a direct look. "Why?"

Brianne was a woman who seemed to ask why a lot, he thought, amused. Unfortunately, he had no satisfactory answers. "Because I hate to eat alone. And because you need a good meal."

Was that a trace of concern? she wondered. Or was she wrong one more time. "Both of those things may be true, Mr. Lassiter, but, you see, there is one problem. I know nothing about you."

He stepped closer, and his voice changed, becoming more seductive. "On the contrary, Brianne, you know a lot about me."

Her eyebrows arched prettily. "Oh? For instance?"

He smiled. "For instance, you know what my lips feel like when they're kissing you."

Her throat went dry, and she swallowed, feeling unaccountably off balance. "That's not what I meant."

As if she hadn't spoken, he went on. "And you know what my body feels like against yours, and how it can make you want things you've never wanted before."

The heat from his golden eyes bore into her, making his words achingly true. She didn't even bother to deny them. "What are you doing in Chango, Sloan?" she whispered.

The fact that without thinking she had called him Sloan gave him an inordinate amount of satisfaction. "I'm on business that will keep me here awhile. As it happens, you also find yourself stuck in this town longer than you anticipated. We're both strangers. And we both need to eat. It makes perfect sense that we eat together."

"Does everything you do make sense?"

"No," he murmured, and after a quick glance up

and down the hall to make sure no one was coming, he moved forward slightly until his body was pressing hers against the door. The contours of her body were no secret to him, but still the feel of her against him was a potent aphrodisiac. "For instance, kissing you makes no sense at all."

His lips touched hers, then his tongue slipped between her lips into the waiting depths of her mouth. Shuddering, Brianne lifted her arms to his neck. They shouldn't be doing this in the hall, where anyone could come along and see them. Her fingers threaded into his hair. What was she thinking? They shouldn't be doing this at *all*. And she definitely shouldn't be enjoying it! Moaning, her arms tightened around him.

He was right. This made no sense. Slivers of desire were penetrating her skin like splinters of fire, and her head was spinning. From inside her somewhere came the sure feeling that she should run as fast as she could from this man. But her knees felt weak and . . .

She was clinging to him, more feminine and desirable than any woman he had ever held. His hands strayed to her breasts, so firm and round. Through the material he could feel her nipple tighten. He groaned, needing to feel her, all of her.

The buttons of her blouse offered him little problem, and his hand was about to slip beneath the fabric to the soft skin, when he heard her small cry of protest. It took him a moment, but he finally remembered that they were standing in the hall of a public hotel, and it was then he realized that if he didn't end the kiss now, he would take her where she stood, up against the door. He tore his mouth from hers with effort, then couldn't help smiling at the dazed and bemused expression on her beautiful face. He reached behind her and turned the doorknob. The door opened, depriving her of its support, but Sloan caught her before she fell. "Wash up and I'll wait for you downstairs. Then you can entertain me with an explanation of how you found Miss Jones."

After Sloan had left, Brianne stood in the middle of the room talking to herself. Her world hadn't always been safe, but it had been secure. She had known exactly who she was and where she belonged. Now her world was turned upside down. Her brother was missing. And her body was choosing this inappropriate time to awaken to a man's touch. And not just any man either, but a golden-eyed, cold-hearted man named Sloan Lassiter.

But he drew her, as light is attracted to darkness, because its natural tendency was to flow toward black places and try to illuminate them. Having dinner with Sloan, with a table between them, and a dining room full of people couldn't hurt anything. And she certainly couldn't do anything more about finding Patrick tonight.

She lifted her fingers to her lips, where his mouth had been just minutes before. She could feel the heat, and it wasn't her imagination.

Sloan Lassiter excited her, there was no doubt about it. But he also troubled her. No matter how simple he made his business in Chango sound, she had a feeling that it was complex. It was more than the gun he constantly wore. And it was more than the fact that he always seemed to be watching for someone or something.

The only time his eyes changed from that particular shade of soulless gold was when he looked at her with desire.

The only time he showed any gentleness was when his hands touched her skin.

So what was she doing having dinner with him? she asked herself. The answer came swiftly. She wanted to.

Brianne's green eyes brimmed with laughter as she gazed at Sloan across their dinner table. The color of her eyes was deepened by the emerald silk of her dress. "Well, apparently Henrietta was so unnerved by what she saw as indecent haste on her husband's part to consummate their marriage, she picked up a good-size pitcher and struck him over the head."

Sloan's mouth twitched, enjoying Brianne's amusement. "What happened then?"

"Luckily, from her point of view that is, she was able to catch a stage out of town before the poor man came to. The problem is, she left so fast, all her belongings are back in California."

"And I suppose she doesn't have any money either."

Seriousness replaced Brianne's smile. "She was a schoolteacher in Philadelphia, and Mr. Bartholomew sent her just enough funds for the fare west. When her own money ran out, she accepted a ride with a group of young women going east. Unfortunately, somewhere along the way she discovered to her horror that the women were not quite as respectable as she had thought; rather, they were the type who, uh—"

"Entertain men for money?"

"I suppose that's one way of stating the case. Without thinking of the consequences, she parted company with them on the spot, out in the middle of nowhere. And to answer your question, no, Henrietta doesn't have any money."

"Isn't it fortunate she found you?"

Brianne tilted her head curiously at the cynical tone of his voice. "Actually, *I* found *her*."

"And now you feel responsible for her, and she's taking advantage of your feelings."

"Sloan, I *want* to help her. The woman is stranded. It will be no problem at all for me to let her rest up here a few days, then pay her way back home."

"Are you always so ready to help strangers?" he asked softly. The candle's glow cast flickering light and shadows over the harsh angles of his face.

"If I can."

"It's not safe."

Neither are you. Without knowing why she was doing it, she rubbed the scarred skin of her left forearm that was covered by the sleeve of her dress. "Henrietta poses no threat to me."

"Maybe not." For a moment he studied her with enigmatic eyes. "So are you going to continue looking for your brother?"

"Of course."

"I was over at Lucky's today. It was interesting. I learned that most of the men over there seem to be afraid of your family."

Her mouth tightened. "Stupid people! They're not even acquainted with fear yet, but believe me, they will be if something happens to Patrick."

"Still, you won't get any help from them."

"That's why I haven't asked them."

"Why haven't you asked me?"

His quietly spoken question made her pause. "It never even occurred to me."

His smile sent shivers skimming along her spine. "I find that amazing."

It was after midnight, and Sloan lay wide awake, his eyes fixed on the ceiling. Staring at the ceiling was a lot better than what he really wanted to do, which was to go next door and climb into Brianne's bed. His blood was running hot tonight, and his loins were aching with a need that demanded to be satisfied.

But Brianne wasn't his answer. What he needed was a woman he could just have and then be done with. Like Janice. Or—in the dark he smiled—like Betsy Spenser, the beautiful young widow of his business associate, Henry Spenser.

In an effort to help assuage her grief, he had escorted her to the theater, where he kept a box. But the production of *Il Trovatore* had not captured his interest, and the glances he had received all evening from Betsy had been enticing. So he had pulled her to the floor of the box with the portiere half hiding them and positioned her on her hands and knees in front of him. Kneeling behind her, he had flipped up her black silk skirt and untied her drawers. Careful to keep his head well below the rim of the box, he had grasped her breasts and roughly taken her. Fortunately, several climactic scenes, including a bombastic chorus, served to drown out her cries of ecstasy.

He could still remember how lush and round her buttocks had been as he had plunged in and out of her. How full her breasts as he had held on tightly. And her red hair—

Squeezing his eyes shut, he groaned with pure frustration as he realized that, in his mind, Betsy Spenser had somehow become Brianne Delaney. His pillow was thrown through the air and hit the opposite wall with a violent force. *Dammit all to hell!*

6

The urge to pace the length of the hotel porch and back was almost overwhelming for Sloan. But he stayed where he was, sitting in the chair.

His body was perfectly still, but inside, his muscles were burning with their need for movement as they slowly coiled tighter and tighter. He hated the feeling. And, more, he hated the niggling sense that had been with him all day that something was wrong.

Casting over the day's events in his mind, he tried to decide what could be bothering him. His investigation into what Wes was up to was going well, and he had learned some interesting things today. No one was willing to tell him much. But someone dropped a piece of information here, another there, and soon he had what amounted to *almost* a whole.

Wes McCord was in Washington, D.C., lobbying to put a deal together so that the railroad could come through Chango. Chango was a thriving town now, but if Wes were successful, the town would boom overnight. And that was why the people of Chango were protecting Wes from nosy strangers. They would be distrustful of anyone who might interfere with Wes and his mission to bring the railroad to their town.

It sounded as if Wes had turned into a civic leader and philanthropist, but Sloan knew better. There was still the underlying fear he heard in certain conversations. Unfortunately, he probably wouldn't learn any more until Wes came back, and he was sure that it was the inactivity that was beginning to bother him.

Yes, that was it. The inactivity.

He stood up and walked to the porch railing, his gaze naturally seeking the direction Brianne had taken this morning. Just past dawn he had watched her ride out of town. The sun had set over an hour ago. Surely she wouldn't be foolish enough to spend the night away from town!

He understood her need to find Patrick. If it were David who had disappeared, he would be turning over every rock in the territory until he found him. But he was a man. Brianne shouldn't be riding alone into a lonely, rugged land, trying to track down four men.

She was so alone. He knew what it was like to be desperate and alone.

Lord, but he wished he had a drink! There was a rawness inside him that a bottle of whiskey would go a long way toward soothing. He hadn't had a drink, though, since that night in New York City, and he didn't intend to. Not until he made Wesley McCord pay for David's death.

But he sure as hell hadn't sworn off women, and, he decided, spending an hour or two driving his body into the softness of a woman might help to rid him of the antsy feelings he had and to satisfy the painful fullness in his loins—especially after the better part of a night spent thinking of burying himself inside Brianne Delaney.

Where the hell was she anyway?

Suddenly alert, Sloan narrowed his eyes against the gathering dusk.

"There is no nobler beast than the horse," Phineas Tooley observed, gesturing expansively toward Dancer as the horse slowly trudged up the main street of town pulling the maroon-painted wagon with cream-colored trim that proclaimed TOOLEY'S MIRACLE RESTORATIVE, A PATENTED CURATIVE on its side in distinctive gold and blue letters.

In the four hours she had been in Phineas's company, Brianne had discovered that his hands often gestured expansively.

"My noble beast appears to be most put out," Brianne said dryly, sighting the hotel up ahead and giving silent thanks. "He's never pulled a wagon before."

"But he's doing an admirable job! Admirable! If I didn't find myself in such reduced circumstances, I would offer for him." He turned toward her hopefully. "Perhaps we could strike a bargain. I still have the contents of the wagon, you know."

"I would never part with Dancer. He was a gift from my uncle."

He gave a wave of his hand that was meant to indicate a philosophical attitude toward her refusal.

"Ah, well, I'm sure I'll find another equally competent animal."

"No doubt." Brianne had just seen Sloan. He was sitting atop the hotel railing with his back supported against a post.

She reined in Dancer and set the brake on the wagon. With a graceful move she jumped down, and Phineas followed her. Nodding to Sloan, she walked to Dancer's head to give him a loving pat. "Get what you'll need out of the wagon," she told Phineas, "then I'll take the wagon on to the stables. I'm sure the owner won't mind letting the wagon stay there until you're ready to leave again."

"Perhaps in payment the good man would take a few bottles of my patented medicine." Phineas waved his hand in the direction of the wagon. "There's not a thing it won't cure."

"I'm sure," Brianne murmured, her eyes on Sloan. She hadn't expected an effusive greeting, but she couldn't help but feel a tinge of disappointment that he hadn't even said hello or asked about Patrick. "Mr. Lassiter, this is Mr. Phineas Tooley. A most unfortunate event left him without any money or a horse. It was lucky I came upon him when I did."

"Lucky," Phineas agreed. "The unfortunate event of which Miss Delaney is speaking was in fact not an event, but a woman of questionable morals. I befriended her, you understand, after searching my soul and deciding I could overlook her dubious character. However, the hussy robbed and abandoned me! Out in the middle of nowhere!" He pulled a handkerchief from his pocket and wiped his brow. "And it couldn't

have happened at a worse time, given the circumstances."

"What circumstances?" Brianne asked curiously.

After a furtive glance over his shoulder he smiled
broadly. "That's a subject perhaps left for another
time, Miss Delaney. Suffice it to say that you are
indeed an angel of mercy."

Sloan remained stone-silent, but Brianne was re-
ceiving the oddest impression of ice-cold fury.

Evidently Phineas received the same impression,
because he took a step closer to Brianne. "At any rate,
I'll have to empty the entire contents of my wagon. I
can't possibly leave such valuable merchandise un-
attended."

Brianne fully expected a scathing remark from
Sloan. Even Phineas cast a cautious glance toward
him. Sloan's continued silence was deafening.

"Phineas." She waited until she had his attention
again. "It just won't be possible for you to take
everything in this wagon into the hotel. Mrs. Potter
would never allow it. But don't worry. I'll pay for
someone to watch your wagon."

A huge smile made Phineas's face fold into a series
of creases, like a half-open fan. "Dear lady, you are too
kind!"

Brianne rescued her hands from Phineas's fervent
grip and watched, puzzled, as Sloan turned on his
heel and walked into the hotel.

The heat from the bath water had eased some of
Brianne's tiredness. But nothing could make her fear
and concern for Patrick go away. If it hadn't been for

the rain washing away all signs right after his kidnapping, she would have found him by now since she was an expert tracker. But tomorrow was another day, and hopefully she could find him. If she didn't, though, she would telegraph Killara. She had made up her mind.

Falcon was in New Mexico, Dominick was somewhere near St. Louis, and Cort and Sean were at Shamrock. Joshua was at Killara, very much a shattered man since Rising Star's death. But all without exception would come at the fastest possible speed. She had no doubt about that.

She picked up a washcloth and squeezed the water out of it. No, the only doubt she had was about Sloan Lassiter.

Sloan might not be the most comfortable person she had ever been around, but he was practically the only person in this town who would talk with her at any length. She had enjoyed having dinner with him last night. Their conversation had been stimulating. *He* had been stimulating. Yet a little while ago he had walked away from her as if she had suddenly become invisible.

It was just as well, she told herself. She had enough on her mind without having to think about a dark, compelling man who revealed next to nothing about himself.

Minutes later she closed the door to her room, then leaned back against it. Sloan was in her room . . . again! He was sitting so still, he might have been dead—except for his eyes. They were blazing with a fiery golden life. She should say something, but for the life of her she couldn't think of a single word.

"Did you get your gentleman friend settled?" he asked in a voice that was very low and quite calm.

"I don't know him well enough to call him a friend. And, yes, he's in his room."

"No doubt in one of Mrs. Potter's finest."

"He's on this floor," she admitted, thinking that she had never known anyone who could manage to convey so much displeasure without allowing a trace of emotion in his voice. "But he's at the other end of the hall."

"I must confess, I'm surprised."

"Oh?" She pushed away from the door and walked to the edge of the bed. "At what?"

"That you can still manage to stand upright with the problems of so many people weighing on your shoulders."

"Henrietta and Phineas are no burden."

He came up out of his chair and was standing in front of her before she had a chance to blink. "You little fool! Don't you know the jeopardy you put yourself into by stopping to help a strange man?"

"I couldn't pass him by!"

Gripping her shoulders, he spoke from between clenched teeth. "Not only should you have passed him by, you should have ridden so wide a circle around him, he wouldn't have even known you were in the area!"

She wrenched out of his hold. "I wasn't going to leave someone who needed help alone out there."

"No, of course you wouldn't! That would have been the sensible thing to do, wouldn't it?"

"Sloan! I was raised to take care of myself. I can put a bullet in the center of an ace of spades at a hundred paces."

"But can you put a bullet in a man's heart?"

"If I have to."

"I don't believe you."

Swiftly, she moved to where her gear was piled and jerked up her rifle. Pointing it straight at his heart, she asked, "Do you want me to prove it?"

He smiled, and his voice quietened. "You wouldn't even get that rifle cocked, redhead."

She believed him. She tossed the rifle down. "Get out, Sloan."

"When I'm good and ready."

Brianne exploded. "I don't understand you!"

He didn't understand himself either. And he didn't understand her. She was standing within arm's reach of him, her hair streaming in wild glory down her back, her skin giving off the sweetly seducing fragrance he had first smelled when he had seen her in her bath.

Angry at her for putting herself in danger, and angry at himself for being angry, he reached for her.

She didn't come to him easily. She pushed against him, fighting with all her might. But his strength was the greater, and so was his need.

His mouth crushed down on hers; his powerful arms pulled her tight against him. Reason wasn't entirely lost, but the rationality that remained was fogged by a pounding desire. He stripped off her robe, then fell with her onto the bed.

Brianne felt the impact of the mattress against her back and was furious. She didn't want to feel the weight of his leg as it lay over hers. She didn't want to experience the rub of his tongue against her own. She didn't want to feel his hand covering her breast. She didn't. She didn't.

Sloan's fingers grasped a ribboned bow over her breast and pulled. So easy. He untied another, and another, until he could lay the edges of the gown back and bare her breasts. He tore his mouth away from her lips so that he could see her, and what he saw nearly took his breath away. No woman could be so perfectly formed, he thought. It had to be an illusion.

He reached out and cupped a long-fingered hand around one generous globe, finding the perfection no illusion. Her body filled his hand, giving him the sensation of cushioned velvet.

Brianne raised her fist and hit against Sloan's chest, but the impact had all the force of a puff of wind. When had she become so weak? she wondered. When had she become so hot?

"Stop," she said in a voice that sounded more like an entreaty than an order. "Please . . ."

Gazing into her emerald-green eyes, he saw that they had softened. He liked that look. "I don't want to stop, Brianne." His warm palm slid over her breast, and his thumb and forefinger closed on one hard nipple. A soft breath escaped her lips, and he tried to capture it with his mouth. "Say please again," he whispered against her lips right before his tongue plunged back to the sweetness.

Desire was a new sensation to Brianne. How easy it would be to give in to it. Heat was exploding everywhere in her. Yet she couldn't surrender. It wasn't in her.

She tried to twist away, but with one strong arm he brought her back. She rolled her head, trying to escape his mouth. "Stop it, Sloan. Now." Her words were soft, but he heard.

He raised his head to look at her, keeping his hand on her breast as if he had no intention of letting her go. "I want you, Brianne."

"But I don't want you!"

He smiled. "I can make you want me, and I won't even have to work at it." To prove his point, his thumb began grazing back and forth across her nipple. A moan escaped from her on an indrawn breath. "See?"

Brianne looked up at him and was immediately confused. How could Sloan's face remain so hard even while he was seducing her, *even while he was smiling*?

Then, as if a flash of light had suddenly sought out and revealed the darkest place in her mind, she remembered why his smile seemed so familiar to her. She had seen that same smile on the only living thing that had ever hurt her—a wolf. He had looked at her with pale gold eyes and a teeth-baring smile right before he sank his teeth into her arm to tear at her flesh.

The memory brought back her strength. In the space of two heartbeats she rolled off the bed, lunged for the rifle, aimed it right at his heart, and thumbed back the hammer. "This is a Model 1873 Winchester forty-four forty," she said, "and it is now cocked, with a bullet in the chamber and fifteen more behind it." A forceful and cool assurance filled her voice.

Her face was flushed with anger, and her gown was gaping open, exposing heaving breasts that were tipped by rigid nipples. Sloan thought he had never seen a more beautiful woman in his life. God, but he wanted her!

"Mrs. Potter is going to be awfully upset if she finds blood splattered all over this room," he said calmly.

"I'll buy this damn hotel if it comes to that! Now, get up, Sloan, and get out of here."

He sat up, slid to the edge of the bed, and stood up. Slowly, he walked toward her, stopping only when the barrel of the rifle was touching his chest. "You're an interesting lady, redhead. You're wealthy enough to buy a hotel, you have guts enough to shoot me, and you're beautiful enough to make me want you as I've never wanted another woman. I'll leave for now, but I'll be back. We're not through, you and I. Not nearly."

Brianne slept badly and awoke later than she had intended. As a result, it was seven o'clock by the time she was ready to leave. Striding past the dining room on her way out of the hotel, she heard, "Brianne, oh, Brianne!"

She stopped and Henrietta appeared in the doorway, her field-mouse brown hair in a neat bun, her high-necked blouse tucked neatly into a brown skirt.

"Are you going out, dear?"

Holding her rifle in one hand and her saddlebag in the other, Brianne nodded. "I don't know when I'll be back, but I've left instructions with Mrs. Potter that you're to have anything you need."

"That's very kind of you, dear." Henrietta wrung her hands together. "You've been so good, and I hate to ask anything else of you."

Brianne glanced down to see that she was impatiently tapping the toe of her boot against the polished oak floor. When had she acquired that habit? "Is there something else you need, Henrietta?"

"No, no . . ."

"Oh, of course!" Brianne exclaimed, upset that she hadn't realized before. "You'll need a few changes of clothes, won't you?"

"Well, yes, now that you mention it. Since I have only the clothes on my back, at least until I'm able to get home and obtain another position teaching school, it would be more convenient—"

"I'm sorry, I've been so busy looking for my brother, I didn't even think."

"Oh, my dear! I know how worried you are about the dear boy, and I hesitated even to bring up the matter. It's just that this skirt and blouse have gotten so dirty, and I don't even have anything else to wear so that I can wash and dry them."

"Don't worry, Henrietta. As soon as I get back, we'll go to Nilsen's Emporium. I've met the young woman who runs it along with her father. She'll be able to help us."

Henrietta gave Brianne a relieved smile.

"Well, good morning, ladies! What a pleasure it is to be greeted by such beauty upon first awakening."

Brianne turned to find Phineas Tooley descending

the stairway, resplendent in a brown and mustard-yellow plaid suit, the jacket of which buttoned at his sternum.

"Good morning, Phineas. I'd like you to meet Miss Henrietta Jones. Henrietta, this is Mr. Phineas Tooley."

"Delighted, delighted." He grasped Henrietta's hand and pumped it, but his eyes were on the rather imposing slope of her bosom. "I could feast on your beauty, madam."

The former schoolteacher retrieved her hand, took a step backward, and gazed at the funny-looking little man as if he were a particularly reprehensible insect.

"You two can keep each other company while I'm gone," Brianne said with a brightness that attempted to smooth over the situation.

"I'll stay in my room until you return, my dear," Henrietta intoned, and turned to make her way up the stairs.

Phineas's gaze followed her stiff-backed ascent. "No doubt the good woman suffers from costiveness."

"Costiveness?"

He swiveled to face Brianne. "Costive habits can be brought on by failure to go to stool at the usual time. I'm sure that must be Miss Jones's problem."

Brianne was sorry she had asked. "Oh."

"Tooley's Miracle Restorative would do the trick." His forefinger punctuated the air. "Two or three bottles, I judge, and the difficulty will be overcome. I'll go inform her of this cure immediately."

Brianne just managed to catch the edge of a brown and yellow sleeve. "I wouldn't do that if I were you, at

least not right now. At any rate, I've got to be going.
I'll see you when I get back."

"Good luck!"

"Thank you."

From behind the outcropping of rocks, Kamanahua, son of King Tanamoro of the Hawaiian island of
Lakahani, crouched his six-foot-seven-inch frame and
trembled with fear at the sight of the woman riding
toward him.

Soon she would find him. He put his hand against
his chest and pressed hard, trying to slow the beats of
his heart. For days he had successfully hidden from
anyone who happened to pass too close to him. But
this woman was riding slowly, and her eyes were
constantly scanning the area around her. She was
looking for him, and if he did not do something, she
would find him.

But what should he do?

He squinted against the bright sun. She did not look
like a missionary, he thought. The missionaries he
knew all wore black and had pinched faces. Her face
did not look pinched. Still, he was sure if he could see
her eyes, they would be stern. But what if he were
wrong? He could be wrong. The missionaries were
always telling him he was wrong.

Just then the sun glinted off the gold cross hanging
at her throat, and he nearly cried out in anguish. She
was a missionary, and soon now she would see his
hiding place.

He must act! If he could jump out and capture her,
he could force her to take him back to the ocean so

that he could sail home. Yes! That was what he would do! He would be a warrior as his ancestors of old. He would be brave.

Looking again, he gave thanks to the king of the gods. At least she was alone. And small.

He leapt out in front of the horse and waved his arms. *"Auwe! Auwe!"*

"What the—"

Dancer reared, and taken by surprise, Brianne fell off the horse to the ground. A sharp twisting pain shot up her left leg, and she screamed.

"Are you in hurt?"

Brianne raised her eyes, then had to raise them higher. Standing in front of her was a giant of a young man. He was as big-boned and brown-skinned as he was tall. Naked to the waist, he had rolled up his trousers to his knees and tied his jacket around his middle. As for his shoes, they were knotted together by their strings and hanging around his thick neck along with an ominous-appearing chain of teeth.

Brianne's first impression was that he was an Indian. Her second made her hold back all judgment.

He was bending over her with an expression of extreme anxiety on his dark-skinned face. "Are you in hurt?" he asked again, his dark eyes brimming with tears. "I am apology."

Brianne made several quick judgments. Her rifle was about twelve feet away on Dancer's back. And there was no way she could run because she could feel her ankle swelling. If necessary, she could use the knife she kept sheathed in her boot. But most of all, she found it hard to be afraid of someone who was

about to cry because he was so obviously worried
about her. She tried to rub her ankle through the
leather of her boot while she took in the strange sight
of the man in front of her. "Your name is Apology?"

"No." He straightened and thumped his chest
proudly. "I am Kamanahua. I am an Alii. My father is
the king of Lakahani. *I* will become the king when he
dies."

"What did you say your name is?"

"You can name me Kamanahua."

Brianne grimaced with pain. Gingerly she began
easing off the boot. The pain from her ankle and the
confusion the young giant was causing were making
her light-headed. "Can I just call you Kam?"

Vigorously, he nodded his head, then took a deep
breath, his eyes staring fixedly at the cross at her
neck. "Are you a religious? Do you believe in the white
man's God?"

Brianne threw him a bewildered glance. "God? Yes,
of course." Setting her boot aside, she gazed with
horror at her left ankle. It was already twice its
normal size. And the pain was terrible. But she didn't
think it was broken.

"Then you are a missionary."

Brianne heard the fear in his voice and saw the
tears in his large black eyes begin to spill down his
broad face. "No, I am not a missionary. Whatever
gave you that idea?"

He choked back a sob and pointed a trembling
finger toward her necklace. "You wear a cross."

"My grandfather gave me this cross on my birthday
when I was fourteen years old."

Feeling somewhat reassured, Kamanahua wiped the tears from his face and tried to look fierce as he imagined his ancestors of old had. "I will not transverse to Boston! I will tomorrow seek the great ocean!" He gazed down at the beautiful lady to see what effect his words had had on her and saw that her small hands were soothing over the swollen skin of her ankle. All at once he felt as if he were going to cry again. "I am so apology for your hurt!"

"You mean you're sorry."

"Yes. I did not mean to pain you."

If her ankle hadn't hurt so badly, Brianne would have smiled. "Where did you learn to speak English, Kam?"

"The missionaries. They invaded our island. They try to teach me much. They were transversing me to Boston so I could learn more."

"Boston?"

"I ran fast away."

"Where were you when you ran fast away?"

"Where men dig in the earth. Nevada, they named it."

"A mining camp in Nevada?" Brianne guessed.

"The missionaries were trying to convict . . . I mean convert the heathens, and I ran fast away. But"—he cast a puzzled glance around him—"I misplaced the ocean."

Brianne uttered a sound that was somewhere between laughter and pain. "Oh, Kam, you really do have a problem, but then so do I, I'm afraid. We're going to have to help each other."

Puzzlement scored long lines into his face. "I must inquiry you," he said. "You were looking for me, but you do not furnish yourself in black. And your face is not pinched. So you are not a missionary." His eyes became fixed on her hair. The color reminded him of the flaming red lava that sometimes flowed from the volcano of a nearby island whenever Pele decreed. *Pele!* He straightened, proud of himself because he had just figured out who the beautiful lady was. "You must be a *goddess* sent to help me!"

"I am not a goddess, Kam, and I was not looking for you. I am looking for my brother. Do you think the missionaries you ran away from are after you?"

With emphatic energy he nodded his head up and down. "Most assertedly."

Brianne sighed. "All right. Don't worry. I'll help you."

"Do you have the power to protect me from the missionaries?"

"I will protect you, Kam, but first we've got to get back to town. You've got to lift me up on my horse. Can you do that?"

"Most assertedly."

"And then you can get up behind me."

Kamanahua didn't want to warn the four-legged animal he was going to look at it, so he turned his head very, very slowly toward it and whispered, "Will he move?"

"We can't get back to town unless he does."

"I will tread beside you," he said a little louder since he was no longer looking toward the animal.

"That's nonsense. You'll ride behind me."

"But I have never before climbed atop a four-legged animal."

"I'll explain, step by step."

"You are most assertedly a goddess!"

7

People swarmed out of the stores and businesses to look with amazement as Brianne came riding into town late that afternoon with Kamanahua perched loftily behind her. Brianne was certain that her activities the last few days and the people she had brought back to town with her had caused a great deal of speculation, some of it decidedly unpleasant, she suspected, but she couldn't find it in herself to be concerned.

Relief was the only emotion she felt as she reined Dancer to a stop in front of the hotel. The trip back to town had been excruciating for her. With each step that Dancer had taken, pain had throbbed in her ankle and radiated up her leg.

A quick glimpse toward the hotel had told her that Sloan was once again sitting on the porch. Deliberately she avoided looking at him. What was the use? She knew his face would be set with that gravestone hardness she had come to expect and that his eyes would be mocking. And she knew he would once again be thinking she had done something wrong by bringing yet another person back to town with her.

"Kam, you get off first."

"I will now fall down," he announced grandly, and proceeded to do just that, toppling sideways to the ground, his great body hitting the dirt with a thud. He scrambled to his feet and looked to Brianne for approval.

She smiled at him and held out her arms. "You'll have to carry me into the hotel."

"I think not," Sloan said, suddenly at her side. Before she knew what was happening, he had her off the horse and in his arms.

"Sloan, I don't *want* you to carry me."

"So shoot me."

He strode with her into the hotel, and Kamanahua, with an uneasy look over his shoulder, scurried after them.

"Miss Delaney! What on earth happened?"

"I had a minor accident, Mrs. Potter. Nothing serious."

Remembering how he had caused the beautiful goddess to hurt herself, Kamanahua was filled with remorse and shame. "Auwe! Auwe!"

Held high in Sloan's strong arms against the warmth of his muscular body, Brianne had momentarily forgotten her new charge. "Oh, Mrs. Potter, this is Kam. He'll need a room."

Mrs. Potter's face showed outrage and shock. "Miss Delaney, surely you can't expect me to house this . . . this half-clothed savage beneath my roof!"

The woman had a pinched face, Kamanahua noted, and stern eyes. And she was upset because he didn't furnish himself from head to toe with clothes that suffocated the body. Kamanahua didn't want to get anywhere near the man with the hard face and the grim eyes, but as the man was holding Brianne, and Brianne had said she would protect him, he had no choice. He sidled over to Sloan and whispered, "That lady is a missionary."

"No, she's not, Kam," Brianne hastened to reassure him. "There are no missionaries in Chango, not that the town couldn't use a few, I'm sure." It was going to be extremely difficult to control the situation, she thought, when her ankle was shrieking with pain and her body was having to cope with the sensations aroused by being held within the circle of Sloan's arms. "Mrs. Potter, Kam is a royal Hawaiian. His father is a king. That makes him a prince. How many hotels can boast that they've had a prince as a guest? I know you'll want to do everything you can to make Kam comfortable."

Mrs. Potter eyed Kamanahua with doubt. She certainly wouldn't want to turn away a prince, but to her he still looked like a savage. And he was so big! Still, he was definitely a foreigner, so she supposed he could be some sort of prince. "What kind of necklace is he wearing?"

Brianne had been trying to decide that for herself.

"Shark's teeth," Kamanahua informed with obvious pride. "I am great fisherman with my spear!"

Mrs. Potter gave a sigh of relief that the teeth weren't human. "Well . . . I guess I could give him a room on the third floor." She wondered if she should curtsy.

"I will sleep with Brianne," Kamanahua announced, having no intention of being separated from the goddess who was going to protect him from the dreaded pinch-faced missionaries.

Mrs. Potter's hand flew to her breast in alarm, and Sloan's arms tightened painfully around Brianne.

"He doesn't mean that," Brianne said quickly. "He just has a little trouble with the English language. And a third-floor room is not acceptable. I know you must have several vacancies on the second floor, and that's where he'll stay."

Mrs. Potter opened her mouth, but Brianne never found out what she was going to say, because Sloan suddenly said, "Enough! Send someone for the doctor immediately. Miss Delaney will be in her room."

"I don't need a doctor! I'm sure it's only sprained."

"Auwe," Kamanahua moaned softly. "I am so apology."

"You've really done it this time, Brianne," Sloan muttered, and started up the stairs with her.

A warm golden glow pooled out from the kerosene lamp on the table beside the bed. Propped up against a mound of pillows, Brianne eyed her ankle with disgust. Just as she had suspected, the doctor had pronounced her injury a sprain, wrapped it with strips of cloth, elevated it on two folded quilts, and told her she had to stay off it for several days.

Sloan had left as soon as the doctor had seen her, and had not returned, but her three charges had been harder to get rid of.

After tactfully declining Phineas's offer of a bottle of

Tooley's Miracle Restorative to use as liniment on her ankle, she had reluctantly dispatched him to the telegraph office to send a telegram to Killara for her, informing Shamus of Patrick's disappearance.

Then there was Kamanahua. It had taken a lot of talking, but she had finally convinced him that he must spend the night in the room down the hall and that no missionaries would bother him. Of course he had insisted that he carry her to inspect the room, just to make sure.

She found the room to be somewhat plainer than her own, but nice nevertheless. The bedstead was made of iron that had been painted white, with the tall headboard made up of straight iron spindles that rose a good eight feet toward the ceiling and were crowned by finials. Even though Kamanahua's eyes had lit up at the sight of the bed, Brianne wasn't convinced he would actually sleep in it.

Henrietta, for her part, had fussed over her until Brianne had thought she would scream, but after bringing her dinner on a tray and helping her into her nightgown, Henrietta had at last retired to her own room.

And now she was finally alone. Brianne shut her eyes, gave thanks, then turned her thoughts to Patrick. She had done all she could, she told herself, but she felt no better for the assurance. As long as he was missing, half of her was also missing.

She prayed he wasn't hurt and that whoever had him would treat him kindly. It was intolerable to her to think that Patrick was suffering in any way. But it had been four days since his disappearance, and there had been no word from the kidnappers, nor had she come across any clue that might lead her to him.

She was frightened. She desperately needed to keep telling herself that Patrick was all right. Brought up to face adversity as she had been, she had to admit that it didn't look good for him. Still, something in her refused to accept that he wouldn't be found. *There had to be something she could do!*

"Are you in pain?"

Brianne's eyes flew open to find Sloan standing at the foot of her bed. "How did you get in here?"

"Don't worry. No one saw me, and you didn't answer my question."

"No, I'm not in any pain."

He shoved his hands into the pockets of his trousers. "To answer your question, I came in through the door."

"But I didn't hear you."

"Maybe you were dozing."

"I wasn't asleep. You just move quietly, *too* quietly. You don't move like a normal person."

"If you say so," he murmured, his eyes wandering over her, noting the way her mass of shining, long hair had been restrained by a green ribbon tied around her head. The color of the ribbon matched the ribbons on her gown. Desire came up in him so fast, he was unable to check it. It made him angry. "An old maid schoolteacher and a snake oil salesman were bad enough, Brianne, but a half-naked man is too much!"

"Oh, for heaven's sake! Kam is just a frightened boy. From the story he told me on the way into town, I gather that he is from one of the outer islands of Hawaii that the missionaries have just recently decided to show some interest in. They want his father, the king, to sign over his land to them, and in hopes of influencing the king, they chose his son, Kam, to attend a missionary school in Boston. He managed to elude them somewhere around Nevada, and he's been wandering around ever since, lost and afraid."

"That's a very touching story, Brianne. Real touching. Just like the stories that the schoolteacher and the snake oil salesman told you. I'm quite sure that a very irate husband is after Henrietta, no telling how many missionaries are after your Kam, and, if I don't miss my guess, your salesman is on the run from someone too."

"You're probably right."

"What are you going to do, Brianne, when all these people show up?"

"I'll think of something."

Sloan shook his head in disgust. "It wouldn't matter to you if the whole United States Army were after them, would it?"

Crossing her arms, she glared at him.

He wanted to shake her. No, he wanted to kiss her. "So you've taken them in and made their problems your own." He paused, and his golden eyes were hard and hot at the same time. "What would you do for me, I wonder, if I told you a touching story?"

"Tell me a touching story and find out."

His lips compressed into a rigid, thin line, and he swiveled away to walk to the window. He pushed the lace curtain aside and stared into the blackness.

There was no getting around it. When he had seen her riding up with that huge Hawaiian behind her and in obvious pain, he had experienced fear and fury. Because he couldn't abide the fear, he had let the fury rule. It was a much safer emotion, and one with which he could deal with infinite ease. Even now, after she had been seen to by the doctor and was safe in her bed, he couldn't understand the fear he felt for her.

David had been the last person for whom he had felt fear. Worrying over someone else was so unlike him. Being totally ruthless and selfish, now, *that* was in character for him. *That* he could be comfortable with.

"What are you going to do about finding Patrick?" he asked.

"I've had a telegram sent to my grandfather."

"So, in about two weeks, all the help in the world is going to come thundering into town."

She eyed his rigid back and wondered what he was up to. "That's right."

He let the curtain fall back into place, then brought his hand up to stroke the pads of his fingers over the patterned lace. "What are you going to do in the meantime?"

"I can't do much of anything for now."

He was silent for a moment. "There is one thing you can do."

"What?"

"You can ask me to look for your brother."

Surprise momentarily robbed Brianne of words. He swung around to face her and raised one black brow, prompting Brianne to finally speak. "You'd help me?"

"On condition."

She might have known. "What sort of condition?" she asked warily.

"I will search for your brother, if, when I find him, you will let me take you to bed."

She was stunned. "What did you say?"

"I'm offering you a deal, Brianne, plain and simple. If I find your brother, you come to bed with me. If I don't, you're off the hook."

"Why are you doing this?"

"I think you know."

Yes, she knew. "You want me."

"I want you," he agreed, both his face and voice expressionless.

Brianne felt helpless. Sloan was offering to find Patrick, something she wanted more than anything, but he was asking an exorbitant price.

The idea of Sloan taking her to bed brought forth emotions that bubbled and frothed like water rushing from an underground spring to the surface. The emotions were turbulent . . . and tantalizing . . . and she didn't know how to deal with them. Sloan was a dangerous man, totally without scruples, yet he excited her as no other ever had. What would it be like, she wondered, to be made love to by such a man?

Could she agree to his deal? Could she not?

He thought he would use her, but two could play that game. The Delaneys lived by their own complicated code of honor, but all the complications could be distilled down to two words: Delaneys first.

What was important here was Patrick. Once he was

found, she could find a way to get out of her end of the deal.

"All right, Sloan. I agree."

His jaw clenched; a muscle jumped in his cheek. "There's just one thing."

"What?"

"I'll need a sign of good faith on your part."

"I don't understand."

"A sign of good faith that will reassure me that once I find Patrick, you'll live up to your end of the bargain."

Had she been that easy to read? she wondered, appalled. "What do you have in mind?" she asked evenly.

"For you to submit to whatever I ask of you, short of actually making love, of course."

Brianne's heart nearly leapt out of her rib cage. What Sloan was asking was absolutely outrageous.

And totally exciting.

And she understood why he was doing it. The word *trust* wasn't in the vocabulary of a man like Sloan, so he was hedging his bet.

For her, agreeing would be a risk, a gamble. Could she handle it? Before the question had time to simmer in her brain, she decided she could. What was the harm of giving a little to gain a lot?

When she lifted her head she saw the golden eyes that had the capability of freezing a person's bones. Before her courage deserted her, she murmured, "All right, Sloan. But we'll have to be discreet."

"I told you. No one saw me come in."

Nodding, she folded and unfolded the edge of the crocheted coverlet. "When will you start looking for Patrick?"

"In the morning."

"Good."

"Tonight, though, I'll want my first sign of good faith."

He had seen emeralds that contained less fire, Sloan decided, noting the reaction that flared in her green eyes. She was definitely angry about having to give in to his condition, but he wasn't bothered. He was confident that without much effort that same angry fire could be turned to passionate fire.

"Untie the bows on your gown."

"What?"

"Untie the bows on your gown, Brianne."

Stubbornly, she held Sloan's gaze as her hand went to the top bow, grasped an end of the ribbon, and pulled. Slowly, her hand lowered down the front of her gown, untying bow after bow until they had all been untied. Then she dropped her hand to the quilt and looked down at it. When had her hand started to tremble? she wondered.

"Now part the gown."

Her gaze flew back to him.

"Pull the edges of your gown all the way back so that I can see your breasts. Every bit of them. I don't want any portion of them covered."

"I—I don't know if I can."

"Do it."

Determined not to falter, she did as he asked.

Sloan let out a long, silent breath. Lord, but she was beautiful. Her breasts were just as he remembered from last night—high, full, and perfectly shaped. Before he could check himself, he said what he was thinking. "You're beautiful."

Brianne started with surprise at his words. Other men had told her she was beautiful, and she had been left unaffected. But for some reason, when Sloan spoke the words, pleasure flooded through her body, and she had to acknowledge that the man had an extraordinary effect on her. He wasn't touching her; he wasn't even standing beside her. But his golden stare was glittering with a passion that was intensely predatory . . . and thrilling. Beneath that stare her breasts began to ache and her nipples began to tighten.

As the rose-colored aureoles of her breasts puckered, and her nipples hardened to enticingly stiff points, Sloan felt heat rush to his loins, where it concentrated, thickening the shaft of his manhood so that it pushed against the confines of his trousers.

Without haste he walked to the side of the bed and sat down. Lifting his hand, he placed the tips of his fingers against the sides of her neck. Gently, he stroked the length of her neck and back again. "You're a virgin, aren't you?"

Because of his touch, because of his nearness, she could barely breathe. But she couldn't let him know how much his touch and the sound of the soft huskiness in his voice could penetrate her control. "Yes."

"It should make a difference. It should make me back away. You're the type of woman who should feel a man inside her for the first time only on her wedding night." He paused to let his fingertips rest on the rapidly beating pulse at the base of her throat. "When I first met you, it mattered."

Brianne had lost command of the rise and fall of her breasts as air rushed in and out of her lungs. "But suddenly it doesn't?"

"It hasn't been sudden, redhead." Casually, he trailed his fingers downward, over the slope of her breast, until they reached the velvety softness of the aureole. "Not suddenly." The pad of one finger began to circle her nipple, and his eyes watched intently as the nipple stiffened even more.

Brianne grabbed his wrist, wanting to push his hand away from her. She tried, but the only effect her action had on him was to make him raise his gaze away from the throbbing tip of her breast and back to her face. And he continued the insidious circular motion of his finger.

Brianne stifled a moan. Heat was coiling through her insides, tying fiery knots in her lower abdomen, making a dampness seep between her legs.

"Your virginity makes things more difficult, of course," he said, his voice low. "It would be so much easier if you were like Janice over at Lucky's, willing to spread your legs and let me enter you whenever I asked."

Without giving her any warning, he closed his thumb and forefinger over the erect crest and began rolling it back and forth. This time Brianne couldn't stop the moan that escaped her lips.

Without ceasing the manipulation of her nipple, he bent his head and pressed his lips against the side of her throat. "But that's all right," he whispered. "I don't mind. It's more entertaining this way. And I'll still get what I want in the end."

Brianne realized she continued to hold his wrist in a hard grip. She released it just as his lips began sliding down the fullness of her breast. "You're an unscrupulous bastard!" she managed to say before he drew the tormented point into his mouth. "A bastard," she repeated with a gasping breath, and tangled her hands in the dark silkiness of his hair.

He sucked hard while his hand firmly cupped her other breast. Sloan loved the feel of her nipple in his mouth, so tight, so distended, so sweet.

Incredible sensations washed through him—hunger, lust, desire. Normal emotions when a man had a woman's breast in his mouth, surely, but what about the life he felt so strongly from her?

That wasn't normal. Could it be that he was trying to feed from her? Was he trying to draw the fullness of the life within her into himself? The thought disturbed him, but he continued sucking at her breast, because he knew, incredibly, that somehow it was working. He could feel his blood singing with what he was absorbing from her.

Worrying the distended nipple with his tongue, then pulling on it again with his mouth, he wondered what would happen if he didn't stop feeding at her breast? If he just continued on and on? Could it be possible that Brianne's energy and spirit were the antidote he needed against the hatred that he felt for Wes?

Wes? How had Brianne and Wes become entangled in his mind? He had no idea. He loved the feel and the taste of her so much, it was hard for him to question himself. And when he realized it, he forced himself to reach for his control.

Pulling his mouth away, he stared down at her. Her chest was rising and falling every bit as rapidly as his. Her breasts appeared swollen, and her taut, reddened nipples seemed to quiver under his gaze. God, but it was hard not to lower his mouth back to her. But he made himself continue his survey. He wanted to see her eyes. Ah, yes. The anger was still there, but behind the anger was the passion. She was angry that she was being forced into submitting to him, but she was also angry that she was responding to him. Her passion made him happy.

Her lips were parted, ready to be kissed—to his mind *asking* to be kissed again. Briefly he complied, crushing his mouth down to hers, thrusting his tongue in and out of her mouth in a rhythm he would soon use to thrust in and out of her body.

Because he felt himself beginning to slip back toward the fire and life he found in her, he abruptly ended the kiss and gained immense satisfaction when he heard Brianne utter a small cry of frustration.

He brushed a knuckle down the side of her cheek. "Don't worry, redhead," he whispered. "I'll be back tomorrow night after everyone else has gone to bed."

She jerked away from his touch. "You had better find Patrick!"

"I will. Sooner or later. In the meantime, I want you to stay right here in your room, with that ankle up."

She yanked her gown into place. "You may control my actions late at night, but during the day you have no say."

He fingered a long red strand of hair away from her face. "You're going to be surprised what passion can make a person do, Brianne. Soon I won't even have to ask. Soon you'll do as I want without thinking."

"I may know very little about passion, but I do know myself. And I could never be made to do something I don't want to do."

"But that's the point, redhead. You *will* want. Oh, how you will want."

8

The minute Sloan stepped out on the porch just before dawn the next morning, he knew Wes McCord had returned. Lights blazed from the windows of McCord Enterprises. Outside the office, men milled about. Inside the office, he could see a silhouette of a man against the shade.

The urge to rush across the street and burst into the office with gun blazing was almost overwhelming. He closed his eyes, willing the powerful impulse to pass.

Since he had been in Chango, an idea had begun to form. He was pretty sure he knew what Wes was up to; he just needed to be certain he was right. With the proof, he could make Wes suffer a lot of pain. And then, when he judged that Wes had suffered enough, he would kill him. As it happened, getting the proof he needed would fit nicely into his deal with Brianne to look for her brother.

Feeling the murderous desire recede, he opened his eyes and stared across the street. He would choose the time and the place of their first confrontation. This time *he* would be the one to have control of the situation.

Deciding that there was no sense in alerting Wes to his presence before he was good and ready, he took the back route to the stable and soon was on his way out of town. He had questioned Brianne on the paths she had taken and the area she had searched, so he carefully chose a different direction. He reasoned that if, after a few days, he didn't find either Patrick or the proof he needed to use against Wes, he would then begin to retrace Brianne's trails.

But it didn't come to that, because early in the afternoon he came upon a small hut. Smoke was curling out of the chimney, but there were no horses in sight. He dismounted in a stand of trees and tethered his horse.

Taking his time, he studied the small adobe building and the layout of the land around it. The hut was simply built and probably contained no more than two rooms, he decided. A garden of sorts grew to one side, but from the looks of it, the soil was producing as many weeds as it was vegetables. A plow had been abandoned in a half-finished furrow, its metal rusted.

The smoke puzzled him. There wasn't any other sign of activity, not even any stock grazing near the place. He supposed a family of settlers could be living in the hut, but that seemed doubtful.

The fifty yards between the stand of trees where he was and the hut offered no real cover. He would just have to take his chances. Grimly, he drew his revolver, cocked it, and cautiously began to advance.

Reaching the building without incident, he flattened his body against the cool adobe and listened.

No gunfire greeted him, but he could hear voices. With his back to the hut so that he could cover himself from three sides, he slid along the wall until he reached one of the two windows. Angling his head over his right shoulder, he peered through the dirty pane of glass.

Four men were sitting around a table playing cards. Three of the men he recognized as those he had seen in Lucky's. He could see only the back of the fourth man, but it was Patrick Delaney all right. He couldn't mistake that chestnut hair. He ducked beneath the window and crept to the porch.

A strong kick to the door had it breaking away from its rusty hinges, and it went crashing down amid a billow of dust. Sloan rushed in. All four men surged to their feet, cards went flying, and the three men from the saloon immediately raised their hands at the sight of Sloan's gun.

The taller one, his eyes big with alarm, pointed at Patrick. "He's *our* prisoner."

"Yeah," the other two chorused, all the while keeping their hands high.

"Delaney, are you all right?" Sloan asked without taking his eyes off the three men.

"Yeah, I'm fine, and there's no need for the gun."

Sloan heard the humor in Patrick's voice and cut his eyes to him. "What the hell's going on? We thought you'd been kidnapped."

"He has been!" one of the three men insisted with such a petulant tone that Sloan's attention was brought back to them. All three dutifully kept their hands in the air.

The tall one spoke up again. "I *told* you, he's *our* prisoner!"

"We're gonna get money for him," another one said.

"What you're going to get is more trouble than you ever thought possible if I don't find out what's going on in the next ten seconds."

All three started talking at once.

"It wasn't never our intention to cause no harm!"

"All we wanted was the money!"

"Farmin's hard work!"

"I told them we shouldn't ask for so much money!"

Patrick put two fingers to his mouth and let out a shrill whistle. Everyone turned toward him. "I think it would be better if I told Mr. Lassiter the story, don't you?"

All three nodded. "Whatever you say, Mr. Delaney."

Patrick gave Sloan a wry smile. "Lassiter, I think it's time you formally met the Grimes brothers. Odis, Hannibal, and Lester. Fellows, this is Mr. Sloan Lassiter."

"Pleased to meetcha," the three mumbled.

"Now, why don't we all sit down," Patrick suggested, "and Lassiter, you can tell me how it is that you're here."

Sloan kept his gun pointed toward the three brothers. "You and I can sit down, but those three are going to stay where they are, with their hands reaching for the ceiling, until I understand what in the hell is happening here."

Patrick glanced at the Grimes brothers. "That sounds reasonable, wouldn't you say, fellows?"

They nodded, their eyes on the gun.

"Would ya like a cup of coffee?"

Odis's timidly spoken question earned him a hard look from Sloan. He chose a chair where he could keep the three men under his scrutiny. "To answer your question, Delaney, I'm here because your sister was under the impression you needed rescuing."

Patrick's expression turned anxious. "Is she hurt? Sick? What's happened to her?"

"Nothing serious. She's sprained her ankle. She was out looking for you yesterday afternoon, when her horse shied, and she fell off. The doctor says she just needs to stay off the ankle for a while." He cast Patrick a curious look. "Why did you think something had happened to Brianne?"

A grin returned to Patrick's face. "Because it's not like Brianne to send a hired gun to do her work."

"Ah . . . of course." Now that he knew Brianne, her brother's statement made perfect sense to him. "You're sure she's all right?"

"She's been worried sick about you. She was determined she'd find you herself, but after she sprained her ankle, she telegraphed your grandfather."

Patrick grimaced. "I was afraid that would happen."

"Rest assured, Brianne sent the telegram only when everything else had failed."

Patrick's wide-set brown eyes thoughtfully studied the man across the table from him. "And then she sent you out looking for me."

"As it happened, searching for you caused me no inconvenience."

"I see. Evidently you and Brianne have gotten to know each other pretty well since I've been gone. Brianne would never have asked you otherwise."

Sloan's answer told Patrick nothing.

"She didn't ask me. I volunteered."

Short, stocky Hannibal dared to gesture toward Patrick. "His uncle Joshua once fired us from a cattle drive. And all I did was shoot at a jackrabbit."

"He missed," Patrick said, "but managed to stampede the cattle."

"Well, hell, I was just tired of eatin' beans," Hannibal whined.

Sloan raised his gun, expertly sighting it between Hannibal's eyes. "Who said you could talk?"

Lester, equally short and stocky as his brother, went to his aid. "He didn't mean nuttin' by it, honest."

Sloan shifted the blue-steel barrel of the gun to Lester. "Delaney, I think you'd better start explaining."

"They did kidnap me, it's true. They paid off that little piece I was having a good time with, and knocked me unconscious with ether they stole from the dentist."

Obviously feeling further information was called for, Odis cut in. "The dentist also gives a mighty fine haircut."

The gun shifted toward Odis, causing the man's Adam's apple to bob up and down as he swallowed hard.

"At any rate," Patrick continued, "they threw me over my horse—"

"We didn't steal that horse!" Hannibal said in a panic. "Mr. Delaney was ridin' him. We ain't gonna be hung for no horse thief!"

Patrick rolled his eyes at their reasoning, but carried on with his story. "I gather they had a hard time finding their way out of town—"

"That t'weren't our fault neither!" Lester insisted. "It t'were rainin' and, well, we was kinda high on them ether fumes."

Sloan's roar filled the cabin. "One more word out of any of you, and parts of your bodies will be found in four counties."

The three brothers inhaled sharply and moaned in unison.

A big grin on his face, Patrick shook his head. "Well, I guess there was a lot of to-ing and fro-ing before they eventually got me here. When I woke up, I was mad as hell and sick as a dog for a long time. I threw up from the effects of the ether and, in sympathy, so did Hannibal."

"I couldn't stand to see him sufferin' like that. 'Sides, I've got me a weak tummy," Hannibal lamented, then immediately regretted it, because Sloan's cold eyes sliced toward him.

"I've also had a hell of a headache the last few days. But during this time I've come to realize two things," Patrick continued. "One, they're completely incompetent."

Odis opened his mouth to protest, but one look at Sloan quickly made him change his mind. "And two, they are also essentially decent men."

The three brothers beamed.

Sloan laid his gun on the table and rubbed his forehead. "So, given all this, why haven't you come back to town?"

"Because in all the excitement one of them forgot to fasten the gate to the corral, and the horses ran away."

Sloan stared at Patrick in disbelief. Patrick shrugged.

Odis said, "They'll come back. They always do sooner or later."

Lester and Hannibal nodded their emphatic agreement.

"The other thing is—" Patrick hesitated, then glanced at the three brothers. "Wait outside, fellows, will you?"

Deep furrows formed in Hannibal's forehead as he considered their predicament. "Can we put down our hands if we go outside?"

"Yeah," Lester said, "all my blood's rushin' to my elbows. I can feel it!"

"You can put your hands down."

Odis hesitated and cast a worried look at Patrick. "You promise you won't escape?"

"I promise."

"Well, I guess that's all right then."

After the brothers had left, Patrick sighed. "You see how they are. They're bungling fools. They've done everything from punch cows to mine for gold and have been complete failures at everything they've tried. They thought they'd farm this place, but they quickly found out that farming is hard work."

"So they decided to kidnap you," Sloan said, still having trouble with the logic of the situation.

"Because they had worked for the family, however short a period of time that was, they had gotten some idea of our financial situation. When they heard my name, they thought they could make some easy money. I can handle them, of course. My own concern in all this has been Brianne. I knew she'd be worried, and I also knew she'd set out to look for me on her own."

"She did both of those things."

Patrick nodded, then held out his hand. "I want to thank you for helping her."

Sloan took his hand but didn't say anything.

"Since I'm feeling better, I had planned on walking back to town tomorrow, but now I'd appreciate it if you would tell Brianne that I'm fine, and I'll see her soon."

"You're going to *stay* here?"

"Until the horses come back. I can't take the chance that my grandfather and my uncles will get hold of these three. I have to protect them."

"What is it with you Delaneys? You seem to have an uncontrollable urge to help people."

"Maybe we understand the underdog."

Irritated, Sloan jabbed his index finger at Patrick. "And maybe you trust too easily."

"Now, *that* we don't." Patrick recalled Brianne's initial distrust of Sloan and wondered if that had changed. After all, the man was helping her. Then he remembered his advice to her to avoid scratching him. Somehow he doubted that she had paid any heed. "Rest assured, no one takes advantage of us. We learned at an early age the difference between sheep and wolves. If we hadn't, we wouldn't have survived." He let that sink in, then asked, "What's Brianne been up to anyway?"

Sloan shook his head. "She seems to collect people."

"Ah." Patrick needed no further explanation. "Anyway, when the horses return, we'll come back into town."

Because Sloan's mind immediately conjured up a picture of the Grimes brothers in the Duke Hotel, his next words were weighted with sarcasm. "Mrs. Potter is going to be thrilled."

Inside Nilsen's Emporium, the aromas of newly dyed cloth and the leather of boots, belts, and bridles mingled with the scents of tea and spices bundled in small burlap bags. Coffee beans, flour, and sugar nearly overflowed from their barrels. Off to one side, two kegs held dark, rich molasses; another held pickles.

On one long wall an assortment of ready-made clothes hung from a rack. Hams, sausages, and an array of cooking pots hung from hooks imbedded into the ceiling. In the center of the store, stood an unlit potbellied stove with chairs arranged around it.

Anna was sitting in one of the chairs holding the newborn baby daughter of Rebecca Hunter. "She's just adorable, Rebecca. You and Keith must be so proud."

"We try not to let it show, but yes, we are. Keith wanted a son, but when he saw little Deborah he changed fast. She immediately became his pride and joy. Besides, I figure next time he'll get his boy."

Anna gently smiled at the baby girl in her arms. She could only imagine the happiness of a husband and wife, very much in love, creating a new life. She tried to push back the envy that insisted on creeping into her mind, but failed. She didn't believe that her life could ever work out so she would know the sort of happiness Rebecca felt. And that sense of loss was a pain that throbbed constantly deep within her.

Handing the baby back to her mother, Anna caught the sound of an old Swedish folksong that her father was humming in the back room as he moved about, checking the new shipment of goods that had just arrived. The sound soothed her pain. His contentment and peace were worth any price.

"I must be going," Rebecca said. "This is the first time I've been out since Deborah was born. I still tire easily."

"I understand. What about your order?"

"Keith will be in later on to pick it up." Rebecca turned toward the door, then let out a loud gasp.

The doorway was being blocked by a half-naked, barefoot giant who held a young woman in his arms.

"Don't be afraid," Brianne said, hastening to reassure the women.

Anna took a few steps forward. "Are you all right, Miss Delaney?"

"Perfectly."

"Move, you big oaf!" Henrietta ordered from behind Kamanahua, treating him much as she would one of her students. "Move! I need to see if there are some chairs so we can make Brianne comfortable."

Kamanahua did as he was bid and lumbered into the store. Behind him came Henrietta, then Phineas.

"Poor child, she's sprained her ankle and she's not supposed to walk on it for a few days," Henrietta explained to the two open-mouthed women as she began rearranging the chairs.

"Isn't it lucky I have Kam?" Brianne asked sunnily from her perch in his mammoth arms.

"Brianne is a goddess," Kamanahua said. "I serve her. She protects me."

"There." Henrietta smiled with satisfaction at the two chairs she had arranged, seat to seat. "Put her down here, Kam, and mind, be careful now. That's right, and put her foot up on the second chair. Good, that's perfect."

"Would you like a pillow for your ankle, Miss Delaney?" Anna asked, watching with understanding as Rebecca Hunter skirted the group and headed for the door, all the while holding her baby tightly to her breast.

"That would be nice, and please, call me Brianne. It looks like I'll be in Chango for a while, so we'll have the opportunity to become friends."

When Anna came back with the pillow and had situated it under her ankle, Brianne said, "Anna, I'd like to introduce my friends to you. This is Miss Henrietta Jones, a schoolteacher on her way back east."

"That's right, Jones!" Henrietta's eyes held the militant gleam that seemed to appear whenever she thought of the man she had left unconscious in a San Francisco hotel room. "And how do you do?"

"And this is Mr. Phineas Tooley, a patented medicine salesman."

Phineas stepped up and took Anna's limp hand. "Charmed, dear lady, I'm sure. I can't help but notice that your shelves are remarkably bare of any patented medicines. Perhaps later you would have a moment for me to tell you of my Tooley's Miracle Restorative. It is guaranteed to cure sixty different disorders, including pleurisy, inflammation of the lungs, female debility, and other irregularities."

"That's very interesting," Anna managed, "but our doctor here in town sells all the patented medicines."

"I see." Phineas rubbed his chin. "Well, then perhaps you could tell me if there've been any strangers in town of late."

Humor warmed Anna's eyes. "There have been a lot of strangers since Miss Delaney came to town."

Brianne smiled, while noting the fact that she must remember to ask Phineas to tell her the rest of his story. "You're to call me Brianne, remember? Now I have just one more person to introduce." She pointed to Kamanahua, who had taken up position beside her, his bare feet solidly planted on the plank floor, his arms crossed over his massive chest. "This is Kam. He's a royal Hawaiian prince, isn't that interesting?"

"Very," Anna said, her dimples showing.

"Kam will need several shirts," Brianne went on.

"Evil vapors cannot escape if you furnish your body with too many clothes," Kamanahua announced.

Brianne stretched around and looked up at her self-appointed bodyguard. "Believe me, I would not let you wear something that wouldn't allow evil vapors to escape."

Anna cleared her throat. "I'm afraid we have nothing that will fit Kam, but I can give you the name of a good dressmaker in town. If he would like, Kam can pick out some material. It's over there." She pointed toward the bolts of cloth stacked on a table.

"I will not depart Brianne," Kamanahua said stubbornly.

"We'll pick it out later," Brianne decided, and turned to Henrietta. "Have you made out your list?"

"Yes." The older woman pulled out a small sheet of paper from her pocket. "I'll need a comb and a brush. Perhaps a skirt and a blouse, something serviceable." She raised her eyes from the list and let her gaze run appraisingly over the rack of ready-made clothes. She nodded, satisfied. "It looks as though you have a nice assortment."

"Choose several skirts and blouses, Henrietta. I insist. And you'll want some lotion, perhaps a nice bottle of rosewater."

Henrietta's stern features softened. "You are so good, Brianne." She leaned down and whispered. "What about the more delicate of ladies apparel? You know . . ."

Brianne smiled. "Just tell Anna what you need."

At that moment a short man who showed the

beginnings of a paunch came bustling out of the back room. What greeted his sight brought him up short. "My, my, vhat have ve here?"

Anna turned. "Papa, this is Miss Brianne Delaney. She and her friends are doing a little shopping this afternoon. Miss Delaney, Miss Jones, Mr. Tooley, Kam, this is my father, Mr. Nilsen."

Faced with the somewhat unusual assemblage, Lars Nilsen rubbed his hands together. "Vell, vell . . ."

"How nice that your business is doing so well, Mr. Nilsen. I couldn't be more delighted."

Everyone swiveled to see the newcomer who had spoken.

He was a tall man and extremely well-dressed, Brianne noted. With his light brown hair, pale gray eyes, and pleasant smile, he was very good-looking. But Brianne could feel the hair at the back of her neck prickling a warning.

Anna cleared her throat. Brianne glanced at her, and saw that a cool reserve seemed to have descended over the beautiful woman's manner.

"Good afternoon, Mr. McCord," Anna said. "Was your trip to Washington a pleasant one?"

He swept his hat off. "Yes, it was. Thank you, Miss Nilsen. Mr. Nilsen." He nodded to Anna's father. "I stopped by to see if my special blend of tobacco came in while I was gone."

"Papa?"

Mr. Nilsen threw his daughter a disgruntled look. "Ya. It's in the back, Mr. McCord. I'll get it."

"I'm Wes McCord," the man said, sending a charm-

ing smile around the room, passing over Henrietta
and Phineas, lingering for a moment on Kamanahua,
and finally settling on Brianne. "I don't believe I've
had the pleasure."

Reluctantly, it seemed to Brianne, Anna performed
the introductions. "This is Miss Delaney, Miss Jones,
Mr. Tooley, and Kam."

Wes McCord looked with interest at the new people.
"Are you planning to settle here in Chango?"

"No," Brianne answered for herself and her friends.
She still wasn't sure what it was about the man that
bothered her, but Malvina had drilled manners into
her, so she tried to be pleasant. "What was intended to
be a brief visit has been extended."

"How lucky for Chango," Wes murmured.

"Here's your tobacco, Mr. McCord. Vill you be
needing any more of the fixings?"

"I don't think so. Not today, at any rate." He
scooped the pouch off the counter. "Can you add this
to my account please, Mr. Nilsen?"

Anna's father nodded brusquely. "Ya."

Wes's smile encompassed everyone in the store.
"Good day."

There was silence until he left, then Anna's father
exploded. "I do not like that man!"

"Now, Papa," Anna soothed. "You mustn't say
things like that."

"I know that he is supposed to be doing a lot for this
town, but . . . *he is a bad man!*"

Anna's troubled gaze went to the wide front window through which she could see Wesley McCord

crossing the street to the other side. "He may be a bad man, Papa, but there's nothing we can do about it. He's too powerful."

"Hmph!"

"Now, Papa, I don't want you to distress yourself. Why don't you go upstairs and have a nice cup of tea? I'll wait on Miss Delaney and her friends."

Nodding his agreement, Mr. Nilsen shuffled out.

Anna turned to Brianne, a bright smile fixed on her face. "Now, where were we?"

9

Clouds obscured the moon, making the path Anna was on so dark she could barely see beyond her next step. But she needed no lamp to guide her way. She knew by heart every inch of the path that ran behind the town, since she made this same trek twice a week.

When she reached the edge of the town, she drew her shawl closer around her shoulders and, as was her habit, paused to look behind her. There was no one to observe her, but she had to be sure.

Turning back, she gazed in front of her and saw it—the house that was her destination. Although she was still some distance away, she could see a light glowing behind drawn shades in two rooms, one on the lower floor, one on the upper. The line of her mouth tightened and she continued on.

Once at the house, she didn't hesitate. She climbed the broad steps to the porch, grasped the brass knob, and opened the door. Inside, her steps led her unerringly down a long entrace hall to the first door on her right. Taking a deep breath, she stepped across the threshold.

Wesley McCord was sitting in a large walnut armchair, a drink in his hand. His head rested against the blue velvet upholstered back, his gray eyes were half closed.

Anna's hands curled into tight fists with such force, her nails cut into her palms. "I was hoping you wouldn't come back from your trip to Washington."

Setting the drink aside, he stood, then crossed the room to her. He lifted a finger and touched it gently to her cheek. "I know," he murmured with a smile, and took her into his arms. "I know."

Minutes later they were upstairs in Wes's bed, naked, and he was moving in and out of Anna, slowly, with great power, and very sure skill.

As always, the lamp beside the bed remained lit. He enjoyed the sight of her long golden hair fanned out over the pillow, and he delighted in seeing her face as his throbbing shaft filled her, eased out of her, then filled her again.

Passion seemed to increase her beauty, making it appear as if she were illuminated from the inside out. *He* did that to her, he thought with satisfaction. *He* could make her cry out with pleasure—even though it was against her will.

Supporting his weight on his elbows, he cradled her face between his hands. "Open your eyes, Anna, my sweet, and tell me how you wished someone had killed me before I could return to you."

Entering, withdrawing, entering, withdrawing— his leisurely, demanding strokes were unceasing and sanity-destroying, Anna thought with despair and deep, deep hunger. Languidly her lids lifted, showing him blue eyes whose color had been deepened and glazed by a potent desire. "I did," she whispered. "I wished you dead."

He chuckled and, at the same time, surged high into her. An involuntary moan came from deep in her throat, making him smile.

"Of all my enemies," he said, his voice soft and thick, "I like you the best."

"I wouldn't . . . be here if"—a soft gasp escaped her lips—"if you weren't blackmailing me."

Feeling her velvet tightness close around him once again, he shuddered. God, how he had missed this! There was nothing like this feeling anywhere else on earth. "Don't expect me to apologize, Anna. I won't."

He nibbled at the fullness of her lower lip, then slid his tongue into the waiting warmth of her mouth. Anna accepted his tongue just as her body accepted his pulsing male hardness every time he pressed into her. She didn't want to, but she couldn't do anything else. The delicate tissue that sheathed him so accommodatingly felt as if it were being seared with each thrust of his fullness. She tossed her head from side to side in a fever of helpless desire. "This is diabolical! I *hate* how you make me feel!"

"Maybe afterward you do, but not now, not while I'm doing this." He groaned, deeply penetrating her, then rotated his hips.

She gave a little cry at the exquisite ripples of pleasure that mounted steadily. Her mind fogged. Unable to help herself, she dug her heels into the bed and arched her hips upward.

"Convince yourself, Anna, that right at this moment you hate this feeling." He gave one hard thrust, reaching to her core, making her burn brilliant and hot.

A cry broke free of her lips. "Oh, God, Wesley! *Again!*"

But he moderated his movements. Sweat broke out over his body as he kept his pace slow and careful, taking both of them to peak after peak, yet always making sure that they slid back down before they could crest. It was a wonderful kind of torment. He had had to do without her for weeks. Now that she was under him, he refused to hurry. Besides, he loved it when she writhed beneath him, wild and out of control. Such a lady at the store during the day; such a wanton in his bed at night.

Stroking his fingers across her damp brow, he soothed her. "My sweet Anna . . . sweet Anna . . . so beautiful . . . so pure."

Just for a moment her mind cleared. "Pure! You took my virginity!"

Possessiveness flared in his eyes. "And God, you were good! You *are* good. Wet! Hot! Tight!" He couldn't hold out much longer.

Anna felt him pull out of her and hover. Her hands reached for his hips and drew him forcefully back into her. She could have withstood violence, but never the careful, exquisite way he went about making love to her. He had studied her body and learned her so well.

"Easy, baby, easy," he urged. "Wait just a little bit longer."

Nails dug into his back. "Wesley, I can't!"

"Yes, you can, my Anna," he crooned, reveling in her desperate need of him, while savoring his command over her at this moment. He slid a shaking hand down to cup her small, rounded breast, and it strained into his palm. "You can wait, because you know how good this is, and because you've missed our lovemaking as much as I have."

"I haven't missed it, and I don't want to wait. I want it *now*!" she cried. "I can't stand it!"

"Shhh. Soon. Soon. I can't end it yet. This is too damned much like paradise! Can you imagine how you feel to me? It's as if your small hand, gloved in a dark, plushly textured material is gripping me tightly." He showered urgent kisses over her face and throat, but always kept moving in and out of her. If someone had walked through the door with a gun and held it to his head, he still couldn't have left her.

He rode her with a powerful rocking motion, expertly finding all the nerve endings inside her, until she felt as if she were going to go up in flames. Wes's lovemaking was like dying of pleasure, but the death went on and on. And God help her, how she craved that death.

In the end Anna frantically grasped the spool-turned spindles of the bed's headboard. Wes's hands slid under her and took hold of her bottom, pulling her hips upward so that he could plunge deeper, and then deeper still. His muscular body contracted as Anna felt her passion soar, and each of them, separately, yet somehow strangely together, reached with their entire being for the blissful, rapturous release.

A long time later, Wes felt Anna stir beside him. "Don't go yet."

"I have to. Papa will be home soon."

"You can tell him you went to see Rebecca Hunter's baby."

"At this time of night? He would never believe me." She eased out of his arms and climbed from the bed. Unconsciously, she sighed at the sight of their clothes heaped haphazardly where they had been dropped earlier.

Wes rearranged the pillows behind him and sat up. Reaching over to the bedside table, he gathered the makings of a cigarette, then noticed that Anna was washing herself.

"If you'll come back over here, I'll do that for you," he said softly.

Color flooded Anna's fair skin, and, embarrassed, she turned away to dress. "Someday someone is going to kill you," she said dully.

"Erase that thought from your mind, Anna." He struck a match and held it to his cigarette, then gazed at her through a veil of smoke. An ironic smile curved his lips. "After all, how could I allow something to happen to me when I have you to look forward to? I rode my horse flat out so I could get here by Thursday night, the night of your father's choir practice."

She buttoned the lace-edged neckline of her camisole, then hesitated. "It would kill my father if you called in his notes of debt. You won't, will you?"

His smile widened, becoming slightly cruel. "I've taught you so much, haven't I? I've taught you pleasure, but I've also taught you to distrust."

"And to lie to the person I love most in the world."

"Lies are nothing, my sweet."

"They are to me."

He exhaled a long stream of smoke. "I know they are. And to answer your question, no, I won't tell him—not as long as you come to me when I ask you to."

Reassured, she slipped her dress over her head and let it settle down around her. Walking around the bed, she sat down with her back to Wes and pulled the entire golden length of her hair forward over her shoulders. "Could you do me up, please?"

He ground out his cigarette and took the two edges of her dress in his hand. "You wear such simple dresses. I wanted to bring you a dozen of the most beautiful ones I could find from Washington."

She glanced over her shoulder at him. "You know I couldn't wear them."

"That's why I didn't bring them to you," he said, and began buttoning her dress. When he got to the last button, he murmured, "Stay with me."

She shifted her position on the bed so that she could look at him. The light from the lamp played over his beautiful brown body, and against her will her eyes strayed downward, past his hair-rough chest, to that part of his body that could so capably drive her to such heights of erotic pleasure. Abruptly she stood up. "I can do the last button." At his dresser she picked up his hairbrush, and with sweeping strokes began to put her hair back into some semblance of order.

Wes looked on, gaining the same pleasure he always did—watching her brush her hair. Although he kept a box of hairpins for her, he had refused to buy her her own hairbrush. He liked the fact that she used his. And after she left him he would go to the brush and find her golden strands. He kept them all and would pull them through his fingers, sometimes until he fell asleep.

She was putting the last hairpin into place when she heard him say, "From now on, find a way to come to me on Monday nights."

Her back stiffened, and she whirled around. "That's impossible! Papa doesn't go out except on Thursday and Saturday nights. You know that!"

"Encourage him to increase his social life. Thursday-night choir practice and Saturday nights playing cards with his friends just isn't enough."

"I can't! I won't!"

"Find a way, Anna," he said very gently.

Her shoulders slumped. "Yes, Wesley."

Sloan stretched out on the velvet sofa in Brianne's room and shut his eyes. On his face he could feel the light breeze that floated in from the open window and knew that it would be gently undulating the apple-green bed draperies behind her head. The green bows on her gown would be tied demurely across her breasts.

Brianne. He wanted to savor her like a gourmet meal. He wanted to drink of all her juices, taste of all her flavors. Even now he could feel the saliva in his mouth begin to flow at the thought of her wonderful breasts, their taste, their feel.

But it was the puzzled expression in Brianne's emerald eyes that kept his own shut.

If he were to tell her he had found her brother, he would most certainly have her tonight. Then he could take her, and keep taking her until neither one of them would be able to move. But at sunup it would all be over. And that was what kept him from telling her that Patrick had been found.

"You're keeping something from me, aren't you?"

Sloan opened his eyes and saw her propped up in bed. "What could I be keeping from you?"

"That you've found Patrick and that he's dead."

A smile slowly curved his lips. "Where is that brave young woman who told me her brother was not dead?"

Brianne threw up a nervous hand. "It's just that he's been gone for so long."

"Five days is not long, Brianne, not in these circumstances. The kidnappers aren't going to harm Patrick. They want the money." At the sight of the hope that sprang into Brianne's eyes, Sloan experienced a twinge of an emotion so strange, it took him a moment to identify it as guilt. He shifted uneasily. It had been many a long year since he'd felt guilty about anything. But he didn't change his decision. Having Brianne to do with as he desired each evening was too great a pleasure.

He stood and walked over to the bed. Sitting beside her, he softly repeated Patrick's words, if not exactly, then in spirit. "Your brother's fine, and you are going to see him soon."

Brianne's smile was weak. "You're right. It's just that it's hard, not being able to do anything for Patrick."

"But you are doing something. You're carrying out

your part of our deal so that I will continue to carry out my part."

Brianne didn't need the reminder of their deal to make a heated surge rush through her. That had happened the minute Sloan had walked into her room. And when he had sat down beside her, the side of his hip pressed against the side of her hip, her skin had begun to quiver with the anticipation of what would come.

"Untie the bows on your gown, Brianne, and from now on don't bother tying them. That will save us a lot of time and trouble."

As she raised her left hand to the top bow, the ruffle at her wrist fell back, exposing part of the scar.

"Wait." Sloan grasped her arm and pushed up the gown's sleeve. "How did this happen?" Bending his head, he studied the puckered white marks that marred the perfection of her skin.

She had been so intent on what would happen after she had finished untying the bows, his question startled her and she blurted out, "A wolf attacked me."

"A wolf! How did it happen? *When* did it happen?"

"It happened years ago, when I was a young girl. One day when I was out riding, I saw this animal caught in a trap. His leg was bloody and exposed to the bone. I thought I saw something in his eyes, like a plea for help."

He uttered an oath, but his fingers were stroking with supreme gentleness back and forth across the scarred surface of her forearm.

Defiantly, she stared into the golden eyes that so

reminded her of the wolf's. "The wolf was accepting my efforts to help him, and it would have been all right, except a distant sound startled him. In his fear, he turned on me." Her voice held sadness as she remembered. "That distant sound was Patrick riding toward me, and he had to shoot the wolf to save me."

"Thank God for your brother."

"If only the wolf had known that he could trust me not to let anyone hurt him."

"You mean like Henrietta, Phineas, and Kam have learned." He shook his head. "I'm surprised you didn't find another needy person to take under your wing while I was gone today."

The disapproval in his voice almost made her smile, and she didn't want to. "The only new person I met today was a man named Wes McCord, and I never saw anyone less needy than he."

Sloan went strangely motionless. When he spoke, the sound of his words reminded Brianne of the growl of the long-ago wounded wolf. "Where did you meet Wes McCord?"

His reaction to her simple comment had Brianne puzzled. "At Nilsen's Emporium. Anna Nilsen introduced us."

"Stay away from him, Brianne."

"Why?"

"Because," he said quite simply, "I'm going to ruin him, and then I'm going to kill him."

Brianne shouldn't have been shocked. All along her intuition had told her that Sloan was an inherently dangerous man. Yet she *was* shocked. She shook the feeling off. "Why?"

"Because fifteen years ago Wes McCord left me and my brother to die on the hellish plains of West Texas."

"But you're alive."

"My brother isn't." In a much softer voice he added, "David was only fourteen years old."

"George's age," Brianne murmured. She understood so much now. Sloan was more like that wolf than she had thought, except Sloan's wounds were on the inside, and they had never healed. Could she take it if, like the wolf, he turned on her? The thought made her uneasy. Sloan meant nothing to her. She was just using him, that was all.

Then she remembered the way the hair at the back of her neck had prickled when she had first seen Wes McCord. He was not a man to be taken lightly. Under any circumstances he would be a formidable opponent, and if Sloan intended to go up against him, Sloan would surely be putting himself in danger.

And she supposed that was why she was shocked. As hard as it was for her to believe, she was actually worried about Sloan's safety.

Unsure of what she wanted to say, she resorted to the mundane. "So you're not from New York after all, you're from Texas."

"My formative years were after David's death. I left Texas and never went back. During the Civil War I was a blockade runner, one of the best. I made a fortune, which I took to New York and doubled and tripled many times over. And now, finally, what I've lived for is about to happen. I'm going to avenge my brother's death."

She fought to keep the dismay she was feeling out of

her voice. "Revenge won't bring your brother back to life."

"No, and it won't bring my own life back to me either. But it doesn't matter, because for now I've found something that at least tricks me into thinking I'm alive." He yanked the ribbons of her bows until they were all undone, then roughly pushed the gown aside. "Your breasts in my mouth as I suck them make me feel as though your life is flowing through my veins."

Brianne went hot and weak. She would have liked to have been able to convince herself that she hadn't been waiting since last night for this moment, but she couldn't.

"Sloan, I'd like to talk some—"

"Not now," he whispered harshly, and grasped both of her breasts, one with each hand. Slowly, he ran his palms around and around them, feeling their identical fullness, weight, and firmness. "Look," he murmured. "I haven't even touched your nipples yet, but they are already pointing for me."

Brianne did look down and saw that the tips of her breasts had become taut.

"See. They want me to suck on them, don't they?" Cupping the sides and bottoms, he gently pressed the malleable flesh so that her breasts thrust upward and outward. "Brianne? They do, don't they? They want my mouth badly, don't they?" His thumbs eased to the now throbbing crests and pressed. Her breath caught in her throat. "Don't they?" he asked quite gently.

"Yes," she admitted with a small cry.

He released the pressure on the nipples, only to lightly graze the pads of his thumbs across them, making the sensitive nerve endings feel as though they had been scraped by sand and fire.

"Yes!"

"Good." He lowered his head and drew one aching tip into his mouth. Greedy, hungry sounds began coming from his throat.

Her fingers dug into his hair, and Brianne threw back her head as ecstasy seared from her nipple, down her belly, to between her legs. Instantly, she made the decision to enjoy, telling herself that she could delight in Sloan's attentions without fear that he would take full advantage of her. The two of them had made a deal that included everything but actual lovemaking. That meant she could allow herself to relax and soak up this wonderful new world of feeling he was introducing her to without fearing that she would lose her virginity. And so she did.

Sloan changed to the other breast, this time, though, instead of immediately seeking the nourishment, he laved his tongue across the stiffened nub, then took the point between his teeth and rolled it back and forth.

"Oh, Sloan!"

"What?" he asked, her nipple still caught in his teeth, his warm moist breath fanning her skin.

"That feels so good."

"Do you want more?"

"Yes." Her hand stroked across his cheek and stopped at the corner of his mouth. One thumb dipped just inside his opened lips and rested. "Oh, yes."

He rolled her nipple again, and she felt the serrations of his teeth even as the muscles in her stomach clenched. "Ohhh!"

"It hurts good, doesn't it?"

She nodded, but he didn't see because he was licking at the throbbing crest.

"I just want a little more to keep me until tomorrow night." He drew her back into his mouth.

She cradled his cheek with her palm, feeling the muscles move as he sucked. Powerful feelings were building inside her, yet she was so empty. She wanted to be filled. Ever so slightly her hips began rising and falling.

Withoug taking a breath, Sloan left her breast, went to her lips, and pulled her tongue into his mouth. With the heel of his hand he pressed hard on the soft mound just above her legs.

A fierce jolt of pleasure leapt downward, so powerful she was left shaking.

"You're pure fire, redhead," he murmured, easing his mouth away and looking down into her bewildered, passion-fogged eyes. "I can't wait until tomorrow night."

10

As Sloan had sat on the porch of the hotel and watched wagons and men head out of town, he had carefully noted the direction they had taken. As a result, a little before noon Sloan reined Demon to a halt atop a rise that overlooked a small city of tents. The hard lines of his face settled into an expression of satisfaction. *This* was what he had suspected all along.

Most men would have waited until after they had received government approval for the railroad to mass together the workers and equipment they needed. But Wes hadn't. He was a greedy man who obviously didn't want to waste any more time than was necessary. In this case, he was going to play right into Sloan's hands, because greedy men always wanted more and greedy men always made mistakes. The mere presence of the tent city below him all but testified to that.

In the center of the little city a large tent had been put up, no doubt the kitchen and dining tent. From there, tents spread out in an orderly fashion, tempo-

173

rary homes for surveyors, graders, engineers, and rail workers.

For the moment, anyway, there didn't appear to be much activity. Men milled about, some playing cards, some lounging beneath trees, some sleeping on bedrolls out in the open. One tent was set up away from the others, and it had a score of smaller tents surrounding it. Here Sloan could see women, women brought in, he guessed, to keep the men entertained until work could begin.

Remembering that this morning he had seen Wes go into his office back in Chango, he slowly headed Demon down the far side of the rise toward the tent where he had seen the women. Men wouldn't reveal secrets to other men, but they would reveal secrets to women. If Sloan could just find the right woman.

Sitting outside her tent trying to put a hem into a new dress, Janice pricked her finger with the needle. Cursing, she brought the bleeding finger to her lips. Maybe if she'd listened to her mama and learned how to sew, she thought in frustration, she wouldn't get such sore fingers whenever she tried anything more difficult with a needle than threading it. But then again, if she had listened to her mama, she would be some dull farmer's wife with a brood of kids and a tired back instead of being in on the excitement of the *actual* building of a railroad!

The sound of a horse had her turning her head, and at the sight of the man riding the big black stallion, she jumped up, her new dress and sore finger forgotten. "Sloan, I mean Mr. Lassiter, what are you doing here?"

"Hello, Janice." He stepped down out of the saddle. "And do call me Sloan, and I might ask you the same thing. What are you doing here?"

"Things were kinda slow at Lucky's"—she cast him a sly glance through her lashes—"especially since you didn't come back. A friend convinced me I should come out here."

As he studied the encampment, he asked, "Do you know who's in charge here?"

Her forehead pleated while she gave his question some thought. "I suppose you mean Mr. McCord." The wave of her hand encompassed the tent city. "All of this is his."

Sloan eyed Janice intently. "But I understand he's been out of town. Who's in charge when he's not here? Does he have a foreman or a supervisor?"

Her forehead cleared. "Oh, that's Dan, Dan Cummings. He's Mr. McCord's supervisor."

"Do you know him?"

"Dan? Sure."

"How well do you know him?"

Janice tried to judge what exactly it was that Sloan wanted. It would be exciting to think that he wanted her! Dan was all right, but no man had ever affected her like Sloan Lassiter. But much as she would like to think there was jealousy in Sloan's question, she knew there wasn't, so she told him the truth. "As a matter of fact, Dan's the one who talked me into comin' out here."

"He wanted to see you more often?"

She nodded. "Yeah. And it pays to go along with

what he says, believe me. Besides, most of the time it's
fun."

He took her elbow. "I need to talk to you, Janice. Is
there somewhere we can go?"

She couldn't stop the hope that leapt into her eyes.
"My tent is right behind us."

Sunlight spilled through the windows of the hotel's
front parlor to splash onto the rose-patterned gold
wool rug. Gazing out the window, Brianne absently
rubbed the olive velvet upholstery of the serpentine-
backed sofa on which she sat. Beside her, Phineas was
babbling about his travels, and over at the piano
Henrietta was pounding out a most energetic version
of "Bringing in the Sheaves." Brianne had no idea
where Kamanahua was. She supposed she should be
worried about him, just as she should be listening to
what Phineas was saying, not to mention appreciat-
ing the hymn that Henrietta was playing. However,
Sloan kept crowding everything else out of her mind.

They weren't going to make love, of course. Instinctively, she knew he wouldn't force her. Adamantly, she
told herself she would never allow it to happen.
Still . . .

Soon Sloan's life would be in terrible jeopardy, if it
wasn't already. He had chosen the perilous path of
revenge and it might very well end in his death. He
knew it, and he didn't care.

She cared. That was the problem. She cared desperately. She didn't want him to die. She wanted him to
live and be with her. She wanted—what did she
want?

She felt her hands taken into a squeezing grip. "Miss Delaney, Brianne, you must listen to me! I'm trying to tell you that my circumstances are a bit more dire than I first led you to believe."

With extreme difficulty Brianne tore her thoughts away from Sloan and tried to focus on Phineas. "What?"

A quick glance over his shoulder assured Phineas that Henrietta was absorbed in her hymn. Nevertheless, he took the precaution of scooting closer to Brianne and lowering his voice. "Well, a while back, not too long ago actually, just before I met you, a certain . . . Mr. Fairfield bought several bottles of my Tooley's Miracle Restorative in order to increase his, uh . . ."

"Yes?" Brianne prompted.

"Flagging virility. Evidently, the gentleman couldn't decide whether to take the medicine internally or to apply it externally. He did both. The results, *he claims*, have rendered him bald in a most embarrassing place." Phineas wiggled his eyebrows up and down in what he considered a significant manner to make sure she was understanding him. "Plus, I'm afraid, he has a lingering case of diarrhea."

Brianne stared at him. "You aren't serious, are you?"

Solemnly, Phineas nodded his head.

Brianne gave a heavy sigh just as she noticed Kamanahua edging his head around the door of the parlor, his black eyes trained steadfastly on the gleaming mahogany upright piano.

"Oh, Kam, there you are. I was wondering—"

Suddenly, he jumped into the room, holding in the air something that, to Brianne, looked like a white iron bedpost, and lunged across the room toward the piano.

"Auwe! Auwe!" he cried, and began beating the piano with the bedpost.

Henrietta jumped back in alarm. "What on earth do you think you're doing?"

"It is the missionaries!" he shouted, bringing the iron bedpost down again and again on the piano, his black eyes wild with fear. "They have found me!"

Brianne hobbled on her one good ankle over to him. "Kam, stop beating the piano!"

"The missionaries have congealed themselves within this wooden box!"

Phineas was fascinated as he hastened over to lend an arm to Brianne. "Congealed?"

"He means concealed," Brianne told him, pulling on Kamanahua's arm. "Kam, stop it this instant!"

"But they torment me with that noise!"

"Kam, listen! The music has stopped."

Apprehensively, Kamanahua looked around the room, his arm halted in midair, ready to deliver another blow. "Where are the missionaries?"

"There were never any missionaries here. The piano is—*was*"—Brianne corrected herself as she glanced at the pile of splintered wood that had once been a piano—"a musical instrument, and Henrietta was playing the hymn on it."

Kamanahua cast a suspicious gaze at Henrietta.

Shaking her finger at Kamanahua in her best

schoolteacher manner, Henrietta said, "We've discussed this before. I am *not* a missionary."

Brianne pulled Kamanahua's arm down. "Let me see what you have there. It looks like—"

"My bedpost!" Mrs. Potter screeched from the doorway. "My bedpost!"

"That's what I was afraid of," Brianne muttered.

Mrs. Potter advanced into the room. "Oh, my God, my *piano*!"

"I do not like a joyful noise unto the Lord," Kamanahna pronounced defiantly.

Brianne squeezed her eyes shut and counted to five. Unfortunately, she felt no better when she opened her eyes, but she pasted a smile on her face and swung into action. "Now, Mrs. Potter, you are not to worry about a thing. Your piano will be replaced, along with the bed in Kam's room."

Mrs. Potter jerked her handkerchief from under her belt and held it to her nose, sniffing. "You can't replace those things! I treasured them!"

"And," Brianne continued doggedly, "I will add enough money into the bargain so that your distress will be amply compensated for."

Mrs. Potter stopped sniffing. "That would take a lot of money."

Brianne nodded. "I realize that, believe me. Now, if you wouldn't mind leaving us alone, I need to talk with Kam."

Mrs. Potter looked up at Kamanahna, then down at the bedpost gripped tightly in his hand.

"I dissembled the bed," Kamanahna explained. "A warrior must have war club and spears."

Brianne called out to Mrs. Potter's retreating back. "He means disassembled."

Phineas watched her go, his eyes narrowed thoughtfully. "It's obvious to me that the good lady's extreme bad humor stems from a suffering of piles. One-half pint of my Tooley's Miracle Restorative mixed with one-half pint of the oil of the oldest and strongest bacon we can find, and applied each night will give her great relief. The cure is highly celebrated, I assure you."

All at once exhausted, Brianne slumped back down onto the sofa and started to laugh.

By dinnertime Sloan was back in town and well satisfied with his day's work. For he had offered Janice a sum of money that would insure a comfortable retirement for her whenever she wished if she would help him. She had agreed, as he had known she would. Whether he could trust her or not remained to be seen.

Sloan washed and changed for dinner. Instead of eating in the hotel dining room, though, he headed for the café down the street. The café was plain in service and decor, but it had something that the hotel dining room didn't—Wes McCord's patronage.

Sloan slipped quietly into the café and stood against the wall for a moment. The room was about half full, the customers mostly men. The few women in the room he recognized as having seen around town. The clinking of knives and forks against plates could be heard along with the murmur of voices. Gingham curtains hung at the night-darkened windows, and square-cut calico cloths covered the tables. A variety of baskets and dishes were stacked on a scrubbed-oak sideboard.

Nothing remarkable, nothing to give Sloan pause, except that Wes McCord sat at a table along the far wall. He was facing Sloan, but he kept his head down as he ate. When he did raise his head, it was to speak to the man who sat across from him. Sloan observed him closely.

In fifteen years Wes's chest and shoulders had filled out, and his facial features had become more sharply defined. There was even a bit of gray in Wes's hair.

As Sloan threaded his way around the tables, an icy calmness settled in him, isolating him from everyone else in the room. In his imagination he had taken this walk a thousand times. He no longer heard the noise of the people or silverware clattering against china; he no longer smelled the food. His senses were all attuned to Wes. He drew up to his table and stopped.

Wes looked up inquiringly. "Yes, can I help you?"

"Hello, Wes. It's been a long time."

Pale gray eyes narrowed on Sloan. "I'm sorry, do I know you?"

There was no reason in the world that Wes should have recognized the man standing before him as the scrawny kid he had left stranded in the middle of West Texas fifteen years before. If he looked at the matter objectively, he could remember that Wes thought he was dead. Still, anger quickly reached the boiling point in him. He waited until Wes had raised his glass of whiskey to his lips. "Yes, as a matter of fact, you do," he said quietly. "I'm Sloan Lassiter."

Surprise flared in the depths of Wes's gray eyes along with something else that he quickly banked before Sloan could identify it. Carefully, Wes set the glass down. "Well, well, just imagine seeing you after all these years."

"Just imagine," Sloan agreed.

Cool and calculating, Wes leaned back in his chair and hooked his thumbs in his belt. "So what brings you to Chango?"

Sloan kept his eye on Wes's hand, making sure it didn't drop to the gun in his holster. He also watched the man sitting across from Wes for any sudden movement. "I have business here."

Light brown eyebrows rose. "Oh? Funny, I haven't heard about it."

"You're hearing about it now," Sloan pointed out.

"So I am." Suddenly, the smile that Wes had used to charm Sloan and David so many years before spread across his face. "We have a lot to catch up on. Sit down."

"I think not, not tonight anyway. I just wanted to come by and say hello."

Wes's smile thinned. "Maybe some other time then?"

"I'm sure we'll be running into each other."

Sloan turned to go, but Wes's words stopped him. "By the way, how's your brother? David, wasn't that his name?"

"Yes," Sloan said quietly. "That was his name. And he's dead."

* * *

"I haven't found your brother," Sloan told Brianne as soon as he walked into Brianne's room that night. "Don't worry," he said in a softer voice when he saw her disappointment. "I'm sure Patrick will be back with you soon."

His reassurance somehow made Brianne feel better. "I know."

Sloan slung the saddlebag he had carried into the room onto the foot of the bed and hung his holster and gun on the bedpost. Then, restlessly, he swung toward the dresser. He picked up her silver-backed mirror and ran his finger over the raised vine pattern. Abruptly, he thrust it away, but then he reached for her brush and again traced the silver pattern on its back.

Brianne watched him curiously. He wore buff-colored trousers and a cream-colored shirt, the sleeves of which were turned back to reveal his forearms. Always a man who gave off an air of raw power, tonight his hard, lean body was fairly bursting with a strange, restless energy.

"How's your ankle?" he asked.

"It's much better. In a day or two, I expect, it will be able to take my full weight."

"I wouldn't rush it," he remarked offhandedly, his attention suddenly caught by her sketchpad. He picked it up and flipped through the pages until he came to the sketch she had done today. It was of him. Studying it, he saw the harsh strokes she had used to draw his face, the lines forming his mouth especially hard and dark. His eyes weren't completely formed yet, but in them there seemed to be a mixture of emptiness, passion, and pain. And then he noticed the tenderness. She was wrong, he thought. There was no tenderness in him. He thrust the pad away.

"I saw Wes McCord this evening," he said.

She was suddenly numb with a cold apprehension, and she remembered how, this afternoon in the parlor, she had admitted to herself that she would care very much if anything happened to Sloan. How could she have come to care for a man who showed no signs of having a soul or a heart? How could she have come to love—love? Love.

She heard Sloan chuckle. "Wes didn't recognize me. Every minute of the last fifteen years has been lived with the day in mind when I would finally see Wes McCord, and the son of a bitch didn't recognize me."

"I—I think that's understandable. After all, you were expecting to see him, but he wasn't expecting to see you."

"Hardly, since he thought I was dead."

"Dammit, Sloan, do you have to go on with this vendetta?"

Surprise crossed his face. "Of course."

"But it's so dangerous. You could be killed."

He sat down on the side of the bed and raised his hand to her cheek. "Brianne, the need to avenge my brother's death by killing that bastard McCord has been in me so long, if it were to vanish suddenly, I don't know whether or not there would be anything left inside me."

"That's not true!"

He smiled and dropped his hand. "You couldn't begin to understand."

She leaned toward him and spoke earnestly. "Maybe I can't understand what you went through all those years ago, losing your brother under those circumstances, and nearly losing your own life in the bargain. But I've seen all sides of death, and I know that taking another person's life is not the answer to anything."

His hand came up again, this time to her hair. Lightly his fingers lifted a portion of her hair away from her forehead. "You're so sure of what you say and do, aren't you? I was first drawn to you because of your laughter, did you know that?"

Mutely, she shook her head.

"Your laughter woke me from a sound sleep and drew me to the window. And there you were, down in that muddy corral. You seemed to be so alive, and when most women would have cried, you laughed."

Brianne found it difficult to swallow.

"You were magnificent," he murmured, and lowered his head to take her mouth in a deep kiss of possession. At the same time, his fingers began to untie the ribbons of her gown. Against her lips he murmured, "I thought I told you not to bother tying these bows."

"I forgot."

Her opened mouth was the receptacle for his soft laugh. "No, you didn't. You thought if those bows were untied when I came here tonight, I would think you were eager for my hands . . . and my mouth."

He was right. She had thought all of those things. And tonight she *had* been eager for him to come to her. All too quickly her breasts had become accus-

tomed to his hands and to his lips on them. He had
only to walk into the room for them to begin throbbing. She couldn't imagine never again having him
take her breasts in his strong brown hands and
caressing them. She couldn't imagine never again
having him suck her nipples.

But now that she knew she loved him, what would
happen, she wondered, when he had found Patrick?
She had originally intended to get out of the deal
somehow. But now, the thought of him thrusting
powerfully in and out of her made her go weak
against him and moan aloud.

Sloan pulled away from her and looked down at her
lips, wet from his kiss. He would give all he possessed,
he thought, to feel those lips around him, pulling,
sucking, and licking. As a matter of fact, he would
give most of what he possessed just to be able to
spend a little more time with her. Soon, though, he
would have to tell her that Patrick was safe. He
couldn't bring himself to deceive her much longer.

But that was for another time. Maybe tomorrow.
Maybe the next day. For the present she was too close,
too soft, too sweetly smelling to let go. He slowly
smiled. "I brought you something."

"What?" Bemused by the expressions she had been
watching come and go in his golden eyes, that was the
last thing she had expected him to say.

He reached behind him for the saddlebag. Lifting
the flap, he said, "I picked some wild strawberries
today, and when I got back, I had someone in the
hotel's kitchen wash them."

Delight lit up her face. "I love strawberries!"

His mouth curved with amusement. "Somehow I knew you would. Here." He held up a plump red strawberry, she opened her mouth, and he put it in.

"Ummm," she murmured, and bit down, finding her mouth filled with a juicy sweet tartness. "It's wonderful."

"That's nice, because I'm hungry." He helped himself to two, and after he had eaten them, he offered her another.

"Didn't you eat dinner?" she asked, blissfully unaware that a small trickle of juice had escaped her mouth.

With his eyes on her mouth, he shook his head, then bent to lick away the juice. "I want you naked to the waist."

Addled by his sensuous gesture, she could only stammer. "I'm n-not sure. . . ."

"Naked to the waist, Brianne," he said, and pushed the gown off her shoulders.

Excitement jumped in the pit of her stomach, and she helped. When at last her breasts and arms were bare, and her gown rested around her waist, she lay back against the pillows and waited.

He scooped a handful of strawberries out of the saddlebag and, closing his hand, crushed them. "This is going to be so good," he murmured, more to himself than to her, and began to spread the strawberries and their juice over her breasts. "So damnned good!"

It was his tongue that touched her first. With his hands planted on the bed on either side of her waist, he bent his head and gave a delicate lick. Then another. Then another. Gradually, the tongue strokes lengthened until he was making hard, sweeping forays in circles around her breast, lapping up the thin layer of strawberries from her skin, leaving behind a trail of damp fire to dry and to cool.

Brianne wasn't cooling. Rather, a steadily building heat was curling inside her like a beautiful flaming-red ribbon. Her hands grasped the bedsheets.

With one breast completely clean now, Sloan switched to the other. He hadn't spread any of the crushed strawberries onto the nipples, and he stead-fastly avoided the taut peaks. Instead, he concentrated on the full round globes that to him seemed alive beneath his tongue. He tilted his head to better get at the fruit on the underside of her breast. Between his legs his hard flesh throbbed hotly and painfully. He longed to release it from the confinement of his trousers and plunge the swollen shaft into her. Only then would he find relief.

"Take off your gown," he muttered roughly. "Take off your gown. I want to see you completely naked. I want all of you and more strawberries too."

A response was almost beyond her, so powerfully was her heart beating, so weak did her limbs feel.

"Sit up, my lovely Brianne, and raise your arms."

Her gown came off over her head and was flung across the room so fast her head whirled. She fell back onto the pillows.

For a long moment he did nothing. He simply looked at her, taking in the vivid wild beauty of her red hair, her emerald eyes, her smooth peach-tinted skin, and her long, enticing legs. His gaze paused for a moment at the triangle of tiny red curls, then skimmed upward to the flat plane of her stomach, and then higher to the rapid rise and fall of her breasts. Her lips were parted, her cheeks were flushed, her eyes pleaded.

Abruptly, he said, "Spread your legs."

She gasped, uncertain yet wanting, with everything that was in her, more of the spiraling, breathless passion from him. She didn't want him to leave tonight. She wanted him. She loved him.

"Spread your legs," he said more gently, and with his hands pushed her legs apart until he was satisfied that they were spread wide enough. He repositioned himself beside her knees. Then, compulsively, he touched the satiny skin on the inside of her thigh. Brushing his hand up and down the satiny flesh, he muttered huskily, "God, you feel like you're on fire."

With each flesh-burning sweep of his hand he went higher until Brianne thought she was going to lose her mind. "Sloan," she whimpered, "please . . ."

There was strain in his voice when he answered her. "You don't have to beg, Brianne. Just ask, ask me nicely."

His hand was at the top of her thigh, his fingers brushing against the outer edges of the soft folds there. "Sloan!"

"Damn!" He reached for more strawberries, crushed them, then coated every inch of the insides of both of her thighs. When he bent to her, gone were the languid strokes that he had used on her breasts. Instead, he made long, powerful, urgent sweeps up one leg and down the other, licking, nibbling, biting, until Brianne thought she would go mad.

When the lower portion of her legs were licked clean of every last bit of fruit, he suddenly dropped to the floor by the side of the bed. Taking hold of her legs, he pulled her around so that her hips were at the edge of the bed and her toes were touching the floor.

She raised her head to see him kneeling between her legs. "Sloan, what are you doing?"

As if he couldn't stand the cloth touching his skin, he shrugged out of his shirt. "I want to be able to get at you better. I *have* to."

Brianne was mesmerized. Golden flames filled his eyes, and the harsh planes of his face had been made even more so by his passion. She dropped her head back to the bed, and when she felt his tongue start an upward trek, she moaned. She was trembling all over in a fever of need, in a frenzy of desire. How much more could she take? She was to find out.

With his hands he reached beneath her and gripped her firmly rounded bottom. As he held her tightly, his rough yet velvet tongue ruthlessly scoured her, leaving her feeling raw, as if he were removing layer after layer of skin and exposing the nerves to the air.

At last all traces of strawberries were gone. Sloan sat back on his heels and looked at her. He was in agony with wanting her. How he was going to get up and leave her now, he didn't know.

Of its own accord Brianne's head rolled back and forth. She didn't want to feel Sloan's tongue stroking her skin. She wanted *him*, all of him. But words didn't come, only a soft, helpless moan.

The unobstructed view he had had his heart pounding with a heavy force. "Oh, God, Brianne, you're so wet," Sloan cried.

"Sloan, oh, God, Sloan . . ."

"Wait, just wait," he murmured. Slowly he bent toward the sight.

Brianne's body jerked with the force of the heat that blasted through her and centered exactly in the spot where Sloan's tongue was probing. Her head went back. Her hands were knotted tightly in his hair and she had no idea how they had gotten there. Desperate cries were coming from her mouth. The ecstasy was almost more than she could bear. "Stop, Sloan, stop."

But Sloan was beyond listening. His tongue invaded, withdrew, then invaded again.

Her body demanded. Thought receded, place blanked out. Sound blurred. Colors went white for her. And the world as she knew it ceased.

11

Hours later Sloan was still awake. The night winds were cool and stirred through the long grass with a soft murmur. Above his head a million stars hung in a black sky. Three feet away from him, a campfire sputtered and flamed as it gradually died away.

As boys he and David had slept out on many a night such as this, counting stars and telling stories until they had fallen asleep. Although three years had separated them in age, they always had been close. Their father had never shown affection to Sloan, and after his mother had died, Sloan had known that David was the only person in the world who truly loved him.

Sloan rolled onto his other side so that he faced away from the fire and out into the darkness. Gradually, his eyes adjusted to the lack of light, and he could begin to perceive shadowed shapes of trees and bushes. Quite often David and he would lie on their blankets and try to guess what lurked beyond their campfire. Sometimes they would convince themselves that there were Indians or menacing beasts just waiting for them to go to sleep. They would scare themselves silly.

Now he was a man. And David was dead. And nothing scared Sloan. Nights such as this had lost their mystery and excitement for him—and in his gut a gnawing, burning pain squeezed and spread with agonizing slowness down into his loins. He knew the reason for his pain, and he knew why he was here, yet there was nothing he could do about it.

Something violent had exploded in his head as he had looked at Brianne and seen her lying there on the bed, so on fire for him, so completely willing. With the taste of her and strawberries mingling in his mouth, he had known he had to get away from her or he would take her there and then, without control, without gentleness. He would take her without stopping . . . ever.

He had almost run out of Brianne's room. Stopping in his own room only long enough to get a fresh shirt, a jacket, and his gear, he had left the hotel and the town as far behind him as he could.

He groaned. When in hell had he developed scruples? When in hell had Brianne become more important than satisfying his own needs? He supposed there was no definitive time. From the first moment he had heard her laughter he had been amused and attracted. Need had quickly followed.

He had thought his heart long dead. But gradually and without him being aware of it her spirit and energy, her enthusiasm for people and for life, her refusal to accept defeat and her belief that she could do anything—all of these things, *Brianne*—had seeped through his wall of hatred, supplying him with something he had desperately needed: life, warmth, laughter.

But they had made a deal. He had told her that he wouldn't make love to her until he found Patrick. By omitting to tell her that Patrick was safe and would be back in Chango soon, he was lying to her.

His body was screaming for release within her, to take with both hands the joy and peace she offered. But he couldn't. At the moment he had nothing to offer Brianne. He was a man bent on a vengeful course of action against a man he knew was perfectly capable of killing him. She couldn't understand. He couldn't change.

He paused as a renegade thought struck him. Maybe to a small degree he had changed. He had stood across the table from Wes as he had a thousand times before in his imagination. But before, as the scene had played out in his mind, he had always drawn his gun and fired, shooting Wes dead. The idea of ruining Wes had come only since he had been in Chango.

And now that goal was almost within reach. When daylight came he would ride back to the tent city and talk with Janice. Maybe today would be the day when he would get the proof he needed, and his punishment of Wes could begin.

He sighed wearily. In the end what did it all matter? Things hadn't changed that much. He would still kill Wes and more than likely die doing it.

If by some miracle he was alive when the dust settled, what would be left? Surely not Brianne.

Living out the rest of his life in happiness seemed a
foreign notion to him. In fact, he was sure it wouldn't
be possible.

Sloan closed his eyes and willed sleep to come.

Up on the rise behind the cover of a cropping of
boulders, Sloan observed the compound below. It was
Saturday, and activity in the tent city was brisk.
Sloan planned to use that activity to his advantage.
With so many men riding in and out, the chance he
would go unnoticed was good.

About ten o'clock he rode down. Janice was waiting
for him.

"You were right, Sloan. Dan had a little too much to
drink last night and talked quite a bit." Her nose
wrinkled with distaste. "When he wasn't pawing me,
that is. According to Dan, Mr. McCord plans, with
some financial jugglin' and downright fraud, to move
large amounts of money from the construction con-
tracts into his own pocket."

Perfect composure covered Sloan's elation. "Are
you sure about this, Janice? Do you think it's possible
that Dan knows you're working for me?"

Her shoulders rose and fell. "How could he know?"

"You're right, I suppose." With his thumb Sloan
pushed his black hat back on his head. "It just seems
that was an awful lot of important information for a
man to give out in bed."

Janice picked absently at her skirt. "It's hard to tell,
but it could be he's tryin' to impress me."

"What do you mean?"

"I mean Dan's tryin' to figure out how he can get in on the profits. He told me that soon he'll be a rich man. Mr. McCord is payin' him good money all right, but Dan is greedy. He's thinkin' that there must be a way to get a share of that extra money for himself."

"Without McCord knowing about it?"

"Absolutely. Mr. McCord isn't a man to mess with."

No, he wasn't, Sloan agreed silently. And he had a hunch Dan Cummings wasn't either. He just hoped Janice was right about Cummings's infatuation with her. He didn't want her hurt.

"Did I do good?" Janice asked, put out that Sloan wasn't showing her what she considered proper appreciation. The money he was going to give her was wonderful, but if she could have him *and* the money . . .

He laid his hand on her shoulder. "You did better than good, Janice, but now I need to ask you to do more."

"What?" she asked a bit warily. Dan might be crazy enough about her to try to get her to say she'd be his woman, but he was not dumb. And he could be meaner than a snake when crossed. There were whispers about him that would flat scare a girl to death if she let herself believe them.

"I need proof of what Dan told you. For instance, I need to look at the ledgers."

"Ledgers?"

"Account books. I'm positive that Wes started his financial juggling before he went to Washington. He's too far along with all of this for him not to have. But I need to see the figures. I have to be absolutely sure."

Baffled, Janice frowned. "But how can I help you with that?"

"I wouldn't have a chance of getting into his office in town undetected, but there's got to be a ledger copy here too. Do you know where Dan's tent is?"

"Sure. I was there last night."

"Good. Tonight is Saturday night. What happens here on Saturday nights?"

Janice laughed. "All hell breaks loose. Everyone has a great time."

"There's a lot of drinking?"

She nodded, a big smile on her face. "Is there ever! Very few people are left standing after midnight."

"That's what I figured, and that's my chance. Can you get Dan to stay in your tent tonight?"

She nodded. "That's no problem."

"Then today you'll show me exactly where his tent is. In the morning I'll be here before daylight. I should have plenty of time to search for those books."

Janice's eyes sparkled. "This is exciting!"

"This could also be very dangerous," Sloan warned. "Be careful."

She ran her hand up around his neck. "You don't have to worry about me."

Sloan hesitated. "Janice, I need to stay here today. Will there be anyone coming to visit your tent?"

She pressed her voluptuous curves against him. "Not if I don't invite them."

"You and I have a business arrangement, Janice, nothing more."

At the sudden glint of ice in his golden eyes she

stepped away from him. "Well, sure, Sloan. Don't worry."

The sun rose and set on Chango without any sign of Sloan, and in her room Brianne was seething with fury. She had no idea how she had managed to get through the day. Vaguely, she remembered visiting with Anna Nilsen for a while. And Mrs. Potter had required great measures of reassurance that her hotel would be left standing on the day when Brianne and her party finally left.

As usual Kamanahua had refused to budge from her side. She had purchased a horse for Phineas's wagon, but he, too, had seemed to come to look upon her as protection, and for the moment, anyway, refused to leave town.

She had spent a long time trying to talk Henrietta into continuing on with her trip back east. But Henrietta was a loyal soul, and she maintained that she would stay until she was certain that Brianne no longer needed her.

What she needed, Brianne thought, was a few less people to take care of for the moment. She felt as vulnerable as a baby bird and as angry as a wounded bear. She was sure that her raw, pulsing desire for Sloan was obvious and that her love for him shone as brightly as the North Star . . . there for all to see.

And Patrick was still missing! Her belief that he was alive remained firm. She couldn't believe anything else and still function. But her worry over his well-being had increased tenfold. She had been so sure that Sloan would have found him by now. Tomorrow, she decided, she would begin again to look for Patrick.

God, what a mess! she had groaned at least fifty times during the long day.

And now with night covering Chango, Brianne was at last alone. Although her ankle was still weak, it would hold her weight, and occasionally she would rise from the sofa, where she sat, and pace to the door and back. The door was slightly ajar so she could hear Sloan when he came in.

Where was he? And how dare he leave her last night when she wanted him so badly! And, oh, dear heaven, maybe he was in danger! He could be hurt or worse. . . .

It was a long time before she heard him pass by her door and enter his. Relief made her weak. He was all right, and soon she would be in his arms. She waited, her foot tapping impatiently, her fingers twisting the cross at her throat. Her heart rate picked up when she again heard the sound of his footsteps, but he passed her door to walk down the hall to the bathing room.

She cracked her door, listened, and heard the sound of George's footsteps coming up the stairway and the squeak of the handles of the buckets he carried. When he entered the bathing room, she heard his young, serious voice blend with Sloan's deeper one. Water gurgled and glugged as it was being poured into the tub. Then came the hollow clank of the tin buckets as they were set on the floor. George left and shut the door behind him. Brianne also closed her door. A little while later Sloan walked back to his room.

When more time went by and still he didn't come to her, she decided to take matters into her own hands.

Sloan answered her third knock. "You shouldn't be here," he said, glancing up and down the hall to make sure there was no one to see her.

"I think I've said the same thing a time or two myself, but it never did any good, did it?" She brushed past him and marched into the room.

He closed the door, leaned back against it, and observed Brianne. Her hair was flaring out from her head in glorious red waves and tumbling untamed down her back to her waist. Her eyes were glittering with emerald brightness. There was a sense that, beneath her gown and robe, her body was resonating with a passionate wrath.

"Why did you do it?" Brianne asked, her voice vibrating with her effort to control her anger.

To Sloan's mind, her wild beauty had never been more vivid. The urge to pull her to the floor and take her was almost overwhelming.

"Why did you leave me last night?" Brianne asked again when he didn't answer.

"We have a deal, remember? I was just living up to the terms of the agreement."

"Damn the agreement! You knew that I wanted you to make love to me last night."

"Yes," he agreed calmly, "I knew." He crossed his arms over his chest so that he wouldn't reach out and grab her to him. He had told himself to stay away until he had settled his score once and for all with Wes. And in fact, there was another hotel in town that he could have stayed at. But he hadn't been able to keep away. He had wanted to make sure she was all right, so he had come back to the Duke but had gone straight to his room, intending to stay there. Whether he would have been able to or not he didn't know.

"Then *why*? And while I'm thinking about it, where have you been?"

He almost smiled at her demanding tone. She was a Delaney princess through and through. "Out at Wes McCord's tent city. I'm very close to finding the evidence I need."

She threw up her hands. "Oh, how wonderful! That means you're that much closer to being dead."

This time he did smile. "You don't have much faith in me, do you?"

His smile infuriated her, breaking through the thin veneer of her control. "You're a stupid, stubborn man, Sloan! How can I have faith in you when you refuse to understand that even if your plan to ruin, then kill Wes McCord is successful, you won't win! You can't!"

All amusement left him. "On this particular subject, you're wrong, Brianne."

"No, I'm not! Besides, I've met Wes McCord, remember? Don't you care that he may kill you?"

"Not much," he said, then realized that he wished he had the promise of a life that was full of loving Brianne. That would make him want to live. But he knew himself. He knew what his life had been before he came to Chango, and he knew what it would be when and if he left.

"How *dare* you not care! How *dare* you risk your life

when it means so much to me!" She whirled away to his dresser, picked up the first thing she saw, which was his hairbrush, and threw it at him.

Just in time he moved his head, and the brush hit the door with a loud thud. "Brianne—"

She grabbed his shaving mug and threw it with an accuracy that would have brought blood to his forehead if he hadn't jumped out of the way. "I wanted you last night so badly, I thought I would die if I didn't have you! Thanks to you and your damned strawberries, I would have *crawled* to you if you had asked!" A heavy glass vase found its way into her hand and she hurled it with such force, it shattered against the door.

He began advancing on her. "Brianne—"

"Don't you realize that I wouldn't make love with just any man? I wouldn't hurt and embarrass my grandparents by becoming someone's mistress on a whim!" Unaware that tears were streaming down her face, she picked up an oval silver-framed picture of dried flowers and flung it as hard as she could. It bounced off the wall and fell to the floor dented.

"Brianne, someone will hear."

"I don't care!"

A porcelain pitcher filled with water hurtled past him, smashing with a terrific crash. The basin followed. Sloan turned to watch as its collision with the wall drenched the blue fleur-de-lis wallpaper with soapy water, and streaks of color began to bleed down the wall.

"I *love* you, you fool!" she shouted.

His body jerked as if he'd been shot. He had lost count of the number of women who had told him they loved him. Some had even cried as they told him. But their avowals of love hadn't touched him in any way.

For most of his life he'd been so alone, and it had never bothered him. Yet now Brianne was saying she loved him, and he couldn't even begin to count the number of ways her shouted, angry declaration was touching him.

Sloan's arms closed around her, and he pulled her sobbing form to his body. "Oh, Lord, Brianne, what am I going to do with you?" Not expecting an answer, he lifted her into his arms and carried her to the armchair in the corner of his room. Holding her, he sat down and settled her in his lap. "Brianne, I'm not worth a single one of your tears. Don't cry."

Her small fists came up to beat against his chest. "Don't you dare tell me what to do!"

He grabbed her fist and gave a little laugh. "How did you ever manage to reach the age of twenty-one? You have no sense of self-protection. A wolf, a motley and highly suspect group of people on the run, or a man who's never seen women as anything other than objects to use, enjoy, and then throw away—we're all the same to you, aren't we?"

Sniffing, she raised her head. "Is that the way you see me, as an object that you'll eventually throw away?"

Taking his time in answering, he curved his hand around her face, and with gentle fingers brushed the softness of her skin, not stopping until all traces of tears were gone. "No," he finally said. "Once I had you, I could never throw you away."

"Then—"

"It can't be."

"Don't tell me that!" she said, indignant, pushing away from him.

"Listen to me and listen well," he said, deliberately slicing sharp, flinty edges into his words. "I set out to get you in my bed. I figured I had all the advantages. After all, every night I had your delectable body to do with as I wanted. But somewhere along the way you gained the advantage. Every time I touched you, it became harder and harder to stop."

"You didn't seem to have any trouble last night."

"Shut up, Brianne, and listen to me. I'm trying to tell you that you're interfering with my plans, and I can't have that."

She sprang from his lap. "Good Lord, no! No one can be allowed to interfere, can they? This mission of yours is close to being holy!"

He tilted his head to the side and wearily rubbed his forehead. "God has nothing to do with this, believe me."

"*You're* the one who's playing God, Sloan! Can't you see that? Yes, your brother is dead, and yes, no doubt Wes McCord is responsible, but haven't you ever heard that according to the Bible, 'Vengeance is mine, saith the Lord'?"

"I can't wait for Him to act."

"Damn you, Sloan Lassiter. Damn you for not caring that I love you. Damn you for—"

He was out of the chair so fast, Brianne didn't have time to retreat. He grabbed her arm and shook her. "I care! I care more than is good for either one of us. But, Brianne, that's as far as it goes."

"What are you talking about?"

"I've been empty for so long that I doubt I'm capable of love."

For the first time since she had entered his room, she smiled. "I'll take the chance."

"I'm not going to let you."

"There you go, dammit, playing God again! Who gives you that right?"

"No one. I'm taking it. I don't want to hurt you."

She fell silent, eyeing him thoughtfully. His hands still held her arms. "I love you, Sloan Lassiter," she said quietly, calmly. "And I waited a long time to find the man I could fall in love with. I'm sorry if you see my love as some sort of obstruction, but you're just going to have to work around it, because I'm not going to go away as you probably want me to." She glanced toward the big black walnut four-poster. "As a matter of fact, I'm going to spend the night here with you."

"Brianne—"

"Don't tell me I can't, because I won't go back to my room."

"I could carry you."

"I'd scream until I woke up everyone in the hotel."

"I could gag you."

"Then as soon as you left me in my room, I'd take the gag out and come banging on your door."

"I could leave the gag in, tie your hands and feet, and leave you on your bed like that all night."

"And when Henrietta came to my room in the morning and undid me, I'd come and find you."

Sloan groaned and took her face between his hands. "You're not going to let me try to do the first gallant thing I've ever done in my life, are you?"

Her expression showed both stubbornness and tenderness. "No."

His blood was heating at just the nearness of her, but he held himself back. "All right then, but you're going to have to let me have my way in one thing. You won't leave this room in the morning carrying my baby."

Brianne sensed victory close at hand, and she slowly smiled. "A Delaney loves a challenge."

"You're incorrigible, Brianne. And so damned desirable, you make even my teeth hurt."

She put her arms around his neck. "I've been hurting too," she murmured.

The rich, strong sweetness of his need for her started to pound wildly through his veins and there wasn't a thing he could do about it. Her robe had come open, and through the softness of the gown he could feel her body pressed into his. He was going to come apart inside if he didn't have her soon. "Let's stop the pain," he muttered, scooping her into his arms.

A moment later they were on the bed tangled up with each other. The need he had kept under control for days now burst free. He was going to have her, and nothing was going to stop him. Not even him.

When his mouth came down on hers it was with a
bruising force and a burning hunger that told Brianne
more than words could about the power of Sloan's
passion for her. She accepted his thrusting tongue
into her mouth, knowing that her body would soon be
accepting another part of him.

She couldn't wait. She knew no fear, only a singing
anticipation. It was all so simple. She had been born
to love this man.

Impatient for what was to come, she pulled at his
shirt, but her efforts to undo the buttons were clumsy.
"Help me, Sloan."

He answered her plea. The buttons went flying as he
wrested the shirt from his body. Moments later her
gown was cleanly ripped from neck to hem, and its
ribbons and fabric lay on either side of her, along with
her robe. Then the rest of his clothing came off with
the same speed and carelessness.

When he settled back beside her, and the flesh of his
hard body touched hers, Brianne gasped. She had
never felt such heat. It seared her skin, it burned
through to her bones, setting fire to every nerve along
the way.

Her gasp penetrated through the thick haze of
desire that descended around Sloan. But his hand had
already closed around one breast, and his head was
lowering toward an urgently tight nipple. His need
for her was potent and raw, something solid in his
gut, an inescapable part of him. He was so hungry for
her that he couldn't stop himself. He closed his mouth
around as much of her as he could and began to pull
and draw from her.

She was the essence of woman—sweet and feminine, untamed and passionate—and without being asked parted her legs. She was giving herself to him without condition, without inhibition. He had to fight the rush of power that came to him at the thought. Rolling to between her thighs, he moved himself against the waiting cradle. Her legs came around his back, her hands dug into his hair. When he switched his attention to the other breast, she clasped him tightly to her.

He felt enveloped by her. As he sucked ravenously from her nipple and felt her silken limbs around him, he realized that her sweetness and wildness was both inside and outside him. His need for a more complete joining was suddenly so urgent, so great, he began to shake.

Holding him as tightly as she was, she felt the tremors. "Sloan?"

He raised his head to look deep into her eyes, even while positioning the head of his shaft at the opening of her waiting warmth. "I'm going to try to be as careful with you as I can, Brianne, but . . . I'm not sure—" He was going to die if he didn't get inside her, he thought. He began easing into her and felt the silken muscles gradually enclose him. "I will be careful," he managed to mutter from between clenched teeth in an effort to strengthen his resolve.

Her hands on his back, she could feel the sweat breaking out on his skin and the rigid tension of his muscles. His restraint was torturing both of them. She wanted him, all of him. "Sloan, don't be careful," she whispered.

"You don't understand. . . ." God, but his inside
felt as if he were being clawed with a fiery pitchfork.
Already he could feel her pulsations, but he had to go
slowly. He would soon be at that thin barrier. He
wouldn't be able to stand it if he hurt her. Yet he
didn't know how he was going to live to draw his next
breath if he didn't sink his entire length into her now.

Her hands slid down to cup his buttocks. "Please,"
she begged, "I want you inside me . . . all the way
inside me . . . deep."

Control broke. He drew his hips back, then plunged
into her with one strong, ramming thrust.

Brianne felt a flash of pain, then a rush of ecstasy
so consuming, the pain was forgotten forever. She
twisted and bucked beneath him, becoming a wild
thing. She took his powerful body and returned the
pleasure he was giving her, completely open to suggestion or action. She was in the grips of a devastating tension. She clung to him, unable to let go.
Something momentous was about to happen to her.

Sloan rode her hard, surging deep into her, knowing
that he couldn't hold out much longer. He gathered
her to him, preparing for the moment when he must
withdraw from her.

Sensing his intention, she gripped him tighter. He
called out her name in a combination of frustrated
surrender and gratification. He lifted her hips and
drove into her. Their fulfillment came very quickly,
powerful, complete, and sizzling hot.

She had defeated him, he thought as he held her
tight to him while she slept.

He had never meant to allow himself to want her so much. He had never meant to lose control so completely that he would empty himself into her. But being inside her had been an ecstasy that he had never before experienced. How could he have deserted her when heaven was within seconds of his reach? To a man used to living in hell, heaven was too strong a temptation to deny.

He pulled her closer into him and she murmured his name in her sleep.

Brianne and heaven . . . one and the same thing.

12

At the house on the edge of town the dresser mirror reflected the images of the two people who lay on the bed across the room, their arms and legs entwined. Anna's skin gleamed white against Wes's darker tone.

Raising his head, Wes gently stroked away damp strands of hair from Anna's face. Through parted, well-kissed lips, her uneven breath came sweet and soft. "You may never admit to me how much you love the way I make love to you," he murmured, "but I can tell. Your sweet little cries tell me. And the way you pulse around me when I'm inside you tells me."

"I despise the way you make me feel," she said softly. "I've told you."

He smiled down at her. "But how can I believe you, Anna, my sweet? You claw and scratch so prettily when I fill you."

"I've got to go, Wesley."

He rolled over on his back and gazed up at the ceiling. "Not yet. Bring me the hairbrush."

After a brief hesitation Anna levered herself up and walked over to the dresser to get the brush. But on the way back to the bed she paused to pick up her dress from the floor.

"No," he said. "Don't get dressed. Come back here just as you are, naked and lovely."

A blush spread across Anna's fair skin, but she returned to him.

He slid into a sitting position, took the brush from her, then pulled her down to sit in front of him. "Considering the things I do to you, and the things I've taught you to do to me, you should be past blushing, don't you think?" He began to gently draw the brush through the long golden fall of her hair. "Hmmm?"

She didn't answer, and he continued brushing her hair.

Anna studied Wes's face in the mirror. She would never understand him, she thought. How could a man be so hard as to blackmail an unwilling woman into his bed, and on the other hand, be so gentle with her when he got her there? He had never, not once, not even when he had taken her virginity, hurt her.

Feeling the brush glide through her hair, she closed her eyes. Brushing a woman's hair was an extraordinary task for such a man as Wes McCord to perform. His gentleness and his attentiveness to her pleasure confused her. With her father's debts over her head, he could have taken her as roughly as he wanted. He didn't have to show her any consideration. No, she thought, she would never understand him, nor did she want to. She hated him with all her heart.

She felt him take her hair in his hands and lift it so he could run the brush beneath it, and she opened her eyes. He looked so utterly absorbed in his task, yet there was something in his face she had never seen before. He almost looked worried. "What's wrong, Wesley?"

He glanced up and met her eyes in the mirror. "Why do you think something's wrong?"

"The look on your face."

He chuckled. "More ugly than usual, huh?"

"You're a very handsome man. You could have practically any woman in this town."

"But I don't want any woman in this town, only you," he reminded her softly. He tossed the brush aside, lifted a mass of her hair into his hands, and began playing with it. "You know that, don't you? Surely I've told you enough times."

"Yes." His eyes were on her hair now, so she went back to watching him in the mirror.

Several minutes of silence stretched between them while he fanned her hair back and forth across her naked back, making designs out of the golden lengths. "There was a man in the café last night that I used to know years ago. I don't know how long he's been in town, but one thing's for sure, he's here because of me."

"Did he tell you that?"

With his hand he swept her hair forward over her shoulder, baring her back to his gaze. "He didn't have to."

She saw his brows draw together in a frown as he softly stroked his fingers across and down her bare back. A shudder went through her at his touch. "Who is he?"

"His name is Sloan Lassiter." He bent and pressed a kiss between her shoulder blades.

"I—I've met him. He's been in the store."

He quickly lifted his head so that he could see her face in the mirror. "Did he question you about me?"

"No."

His attention returned to her back. "Good, tell him nothing." He drew a finger down her spine, then back again.

In a helpless reaction Anna sucked air in between her teeth. Hoping he hadn't heard, she asked, "What does he want?"

"I don't know, but I'm going to find out. In the meantime, I know what I want." He touched his lips to the side of her neck.

"Wesley, don't! I don't have time."

He turned her around so that she lay in his arms. In that position her hair completely covered one breast. "Yes, you do," he whispered, smoothing his hands down the cascade of her hair, contouring the length of it over her nipple and down her stomach. "Yes, you do."

"No! Wesley, I can't stay!"

Where her hair fell below her breast, he took a bunch of it in his hand. Slowly, he moved the glistening length back and forth so that it seemed as if hundreds of silken threads were sensuously stroking her breast and rigid nipple. When at last he lowered his mouth to hers, she raised up to meet him. Moments later he deliberately ended the kiss. "You can stay, can't you?"

A sob of desire tore from her throat as she pulled his mouth back to hers. "Yes, damn you, yes."

Several hours before first light Sloan made his way through the quiet tent city and slipped into Dan Cummings's empty tent. Befitting Wes McCord's supervisor, the tent was well outfitted. Besides the bed, there was a small bureau, a table, and four chairs, and, against the far wall, a desk.

Fifteen years of hell could come to an end, depending on what he found in that desk, Sloan thought.

Two drawers of the desk were locked. Without compunction he drew a knife, and moments later the locks were opened. The first drawer yielded nothing of interest. The second drawer did, however.

A pulse throbbing in his temple was the only sign of the tension he felt as he pulled a thickly bound ledger out and set it on the desk. Bending over, he opened it and began flicking through the pages. As he scanned page after page of entries, his elation built and grew, until at last he closed the book.

He straightened, the book in his hands. *This was it.* This book was going to give him everything he wanted. Maybe he wouldn't have to kill Wes McCord after all.

The cold steel of a gun barrel bit into the flesh at the base of his skull. "Draw a breath, Lassiter, because it's going to be your last."

Sweet, soft dreams floated through Brianne's head as she slept. When the pounding at the door began, it registered only vaguely. A smile curved her lips as images of Sloan making love to her curled gently around her. The pounding came again. Her smile faded and she reached out her hand for Sloan.

He wasn't there!

Her eyes opened as she felt a stab of disappointment. Where was he? Why had he left? She had never meant to fall asleep, but then she had never before experienced the extraordinary intensity and pure energy that passion demanded.

The pounding on the door broke through her sleep-hazed thoughts and brought Brianne's head around. Sloan! He must have gone out for some reason and couldn't get back in. She slid out of bed and grabbed up her robe. Making her way across the darkened room, she slipped the robe over her naked body, already anticipating the next few minutes when Sloan would again take it off her.

Smiling happily, she flung open the door, but the name of the man with whom she had shared such incredible lovemaking died on her lips as she saw a sobbing Janice standing before her. Concern immediately replaced her unhappiness that it wasn't Sloan.

"Janice, for heaven's sake, what's wrong?" The girl was covering her face with one hand and quietly crying. With her other hand she was tightly clutching some sort of book to her middle. "Come in," Brianne urged, pulling her into the room.

Brianne hurried around the room, lighting two of the lamps. When she turned back, she let out a gasp. Janice had been beaten up. Her lower lip was cut and swollen. There was an ugly bruise that covered almost the entire area of her left cheek. And above her brow a nasty cut showed signs of oozing blood. Brianne went to her immediately and led her across to a seat. "God, Janice, who did this to you?"

Janice collapsed into the chair. Her hair was wild around her head, and with a shaky hand she swiped tears from her face. "It was Dan." She cast a somewhat disoriented gaze around her. "Dan Cummings. I hope you don't mind me coming here, Miss Delaney, but when you weren't in your room, I guessed you might be here. It was plain Sloan's affections were elsewhere. Not with me," she added vaguely. "I decided you were the one. I did try to attract him though, but I had to give up. He has the coldest eyes, have you ever noticed?"

Brianne had followed Janice's ramblings as best she could. She knelt beside the girl and took her hand in hers. "Tell me why you're here and how I can help you. Do you need a doctor?"

"No, no. I wanted you to know—that is, I thought you should know about Sloan."

Confusion knit a line in Brianne's brow. "You mean what you were just telling me?"

Janice shook her head. "You can't help him now. But I brought you this." She handed Brianne the book that she had been clutching so tightly. "It's the ledger Sloan wanted. It won't do him any good now though."

A cold chill crept down Brianne's spine. "Where is Sloan, Janice?"

The girl gave a sob-racked laugh. "I thought I was foolin' Dan. I thought he wanted me bad enough that I could fool him." She turned bewildered eyes on

Brianne. "But he had it all figured out that somethin' was up. He was waitin' for Sloan."

Brianne took Janice's face between her hands and willed the girl to focus on her. "Where is Sloan?" she asked again slowly, clearly.

"But I thought you knew! He's out at the tent city. They've beaten him up pretty bad. They're gonna kill him once they find out what he knows. Might already be dead." Hysteria edged into her voice. "I've got to get out of Chango."

Brianne fought to push back the sheer panic that rose so swiftly it threatened to black out her reasoning ability. "You're in no condition to go anywhere," she said firmly. "I'm going to get someone to take care of you. But first, you've got to tell me where this tent city is."

"Why?"

"Janice, this is important!" Brianne snapped, her control hanging by a thread. "Tell me where the tent city is."

The girl gestured listlessly. "North of town."

"Good." Brianne stood up. "Now, I want you to stay right here. You'll be safe, and you won't be alone for long. I'm going to go get a very nice lady to look after you while I'm gone. Her name's Henrietta."

For the first time since she entered the room, Janice's eyes cleared and she spoke lucidly. "Miss Delaney, you've gotta know that Sloan can't be rescued, and if you're thinkin' of going after him, you won't be comin' back either."

"Just tell me where Dan Cummings's tent is, Janice."

* * *

In her room Brianne hastily dressed in her riding clothes, all the while making plans. Since birth she'd been taught that the difference between living and dying very often was determined by one thing—being prepared. Fortunately, her saddlebag was already packed for the trail. Her rifle and gun were always kept loaded, and her knife was hidden in its sheath in her left boot. If she could find it, Sloan's horse would undoubtedly be carrying a certain amount of supplies, ammunition, and a bedroll. Everyone knew that you never rode out of a western town without being ready for anything.

Strapping her gun around her hips, she decided that on the way out of the hotel she'd invade the kitchen and throw together a sack of grub. Now, if she could just think of a diversion.

The door flew open, and Henrietta entered the room like a ship under full sail. "That girl was gone, Brianne. But never mind. Her kind can look after themselves. The important thing is that you be talked out of this most dangerous plan."

Brianne stooped to pick up the saddlebag, slung it over her shoulder, then reached for the bedroll and rifle. "I don't have time for discussion, Henrietta. Look after Kam for me. He's going to be scared when he finds out I've gone."

"*He's* going to be scared! I will be, too, if you persist in this madness. My dear, the thing to do is to get help from the law of this town."

"I tried that once. Not again. Now, about Kam."

The older woman snorted. "I can handle the boy. Don't worry about that. But—"

Brianne had no time or spare energy to argue. She held up one stern, silencing finger, as if she were the schoolteacher and Henrietta the pupil. "My family will be riding into town in about a week's time. If I'm not back, give them two names—Wes McCord and Dan Cummings. They'll do the rest."

At a knock on the door Brianne strode across the room and jerked it open. Phineas stood there.

One look at him and Brianne knew she had her diversion.

The sky had barely begun to lighten when Brianne dismounted. Dan's tent had been easy to find. It took her a little longer to locate Sloan's horse. Sloan had left his horse in an easily accessible spot, so she hobbled Dancer beside the big black. Then, taking the extra saddlebag off Dancer, she started threading her way quietly through the still-sleeping camp.

Her heart felt as if it were in her throat. Never in her life had she been so frightened. But her fierce determination that she would find Sloan alive and be able to get him to safety kept her going.

At each tent she knelt and pulled from the saddlebag a bottle of Tooley's Miracle Restorative. Quickly, she unscrewed the cap and stuffed a long length of cloth into the opening. Then she lit it, shoved the bottle with its contents of ninety-proof alcohol beneath the flap of the tent, and moved on to the next one. By the time she reached Dan's tent, the tent city was already beginning to burn.

She hid and waited.

* * *

"Come on, Lassiter. Make it easy on yourself. Just how much pain do you want to suffer before you die?"

Over the last two hours Sloan had learned that Dan Cummings was a straightforward man with a simple-minded doggedness. It didn't bother the man that despite the heavy beating, he hadn't told him a thing. In Cummings's mind, a beating would equal a confession sooner or later. And once he had his confession, he would kill him.

He was going to die, Sloan thought, but he sure as hell wasn't going to make it any easier for Cummings or Wes. A man on either side of him held him upright and still. He squinted his eyes and tried to focus on Cummings. "Go to hell."

A blow landed squarely in his gut. Hot sharp pain lanced through his body. Nausea rose in his throat.

"Hurts, doesn't it?" Dan asked almost sympathetically. "All you gotta do is tell me how you found out about our operation and who else knows, and I'll end your pain."

"What about that bitch Janice?" a voice belonging to the man holding Sloan's left arm snarled.

"I've got someone after her now. She made a big mistake when she took that ledger. She'll pay."

"Leave her alone," Sloan managed to say. "She's not involved. And having to sleep with you should be payment enough."

Sloan felt something slam brutally into the side of his skull. He fought to retain consciousness, but it was a losing battle. Blessed darkness overtook him.

He had no idea how long the darkness lasted, because the next thing he knew, cold water was being thrown in his face. For a moment he thought he would drown.

"Lassiter, I'm gettin' mad now. You turned my girl against me. You broke into my desk. The ledger's gone. I've gotta come up with some explanation for McCord. He's not gonna be a happy man."

Sloan coughed, then groaned because it felt as if the muscles of his stomach were tearing. "That breaks my heart."

"Damn you, Lassiter!"

"Fire! Fire!"

Suddenly, people could be heard running and screaming.

"God, the city's on fire!" the man on Sloan's right muttered, fear in his voice.

"Go find out what's goin' on," Cummings ordered.

With one half of his support gone, Sloan slumped to the ground.

"Frank, get him on his feet!" Cummings barked.

Brianne stepped into the tent, her rifle pointed at Wes, the pistol aimed at the man he had called Frank. "Don't touch him."

Sloan could hardly believe his eyes. "Brianne."

Frank whirled, reaching for his gun. Brianne fired twice. One bullet knocked his gun out of his hand; the other bullet hit him in the leg. He went down, clutching his leg. Blood was already spreading down his pants leg.

Out of the corner of her eyes Brianne saw Sloan try to get up. "Don't try to move yet," she told him. Dan Cummings wasn't armed, but Brianne's steady gaze had been off him only seconds. "Drop to your stomach and hold your hands behind your back."

With the hammer of the rifle cocked and its muzzle pointed directly at his heart, he did as she ordered. He'd never seen a woman with such fiery green eyes. He'd also never seen a woman that was as good with a gun as she was. If Frank didn't die from blood loss, he was going to be out of action for a long time to come.

When he was prone, she walked to him, jabbed the rifle at the back of his neck, then reached for the rope that she had tied at her belt. It already had a slip knot in the end of it. She lengthened the loop, dropped it over his hands, and pulled tight.

"Ow! That hurts, you bitch!"

"Hold up your feet," she demanded, yanking tighter on the rope. He did, and she secured his feet. Lastly, she jerked the neckerchief from around his neck and tied it around his mouth.

She gave the other man the same treatment, slightly more gentle, because he was in such obvious pain. Then she went to Sloan.

"Can you stand?"

"Brianne, you shouldn't be here."

"And you shouldn't have been gone when I woke up either!" she snapped, so glad to see him alive she had to fight back tears. Now was not the time to break down. "Never mind. We've got to get out of here." She bent to him and helped him to his feet, turning pale when she heard his groan of pain. "Lean on me. The horses aren't very far away."

The air was thick with smoke when they stepped outside the tent. Flames were everywhere, and it appeared that the gray dawn sky was on fire. From somewhere close she could hear the frightened sounds of the livestock and made a mental note of the direction. When she sighted their horses, she gave thanks that both animals had been well trained and hadn't bolted at the first smell of smoke.

"We're going to use my horse," she told Sloan. "I know him, and I know he'll carry double. I can keep you in the saddle once you're up, but you're going to have to mount by yourself. Can you?"

Grim determination entered his pain-lined face. "Yes."

She leaned over to guide his foot into the stirrup, and in the end had to put her weight under him to help him into the saddle. She molded his hands around the saddle horn, then tied his horse behind Dancer. After she mounted behind him, she took hold of the reins with one hand and wrapped the other arm around him. "Stay with me, Sloan. Don't pass out." The fact that he didn't answer her added to her fear.

She kept to the edge of the camp only long enough to find the corral the cattle were kept in and open the gate. The remuda was nearby, and she reached over to cut their lines. Crazed with fear, the animals bolted. She reined Dancer in behind four or five head of cattle, taking advantage of their wake of churned-up ground, and began to drive them, heading west into the hills.

But staying behind them, she could go only so fast. When she sighted the brush, she headed for it. "Sloan, I'm going to tie some brush behind your horse to wipe out our tracks. Will dragging it bother him?"

She barely heard his whispered "No," but it reassured her.

She pulled Dancer to a halt and dismounted. Laying her hand on Sloan's thigh, she murmured, "I won't be long. Just hang on. I'm going to get us to safety."

Minutes later she was behind him again, one arm holding him tightly. "Lean back against me, Sloan. We're going to go faster now. The sun's coming up and we need all the time we can get." She kicked Dancer into a lope.

The ride was agony for Sloan. The pain came at him in endless waves. The fight to hold on to consciousness was constant. Brianne talked to him continuously in a calm voice meant to reassure him, yet keep him conscious. Tenaciously, he fastened onto her words, forcing himself to listen carefully, certain that they were the only thing between him and oblivion. The other thing he tried hard to do was to make his mind work, to be as aware as he could of what was going on, even through the fog of pain.

He wasn't always successful. There were times when the pain would become too much and he would give in to the urge to close his eyes, to moan, and to let the pain take him where it would.

But at all times a small, distant part of him remained amazed.

Brianne used terrain and cover like an Indian. At one point she had found a stream and they had ridden a couple of miles in it. When they came out of the stream, she had chosen rock. Then when the rock ran out, she somehow managed to find the hardest ground.

When he had first seen her in Dan Cummings's tent, he had been horrified that she had put herself in such danger. He was still afraid for her, but now he realized that if anyone could pull off a miracle, it just might be Brianne Delaney.

Wes slammed the drawer of his desk shut. Damn Sundays! He hated them. Sundays were the one day of the week he couldn't see Anna. The Emporium wasn't open, so he couldn't make an excuse to drop in for some item or other. And he wouldn't have her all to himself again until Monday night.

Damn! He stood up and strode to the window.

"Mr. McCord, is there something I can do for you?"

He heard the tentative voice of Ralph Mahoney behind him and silently swore. "Yeah. Go over to the café and bring me back a fresh cup of coffee."

"Sure thing."

He didn't really want any coffee. He just wanted to be alone. To think of Anna. Three nights a week wasn't enough. But three nights a week was pushing the situation and he knew it. Any more, and her father might get suspicious. To have her father know that she was his woman would hurt Anna beyond belief, and he would never want that.

Still, he couldn't help but daydream about having her sleeping beside him seven nights a week. And waking up with her seven mornings a week.

A rider turned his horse into the hitching post in front of Wes's office and swung down. Wes recognized him as Dutch Howard, one of Cummings's men. He jerked his mind back to matters at hand and went out to meet him.

"Mr. McCord, Dan asked me to deliver a message."

Wes nodded. "What is it?"

Dutch glanced up and down the street. Even though it was Sunday, people were visible, out for a morning stroll or on their way to church. "We best go inside, Mr. McCord."

Wes turned on his heel and reentered his office. Dutch followed. Minutes later, Wes was looking at Dutch in disbelief. "How much was destroyed?"

"Just about all the tents and everything that was in them. Fire caught some black powder. It went up and took a flatbed load of rails up with it. We was able to save most of the rest of the supplies."

Fury fast replaced disbelief. "And Cummings thinks that Janice got away with the ledger?"

Dutch squirmed in his chair. "She's the only one that could've. Dan had slapped her around and thought she'd be quiet for a while. We turned our 'tention to Lassiter, and next thing you know, she's up and gone. And so's the ledger."

Wes's fist came down on top of his desk so hard, the wood rattled. "And so, goddammit, is Sloan Lassiter! Just how in the hell did you people manage to let so many things get destroyed and so many people get away?"

Dutch gazed nervously around the room. "It was the fire and all. Nobody was expecting no fire."

"Apparently, that wasn't all you weren't expecting,"

Wes snapped, thinking of Brianne Delaney. Suddenly, he jabbed his finger at Dutch. "You tell Dan Cummings I want those three people. Find them and take them back to the tent city."

"Wes and four or five of the boys have already lit out after that lady and Lassiter. He sent a couple of others after Janice."

"Good. We've *got* to find that ledger! In the meantime, I'll make arrangements for new tents for the men. We can't let this delay the building of the railroad any longer than necessary."

13

The sun had been beating down on them all day. By its angle, Brianne judged the time to be about four o'clock in the afternoon. They had been in the saddle since early morning, and Sloan had long ago stopped giving her even monosyllabic answers. She was frantic with worry about him, but they couldn't afford to stop until she found some sort of shelter for them that would offer concealment and that would be defensible.

Using every evasive maneuver she had ever learned, she had kept them riding west away from the tent city until noon. Then she had doubled back, keeping in mind something her uncle, Dom, had once taught her—the best place to hide from your enemy is somewhere close to his own home ground, because that's the last place he thinks to look.

Up behind the tent city there was a butte, and she had had them climbing the back of it for the last two hours. She was practiced at reading the lay of the land, and she was betting their lives that she would be able to find them shelter somewhere on the butte.

She knew that the natural formation of land could

be deceptive. So she was going on instincts, that and her knowledge of animals. She had found an old cattle trail. It was narrow, and by its overgrown state she judged it hadn't been used in years. But she had decided to follow it, gambling that it would lead her to water and perhaps good grazing for the horses.

Giving Dancer his head, she swiveled around to carefully scan their back trail. "Still clear," she said to Sloan, no longer sure he heard her but needing to talk to him anyway. "I've been as slippery and cunning as I know how. And I've used every damn thing that Rising Star and Silver Dove taught me. Oh, Cummings and his men may be able to track us, but we'll sure as hell slow them up and make them work to find us." She laughed. "I shouldn't cuss, should I? If Patrick were here, he'd tell me Malvina would wash my mouth out with soap." The laughter died out of her voice, leaving a sudden deep sorrow. "I wish Patrick were here."

Sloan stirred. Her arms trembled and ached from holding him in the saddle all these hours. Because they were climbing, he was leaning back against her, and every torturous breath he drew was transmitted to her. The tension she could feel in his muscles told her the tremendous effort he was exerting to stay upright. She was so afraid for him. She had no idea how extensive his injuries were, but she knew he wasn't going to be able to last much longer. She had to get him to a place where he would be safe and she could nurse him.

"It won't be too long," she murmured, hurting for

him. "I promise you. Just hang on a little while longer."

Dancer stepped off the trail and turned toward a wall of brush that was growing against the side of the butte. She reined him back. When he persisted in pulling in that direction, she decided to let him have his head. In some ways animals were smarter than people, and they had the ability to sense danger or to smell water.

As they drew closer, she saw that behind the brush there was a narrow opening in the side of the butte. Further scrutiny revealed that the opening would be just wide enough for the horses to go through single file.

Two choices occurred to her simultaneously. Either she could dismount and investigate the opening on foot, or she could go ahead and lead the horses through. Quickly, she chose the latter. She didn't feel that she could risk leaving Sloan alone for even a few minutes.

"This may be our answer," she told him. "Hold on tight." She directed the horses through the brush and into the opening. There was no space to spare on either side of them. Their boots grazed the sides of the rock walls that rose high above them. But when they finally made it through, she permitted a smile of satisfaction to spread over her face.

They were inside a box canyon. On the floor of the canyon a meadow of green grass flowed into and out of deeply carved arroyos and around huge boulders. At the far end of it was a stand of trees. To her left and perhaps twenty-five feet above the meadow an overhang jutted out over a ledge. Water, she guessed, had worn the rock back until a small cave had been created. A shelf edged the mouth of the cave then began to curve downward to the floor of the canyon. To the right of the cave a fall of rocks and boulders blocked the shelf ledge, but the other side was clear.

She walked the horses to the beginning of the rocky footpath, then slid off Dancer and hobbled him. Sloan's eyes were shut and his breathing was shallow.

His hands were clutched tightly around the saddle horn. She covered them with his. "Listen to me. You're going to have to walk up an incline, but once you're there, you can rest and I can take care of you." He didn't answer or respond. She began prying his fingers away. "You've got to get down. You can lean on me while we're walking. I'll take as much of your weight as I can."

When he still didn't move, she reached up and took hold of his arm. "Sloan, I know you're in a great deal of pain and that you've endured a lot, but you're going to have to do one more thing. You're going to have to help me!"

Sloan heard the urgent plea in her voice. His dismount was part fall, part slide.

The impact of his feet hitting the ground made Sloan groan aloud with pain. It felt as if red-hot spikes had imbedded themselves in his head and in his stomach. He would have collapsed if Brianne hadn't quickly thrust herself under his arm and steadied him.

"I know this is hard, Sloan, but you've got to do it."

"I can't."

"Yes, you can, and you're going to. I'm not going to let anything happen to you." She had to ignore the fact that his skin was almost white, she told herself.

"Bri—"

"Don't talk. Save your strength." Slowly, she walked him onto the ledge path. "Take it one step at a time."

Sloan couldn't see. The pain had blinded him. So again he fastened on to her voice. And she never stopped talking, encouraging when he faltered, giving him courage when he could find none within himself.

Once he fell. He didn't want to get up. But he heard Brianne frantically calling his name, pulling at his arms, and somehow he managed to get back to his feet and begin walking again. He wanted to stop. He desperately needed to. Just when it seemed to him that he couldn't take one more step, though, he'd take another. He didn't know how. He didn't know where they were going. He didn't care.

All he wanted to do was cease his motion, lie down, and let the tormenting pain take him toward the blackness that had been pulling at him all day. But Brianne's voice wouldn't let him go. He listened carefully, wondering where her laughter had gone.

At last, with a sob of relief, Brianne guided him into the little cave. At its deepest point it was sixteen or seventeen feet. She led him to the back of it. "Here . . . sit down here and rest." Her arms were around his back and his waist, holding him tightly, supporting him as best she could. When he went limp and slipped out of her arms, she wasn't prepared. "Sloan!" She dropped down beside him and rested his head on her lap. Tears were running down her face, but she ignored them. "Sloan," she said again, this time more gently.

But he didn't answer. He was unconscious.

Jake Koller shoved Janice backward onto the bed in Dan's tent, one of the few tents that hadn't been completely burned to the ground. He grinned crookedly as her skirts flew up to her knees and he spoke to the man standing next to him. "Dan told us we should find her and bring her back here, but he didn't say what we should do with her, did he?"

Malcolm Williams's gaze was on the torn neckline of her blouse. She'd fought like a wildcat when they'd caught up with her, he remembered with considerable pleasure. During the struggle he'd been the one who'd torn the blouse, and he'd had a feel of those luscious breasts. But dammit all if he didn't want more now. He went to sit on the edge of the bed. "We're supposed to get out of her where the ledger is."

"Did he say how we was supposed to do that?" Jake asked, never taking his eyes off Janice. If it'd been up to him, they wouldn't have brought her in at all. They'd have set up camp and just kept her to themselves for a while.

"Nope," Malcolm answered.

Pulling the two sides of her blouse together, Janice squirmed to the head of the bed and sat up. Malcolm and Jake were two of Dan's men, and she'd never liked them. But at least they'd left her alone in the past. Now it was clear what was on their mind. They were fairly panting with lust. "I'm not tellin' you nothin'! Where's Dan?"

Malcolm reached out and thrust his hand beneath her skirts to stroke the back of a calf with his fingers. "Now, honey, why would you want him? He's just liable to beat you up again."

Repulsed by his touch, she tried to shrink away from him, but his caressing fingers turned hard and bit into her flesh. Tears sprang into her eyes, but, she decided, she wasn't going to give these bastards the satisfaction of crying. "He'll kill you if he comes back and finds you've laid a finger on me!"

At that Jake gave a snort of laughter and pointed to her battered and bruised face. "Who're you kiddin', girlie? Any man that'd do that to a woman doesn't care what happens to her. He sent us after you. We found you. Now you're ours!"

Malcolm had shifted his position on the bed so that he had her trapped against its back. "All you got is us, honey. Now what we want to know is, where's the ledger?"

For probably the first time in her life Janice forced herself to face some ugly truths. No one would come if she screamed. Everyone thought of her as nothing but a whore. No one saw that she had a heart that hurt occasionally. No one was ever kind to her unless it was in bed—and then not always. And lastly, Dan was going to kill her when he got back. She needed to play for time. "If I tell you, will you let me go?"

Jake sat down on the side of the bed and slapped her hands loose from the material she was attempting to hold over her breasts. "Sure, honey, tell us."

Janice's resolve not to cry was fast fading. Her face was hurting, and she knew they were lying to her. They wouldn't let her go. Why had she ever thought that being in on the building of a railroad would be fun? For that matter, why had she ever thought men were fun? Malcolm and Jake were ugly and dirty. She didn't want them to touch her. She never wanted any man to touch her again! Suddenly, she couldn't take it anymore. She kicked out with her feet and caught Malcolm squarely in the stomach. "Leave me alone!"

While Malcolm grabbed his stomach, Jake snatched a handful of her hair and pulled her head back. "Now, that's not nice, girlie." Rotten teeth showed through parted lips. "Malcolm, you all right?"

"How'd you like some of her?" Malcolm asked, grunting.

Jake pressed his hand against the uncomfortable bulge in his lap. "What d'ya mean? I can have her?"

Malcolm shoved one big hand under the torn material of her blouse, brutally grabbed one of her breasts, and began squeezing. "She's not gonna tell us nothin', so let's have a little fun."

Janice tried to push the men away, but they were all over her and it seemed like their hands were everywhere. "Stop! Stop!"

"We could divide her up!" Jake suggested generously, already reaching for the buttons of his trousers. "I'll use her top half and you can use her bottom half; then we'll switch."

"Good idea," Malcolm said, grabbing her legs and pulling her down on the bed until she lay full length.

He shucked his pants down around his knees and squirmed himself between her legs.

In the meantime Jake began to arrange himself over her mouth.

Janice was screaming and screaming.

Two gunshots were fired, so close together they sounded like one.

"Get off her!" Wes McCord said, his voice cold yet soft, ominously so.

Just the sight of him frightened Malcolm and Jake more than the sound of the two shots being fired had. They scrambled to their feet, falling several times in the process.

"We were just tryin' to get her to tell us where the ledger is," Malcolm said, hastily pulling up his pants.

"Yeah," Jake chimed in, his fingers shaking so badly he couldn't even grasp a button, much less do one up, "the bitch wouldn't cooperate."

"Wait for me outside," Wes said.

It didn't matter that neither of them had their pants fastened yet. They left the tent so fast, they stirred up dust.

Janice's sobs were calming now. Wes walked to the side of the bed and stood looking down at her. What he saw made his jaw clench. Her breasts had angry red whelps where the men had grabbed her. The inside of her thigh had three long, bloody scratches running the length.

Leaning over, he pulled her skirt down to her ankles. Before he straightened, he gently touched one finger to the side of her face. "Did they do this too?"

Like everyone who knew of him, Janice was afraid

of Wes McCord. She had never actually been this close to him before, and now that she was, she could see the cold anger burning in his eyes. She swallowed hard. "Dan Cummings."

Wes cursed silently. He'd heard that every so often Cummings liked to hurt a woman just for the fun of it. There'd even been a rumor that he'd killed one of the girls at Lucky's Saloon awhile back, but no one had been able to prove anything. As soon as Cummings got back to town, he was going to fire him, something he obviously should have done a long time ago. His only excuse was that he'd had so many other things on his mind.

He glanced around, locating the small bureau. He opened a drawer, pulled out a shirt, and handed it to Janice. "Put this on." Then he sat down.

Hastily, Janice sat up and pulled the shirt on over her dress. Because she was shaking so badly, it took her a long time to button it.

Wes sat patiently, waiting. Finally she was finished. "Can I get you anything?"

Warily, she shook her head. Even though he was speaking softly, she thought his voice sounded as cold as a knife's blade and just as dangerous. She'd be better off with a dozen Malcolms and Jakes, she thought, than with one of Wes McCord.

He crossed his legs and leaned back in the chair. "All right, Janice. I want you to tell me what you did with that ledger."

She hesitated, thinking of Brianne Delaney. Miss Delaney had been nice to her. She'd spoken to her on the street, and when she'd been hurt, Miss Delaney had been concerned.

"The ledger is my property, Janice. I have a right to know."

Janice felt a chill skip down her spine. His voice reminded her that this was a man she did not want to cross.

"Janice?"

"I gave it to Miss Delaney."

There was a short silence. "Do you know what she did with it?"

She shook her head, not daring to look at him.

"Do you know where she is now?"

She shook her head again.

"Are you telling me the truth, Janice?"

He was a compelling man, and being a woman, she couldn't help but finally look at him. "Yes."

He nodded and stood. "All right. Someone will bring in some soap and water. After you've cleaned up, you're free to go."

"Go?" Her bewilderment showed in her face. "You mean you're going to let me leave now?"

Already at the opening of the tent, he paused briefly to throw a last glance at her over his shoulder. "Your horse will be waiting for you."

Janice's legs gave out and she sank to the bed. In an instant she made the most important decision of her life: As soon as they brought her horse to her, she was going home to her mama!

Over the years pine needles and leaves had blown into the cave. Brianne formed them into the shape of a mattress, and then spread one of the blankets over the mound. Looking back at Sloan, she saw the huge welt on the side of his head that was caked with blood. There were other bruises on his face, and she imagined his body had taken a battering too. Her stomach turned over as she thought of the pain he must have suffered today. But he had never complained. And somehow he'd managed to stay strong long enough for her to get him to shelter. As gently as she could she rolled him onto the makeshift mattress and covered him with another blanket.

"I love you," she whispered to him, and ran a hand across his forehead. "I've got to leave for just a little while. I hate to, but if we're to survive, I have some more things I've got to do." She bent and pressed a kiss on an unbruised portion of his cheek. "I'll be back soon."

During the next few hours she set out to increase their chances of coming out of this whole thing alive. She went back to the opening of the box canyon and rearranged the brush as best she could, so that, hopefully, a person passing by might not notice anything out of order.

Having already taken one bedroll up to the cave, she now stripped the saddlebags, guns, and canteens from both horses, plus the remaining bedroll. It took two trips, but she managed to get everything transferred up to their shelter.

Then she set about exploring the rest of the canyon. At the far end of the meadow she discovered a small creek that meandered through the stand of willows and cottonwoods. The grass grew lush and thick there. She unsaddled the horses and tethered them so that they could graze and water but so that anyone coming through the narrow passage into the canyon wouldn't be able to see them.

She was eager to get back to Sloan, but before she did, she thoughtfully scanned the back wall of the canyon and discovered another way out. A steep, rocky path led up its face to the top of the butte. It was already getting dark and she couldn't see very well, but unless she missed her guess, the summit would overlook the tent city.

Impatiently, she glanced toward the overhang where she had left Sloan. She'd climb up to the summit tomorrow. For now she'd been away from him long enough.

All night long he tossed and turned. Two times he was sick. Brianne cleaned him up and soothed him, bathing his forehead.

She slept when she could. When she couldn't, she huddled close beside him under the blankets and talked quietly to him.

She told Sloan about growing up on Killara and about how wonderful it had been. She told him a story about each member of her family. Often she'd find herself smiling as she talked; once she was surprised to find a tear sliding down her cheek.

She saved Patrick to talk about last. She told Sloan about how, when they were young, they would play "hide-and-track." They got so good at it, they finally had to stop playing the game because they couldn't find each other.

Those days were gone now, and for the first time in

her life, there were no Delaneys to help her. Men were trying to track her, but not for any game. She was all alone. And if she and Sloan were going to survive, she was going to have to call upon every bit of Delaney know-how she'd ever learned.

The soft voice floated around Sloan, but he heard no words. Waves of heat and cold broke over him. And always there was the pain. It lanced through his head, pulsing, pounding.

Images of a smiling young Wes McCord swam through the blackness of his mind. "Water," the image said. "Just follow my directions and you'll find water." Then he saw his brother. Agony scored David's face. His leg was swollen to grotesque proportions. "Go on without me," he said.

Once the pain stopped, and he saw Brianne. Her beautiful face was pale, and her eyes looked tired. He tried to speak, but his mouth wouldn't move. She smiled down at him, and he felt her hand gently stroke his brow. "You're going to be all right," she said. He shut his eyes then, the blackness and the pain coming again.

Brianne climbed up to the summit of the butte and eased over until she could see the tent city. Lying on her stomach, she looked down. Distance made the people working near the tents appear as ants, and the burnt-out tents as black spots. There was a lot of activity. That they were reconstructing the city was obvious, but she couldn't see anything in detail.

She made her way off the butte and back down to the meadow. She changed the position of the horses, then checked the hidden entrance Dancer had found.

Nothing appeared disturbed. Gingerly, she made her way out until she could check the trail. Nothing so far.

Back in the little cave she added aspen leaves to the smokeless fire and boiled beef jerky for a broth.

Sloan felt the hot liquid in his mouth and swallowed. It tasted good. When in a few minutes he again felt the spoon against his lips, he opened his mouth for more. He heard Brianne's soft voice say, "That's the way!" and then the blackness claimed him again.

He opened his eyes. The first thing he saw was Brianne. She was sitting just beyond him, staring away at the distance. He let his eyes focus on her and he remembered.

He remembered being beaten, and Brianne shooting one of the men, and tying up Cummings and the man she had shot. He remembered that awful ride, her constant encouragement, and her resourcefulness and cleverness. She had saved his life.

"Brianne."

Her head jerked around, and at the sight of his open eyes her face lit up. "Sloan!" She crawled to his side and placed her hand on his cheek. "I'm so glad you're back with me. How're you feeling?"

"I'm either feeling better or I'm dead."

She sat back on her heels. "Humor. That's good."

"It's not humor. It's the truth." His voice was weak, raw.

She was so happy that he was talking to her, she had to touch him. She combed her fingers through his hair. "I understand," she crooned. "You've been through hell, haven't you? But you're going to be all right now. I'm going to take care of you." She paused. "Are you hungry?"

He thought for a moment or two, his gaze steady on her. "I don't think so."

She glanced over her shoulder at the fire over which a spit turned. "I trapped a rabbit, but it's got a way to go yet before it'll be ready. In the meantime, you should have water." She reached behind her for a canteen, held it to his lips, and waited while he drank. When he finished, she set it aside and smiled down at him. "I'll give you some broth in a minute."

"I remember having had some."

She nodded, thinking that his voice was getting stronger. "You've been so sick. It was the head injury."

"Cummings did a job on me." His eyes roved over her. "There were times when the pain was so bad I thought I was going to die and I'd never see you again."

With an expression of tenderness on her face, she leaned over him. "I wasn't going to let you die."

He brought a somewhat unsteady hand up to touch her cheek. "You were wonderful." He saw something like surprise come and go in her eyes, and he continued. "I can't think of another person, or for that matter an army of people, who could've done what you did."

She was suddenly uncertain. They weren't making love, and yet he was looking at her as if— "I did what I had to do."

"I've never been so scared in my life as when I saw you step into that tent, Brianne."

"Nothing was going to happen to me."

"Of course not. You're a Delaney, right?"

"Right," she said softly.

"I hadn't realized how much life had come to mean to me until I nearly lost it." He paused. "I hadn't realized how much you'd come to mean to me."

She felt the faint stirring of hope, but she was still hesitant, realistic, because he was badly hurt and he needed her . . . for now. "Do you really mean what you just said?"

"I'm very much afraid I do."

"But for how long, Sloan? Until you've recovered? Until you go back east? How long?"

He smiled tenderly. "Redhead, I suspect that eternity may be too short for the loving we've got to do."

**Don't miss the enthralling sequel to this book,
Silken Thunder, also by Fayrene Preston, and part of
the concluding trilogy of THE DELANEYS, THE
UNTAMED YEARS.**

THE DELANEY DYNASTY

Three of Bantam's bestselling romance authors, Kay Hooper, Iris Johansen and Fayrene Preston, have established a unique event in romance publishing—the creation of the Delaney Dynasty—a family filled with fascinating male and female characters whose love stories are deeply sensual and unforgettable. Each author's work stands alone, but read with the other books is part of a panoramic picture of a colorful, exciting, and heartwarming family.

The stories of the members of the Delaney Dynasty began with the publication of THE SHAMROCK TRINITY, the first trio of contemporary love stories of the Delaney brothers—*Rafe, The Maverick* by Kay Hooper; *York, The Renegade* by Iris Johansen; and *Burke, The Kingpin* by Fayrene Preston. These three romances received such wide acclaim and generated such a clamor for more stories of the Delaneys that our authors soon gave us the next three contemporaries—THE DELANEYS OF KILLAROO: *Adelaide, The Enchantress* by Kay Hooper; *Matilda, The Adventuress* by Iris Johansen; and *Sydney, The Temptress* by Fayrene Preston.

The authors' fascination with the Delaneys grew and, particularly, they were captivated by the daring and romantic ancestors who started it all. Thus, the Delaney historicals were created, one of which you have just read.

Setting the stage for the trilogy THE DELANEYS, THE UNTAMED YEARS, though, was THIS FIERCE SPLENDOR by Iris Johansen. In the pages that follow we are giving you excerpts of THE DELANEYS OF KILLAROO, THIS FIERCE SPLENDOR, and two of the other books of the trilogy THE DELANEYS, THE UNTAMED YEARS. We hope these excerpts will tempt you to get any of the books you may have missed . . . as well as to look forward to the second and last set of historical novels that will follow up THE UNTAMED YEARS and be published in the late fall of 1988.

ASK FOR THE BOOKS OF THE DELANEY DYNASTY SERIES AT YOUR LOCAL BOOKSTORE OR GET THEM THROUGH THE MAIL BY USING THE COUPON AT THE BACK OF THIS BOOK.

The Delaneys of Killaroo:

Adelaide, The Enchantress

by Kay Hooper

He probably wouldn't have noticed them except for the koala. It wasn't, after all, unusual to see a horse at a racetrack, or even a girl walking beside a horse. And it wasn't that unusual to see a koala in Australia.

But he'd never seen one with four leather gloves covering its paws and riding a horse.

He didn't know much about koalas, but this one seemed a fair example of the species. It looked absurdly cuddly, with tufts of ears and a round little body, button eyes, and a large black nose.

Shane Marston turned his astonished eyes from the koala to the horse that walked quietly, obediently, beside the girl holding his lead rope. He wore no blanket or leg bandages, and seemed not to mind the koala clinging to his back.

The girl stopped just inside the wide barn hall and dropped the lead rope, and while the horse stood calmly she held out her arm toward the koala, calling, "Sebastian."

The little creature reached a gloved paw toward her, not completely releasing the horse's mane until he could grasp her arm. Then he left the horse in a smooth transfer to the girl's back, his limbs firmly around her neck.

Shane stood very still, gazing at the girl and feeling the shock of her voice still echoing in his mind. It was the sweetest, most gentle voice he had ever heard, and it touched something inside him, something that had never been touched before. His throat felt tight and his heart pounded, and he was bewildered because suddenly he couldn't breathe very well.

She was not thin, but she was small and looked amazingly fragile. Her skin was very fair, almost translucent. The only color she could boast of was the vibrant red of her short hair; and though that hair was a badge of passion and temper, in her face was reflected only gentleness and calm.

She was not, he realized on some uncaring level of himself, a beautiful young woman. Her mouth was too wide for beauty, her eyes too large. Yet that tender mouth would always draw the gaze of a man, and those dark eyes would haunt his dreams.

"You want to meet her?"

Shane started at the sound of Tate Justin's voice. Tate didn't wait for an answer, but started walking forward.

Shane fell into step beside him, eager to meet the girl with the soft, gentle voice and the fiery hair.

"Addie." Tate smiled rather sardonically. "A guest of ours wants to meet you; he's an American horse breeder. Adelaide Delaney, Shane Marston."

Shane, peculiarly sensitive to undercurrents, saw something flash between them, something genuinely humorous on Tate's part and somewhat pained on hers.

She turned to Shane, looking up at him. "Mr. Marston."

Shane held the small hand, instinctively gentle, his fingers tingling again while a faint shock registered at the back of his mind. Her name . . . Was it possible? No . . . half a world away . . . "A pleasure, Miss Delaney," he said, releasing her hand when it occurred to him that he had held it too long.

"I'll leave you two to get acquainted," Tate said, and then walked away.

She gazed after him for a moment, then gave Shane an easy, friendly half smile. "You're interested in Australian horses, Mr. Marston?"

"Shane. And yes, I am."

"Breeding stock, or racers?"

"Primarily breeding stock." Shane reached out to pass a hand down Resolute's sloping shoulders. "He's a fine animal."

"Yes, he is." Her voice gentled even more with the words.

Shane chuckled suddenly and gestured to the koala asleep with his chin on her shoulder. "And unusual, since he allows the koala to ride him."

"Sebastian's the unusual one." She reached up to trail a finger along the koala's foreleg, and a tufted ear twitched sleepily. "He was orphaned young, and instead of climbing trees he took to people and horses. Some people, mind you, and some horses. He's a bit temperamental—but then, so is Resolute." She smiled. "I believe American racehorses sometimes choose odd stable companions?"

"They certainly do," Shane said, remembering the moth-eaten cockatoo at his stable.

Shane looked down at her lustrous coppery curls and felt his heart turn over. He was conscious of an abrupt sense of urgency, a fiery prodding along his nerve endings.

Addie frowned a little and touched his arm in a seemingly instinctive gesture. "Are you all right?"

He looked down at her, feeling her touch clear through to his bones. "Yes. I suppose I haven't recovered from jet lag yet, that's all."

The dark eyes searched his briefly, but she nodded and dropped her hand. "It was nice meeting you—" she began.

Shane smiled broadly. "Oh, I'll be around for a while," he said. "In Australia—and on the tracks. You're riding this afternoon?"

Addie nodded. "Yes, and tomorrow." She didn't seem surprised that he knew she rode. "Then up to Sydney with Resolute for the weekend races."

Shane bit back what he wanted to say. "I see. Well, I believe I'll watch you ride today." He grinned. "Should I bet on you?"

Seriously, she said, "I intend to win."

"Then I'll bet my kingdom."

She laughed a little, the sound once again running through Shane like a haunting song, then waved casually and walked away. He stood stock still for several minutes, gazing after her. Suddenly aware of the increasing noise that heralded the beginning of the afternoon races, he headed toward the track.

Addie had just won the last race on a horse improbably named Catch Me If You Can. She went through the routine of unsaddling, weighing out, and speaking to a delighted owner and a somewhat stunned trainer. Then, tiredly, she headed back for the changing room. She showered and changed into jeans and a light blouse.

Shane was outside, waiting for her.

"I won some money," he said, smiling at her. "And I was hoping you'd go out with me somewhere to celebrate."

"I'd like that." Addie was a little surprised by her instant acceptance, and frowned briefly. "Let me check on Resolute first, all right?"

"Where would you like to have dinner?"

Addie started a little. "Oh, wherever you like. Somewhere casual, please; I travel light on the circuit, so I never pack dressy things."

"Fine. We can go in my rental car, and pick up your Jeep later."

"All right then, and thanks."

"My pleasure." He watched her lock up the Jeep and pocket her keys, then took her arm courteously as they headed toward the parking area near the stables.

Shane didn't try to fool himself into believing that manners had compelled him to take her arm; he was, in fact, very well mannered. That had little to do with it, however. He had taken her arm because he knew he'd go out of his mind if he couldn't touch her even in a polite and casual way. And though it might have seemed just that outwardly, he was very conscious that there was nothing casual in his reaction to the touch.

He felt a sizzling jolt when he touched her, his breath catching oddly and his head becoming curiously light. The strength of his own feelings distrubed him, not in the least because she seemed almost too frail to withstand the powerful force of such vital desire. And it did no good at all to remind himself that she was quite obviously a strong woman; her soft voice, her shimmering halo of silky red hair, small size, and magical gift with animals made her appear ethereal, and all his male instincts urged him to believe in frailty rather than strength.

Shane had always taken his attraction to women lightly in the past; he enjoyed their company, whether casual or intimate. He had a great many female friends, and the lovers in his past tended to remain firm friends after the affairs had ended. Though in a position of comfortable wealth and gifted with blond hair and green eyes that caused the American tabloids to persist in referring to him as "the sleekest, sexiest Thoroughbred in racing circles," Shane had never cared much for casual sex.

Not since his experimental teens had he taken a woman to bed without first having genuinely liked her—and if those invited declined, they never lost Shane as a friend.

What he had seen and heard of Addie, he certainly liked. He liked the frank gaze of her dark eyes, her quick smile and fluid grace. Her voice held a strange power to move him; and her gift with animals and—apparently—people fascinated him.

Yet, for all that, he knew almost nothing about her. Nothing to explain why his very bones seemed to dissolve when she looked at him or spoke to him. Nothing to explain the rabid fear he only just had managed to control while watching her race. Nothing to explain this urgent, driving need to touch her.

Shane knew what desire felt like, and he had even known the feeling to occur spontaneously when first meeting a woman—but that was like comparing the rumble of thunder to the violence of a hurricane.

You'll frighten her to death, he told himself fiercely. If he let go. If he gave in to desires urging him to tumble them both into the nearest bed and violently explore these feelings he had never felt before . . .

She was too gentle and frail, he told himself, to respond to that kind of savagery. Too magically ethereal to want anything but tenderness and gentleness. She was sheer enchantment.

Shane knew dimly that he was already placing her on a pedestal, already setting her like some Greek goddess on an Olympus where an earthy hand could never mark her.

And he hardly heard the inner voice reminding him that the ancient gods and goddesses, for all their divinity, had been remarkably human at heart and quite definitely earthy in their passions.

Beneath the magic.

The Delaneys ouf Killaroo:

Matilda, The Adventuress

by Iris Johansen

"What the hell! There's a woman standing in the middle of the road!" Roman's foot stomped on the brakes of the Jeep. The vehicle swerved and then skidded to the side of the road. He could hear the screech of brakes from the long column of trucks and trailers he was leading. The sound was immediately followed by the blistering curses of the drivers.

"Well, there goes tomorrow's shooting." Brent gingerly touched the bruise he'd just acquired on his forehead from banging his head on the dashboard of the Jeep. "Unless you'd care to write in a barroom brawl. I'm going to have a devil of a bruise on my matchless profile."

"Are you all right?"

The breathless question came from the woman who had run up to the Jeep as soon as it had come to a halt. Her tousled cinnamon-colored hair, sparkling as though touched by a golden hand, shimmered in the headlights; Roman was fascinated for a fleeting instant by that brilliant halo of color. He shifted his gaze to her face. "What the hell did you think you were doing? I almost ran over you."

"Lord, I'm sorry. I didn't realize you were going so fast. I just wanted to . . ." Her eyes widened in amazement. "You're Roman Gallagher. How wonderful. I've always wanted to meet you."

"Yes." Hell, not another would-be starlet, he thought. He'd had his fill of actresses throwing themselves into his path in the hopes of getting a part in one of his films. As his gaze touched her he was startled to feel a swift and incredible desire for her. It didn't make a damn bit of sense to him. She wasn't even sexy. Yet his reaction had been undeniable. A tingle of annoyance went through him.

She smiled, and he inhaled sharply. Warmth. Lord, her

smile illuminated her thin face like the Southern Cross illuminated the night sky.

"I love your films," she said. "I thought *Fulfillment* was terrific, and I've seen all your documentaries. My favorite was the one you did on the Barrier Reef."

He tried to mask his surprise. She had clearly done her homework. He hadn't made a documentary in seven years, and at that time his audience had been extremely small. "Thank you. I enjoyed filming it, even though the subject of the reefs had been done a hundred or so times before."

"But not like you did it. The underwater scenes were . . ." She took an eager step closer, her brown eyes shining in the reflected beam of the headlights. She met his gaze and suddenly her eyes widened in curious surprise, and she forgot what she wanted to say. Then she shook her head as if to clear it and laughed uncertainly. "There aren't any words to describe that film. I wanted to hop on the next boat to the reef."

"I'm surprised you didn't."

She whirled to her left, and faced the man who had just stepped down from the truck directly behind the Jeep. She squinted into the shadows as she tried to match a face with the familiar voice. "Dennis?" Then, as the man came into the perimeter of the headlights, his gray-flecked sandy brown hair and rough-hewn features became clearer. She flew across the road and into his arms, and gave him an enthusiastic hug. "Dennis Billet, what on earth are you doing here?"

"I could ask you the same thing." His hazel eyes were twinkling down at her. "Except I've given up being surprised at the places you turn up. Nowadays I just accept the fact that if there's excitement or trouble or danger around, sooner or later you'll be there."

"I hate to interrupt this reunion, but I have a location to set up." Roman's tone was caustic. For some irrational reason he was displeased at the sight of the golden-haired woman in Billet's arms. "You know this woman, Dennis?"

Dennis nodded. "We go back a long way." He placed his arm companionably around her waist as he turned to face Roman. "Manda Delaney, this is my boss, Roman Gallagher."

Manda was frowning. "Location? You're going to set up a movie location here? But you can't do that!"

"I have a drawerful of permits back in Sydney that says the opposite." Roman's lips tightened. "I'd damn well better be able to do it. Are you saying you have a prior claim?"

"No, not exactly." She ran her fingers through her shining hair. "I tried to get one, but the authorities said the entire area had already been leased. I thought it was a mistake. No one comes to Deadman's Ridge anymore. There haven't been any opals found in this field for over twenty-five years."

"Which is why I had no trouble obtaining a three-month lease on the ridge."

"You're going to be here for three months?" The dismay on her face was unmistakable. "Look, can't you go somewhere else? I know I don't have a legal permit, but I was here first, and my business is very important."

He was staring at her in disbelief. "Do you realize how much money I'd lose per day looking for another location?"

She made a face. "No chance?"

"No chance." His eyes narrowed. "May I assume you're not an actress then?"

"Me?" She was astonished. "Why would you think I was an actress?"

He stiffened. "What's your business here? Are you a newspaper reporter?"

"What is this? Twenty questions?"

His lips twisted. "I know you people consider questions the prerogative of the press, but you should have thought of that before you decided to trespass on my land. Lord, I thought I'd gotten away from vultures like you."

"I'm *not* a reporter."

"Then just what is your business here, Miss Delaney?"

"Manda." She smiled and again he felt warmth radiate through him. "I'm afraid my business is of a private nature. However, I assure you it's most urgent. I promise I won't get in your way if you let me stay." Her voice dropped to wheedling softness. "I know you'll understand."

Dennis Billet suddenly burst into laughter. "Manda,

you never change. Be careful, Roman, she'll be talking you out of your mobile home in another minute."

She had come very close to getting what she wanted from him. Roman felt a flare of anger when he realized that if he hadn't been jarred by Dennis's obvious amusement, he would probably have let her stay. "I can't help you. I've made it a rule to close my set to outsiders." Roman got back into the Jeep and started the ignition. He noticed Dennis's arm still held the woman in a casual embrace, and he found his pilot's familiarity with Manda Delaney oddly annoying. The woman was obviously an accomplished charmer and accustomed to getting her own way with men. Well, she would find he distinctly disliked being used by anyone, women in particular. "I'll give you one day to pack up and get off the property."

"But you don't understand. I can't—" The rest of her sentence was lost as he revved the engine of the Jeep. "I *have* to stay here. There are reasons. . . ."

The Jeep jumped forward as he pressed the accelerator. A few seconds later he'd driven several yards down the road.

"You weren't very polite," Brent drawled. "You didn't introduce me, and I got the distinct impression that something about the lady annoyed the hell out of you. Pity. She could have been very entertaining to have around. You could have thought about *my* convenience, Roman. You drag me out here in the wilds with an all-male cast, forbid me to seduce any of the women on your production crew, and then send packing the only alluring woman who crosses our path. How inconsiderate can you be?"

"I'm sure you'll survive. Besides, she wasn't all that pretty."

"You don't think so? Personally, I prefer the unconventional type."

"Too thin."

"But she really fills out a T-shirt."

"I didn't notice," Roman said.

Brent glanced sidewise at him, and then smiled. "Oh, yes, you noticed all right. Is it okay if I go after her and offer her my sympathy, my gorgeous body, and anything else she'll accept?"

"Why should I care? She's nothing to me." Roman's hands tightened unconsciously on the steering wheel. "Though I don't think it's worth your while. She'll be gone tomorrow."

"Long enough. Haven't you heard I'm irresistible? All my press clippings say so." The amusement was abruptly gone from Brent's expression. "If you want her yourself, I'll back away, Roman. My role in your film means too much to me to jeopardize our professional relationship over a woman."

For the briefest instant Roman was tempted to tell him to back off, to keep away from her. The instinct was brutally primitive. Lord, what had gotten into him tonight? There was no way he was going to involve himself with Manda Delaney. Her appearance in his life had been entirely too coincidental, and her reluctance to tell him the purpose of her business in the opal field was distinctly suspicious. She could be anything from a con artist on the make, to one of the paparazzi out to get an exclusive interview. This was sheer madness. He forced himself to relax and the moment of insanity passed. He shrugged. "Do what you like. She doesn't appeal to me."

Manda laughed softly as she stood in the middle of the road watching the receding taillights of the vehicles of the caravan. The desert was no longer tranquil, and the entire situation was fraught with complications. Yet she was still feeling a familiar shiver of excitement. Change. Things were changing, events were going to occur, people would act and react. How she loved adventure and change and this time the potential was more exciting than ever before.

Because a difficult, sensual man named Roman Gallagher was leading that caravan and she had suddenly realized he just might be the greatest adventure of all.

The Delaneys of Killaroo:

Sydney, The Temptress

by Fayrene Preston

One floor above the casino, from behind the one-way glass, Nicholas Charron watched her, as he had every night for the past three nights.

Her name was Sydney Delaney. He had gotten this information from the registration card she had filled out when she had arrived on the island three days ago. Alone.

With each night that passed his curiosity about her grew. She seemed intensely interested in the games, but she had yet to place a bet. And he had seen several men approach her, but with scarcely a look she had sent them on their way.

From his remote observation post he had a complete view of the entire casino. Men and women dressed in their evening finery milled below him in a rhythm of bright color and swirling motion, uncaring that just beyond the casino's wide expanse of windowed walls lay the wonder and the glory of the Great Barrier Reef. Their disregard of the natural beauty of the reef and the star-brilliant night above it amused him. While most casinos were windowless, his was not. He deliberately had had the windows included in the design as his own private joke—just as he had giant seawater aquariums set in the long wall that ran across the back of the casino. Although the aquariums featured the vividly patterned fish that swam in the waters of the reef, he knew that to the majority of the people in the casino, the fish provided little more than an exotic backdrop for the real reason they had come to the island—the gaming.

He understood people, their vices, their greed. Soon, Nicholas promised himself, he would understand Sydney Delaney.

He turned away from the window and walked to the long row of monitors that provided coverage of the entire casino. With a quick flick of a series of switches, four screens glowed simultaneously with her image.

Sydney Delaney was clearly beautiful, but there were many women in his casino tonight who were as beautiful, if not more so. Yet there was something about her that had drawn his attention to her and had kept it there. Unprecedented for him.

Once, a long time ago, he had seen a figurine of a young girl in a Chicago store window, so fine and delicate, she appeared translucent, so fragile and expensive, a glass dome had protected her. He had wanted the figurine. The woman below reminded him of that figurine.

He looked closer, trying to decipher, to take apart, and thus explain, the pull she was exerting on him. Her hair seemed a dark burgundy and hung in a lustrous mass to below her shoulders. He frowned, for the color seemed to contain a depth that the screen of the monitor couldn't satisfactorily register.

In the monitor that caught her profile he saw a straight nose and a clean sweep of jaw. Another monitor showed him finely shaped brows arched over wide, light-colored eyes of an undiscernable shade and a disconcerting mouth, full and perfectly formed to fit under a man's lips.

A third monitor revealed a full-length picture of her. The long dress she wore was of cream-colored slipper satin. The neckline was high, but the back dipped to the waist, exposing skin that, on the monitor at least, appeared flawless. In involuntary anticipation of the time when he would touch that flawless skin, his fingers curled one by one, into his palm.

Experience told him that most of the gowns on the women in the casino revealed more and cost more than the one she wore, but it didn't matter. Any clothing would look marvelous on her, he concluded.

There was an elegance about her and a grace, even as she remained still, and motion and noise swirled around her—like the sea that surrounded the island . . . his island, the Isle of Charron.

Did she have that much command over her emotions and nerves? he wondered. The question intrigued him.

His mind returned briefly to the glass dome that had surrounded the fragile figurine years before. Glass could be broken.

If a panther could live on a tropical island, his name would surely be Nicholas Charron, Sydney decided. She had never seen him, but she could *feel* him—like a violent disturbance in the atmosphere.

Strangely, she never questioned why she felt he was there above her, watching. She just did. She knew that he paced in his control room above the casino, and she sensed his eyes on her, like a warm breath across her skin.

The fact that he was observing her from behind a one-way mirror made her feel exposed, unprotected, and it was a feeling she hated above all else. But she dealt with the vulnerability he was opening up in her as she always did—with absolute control over her body and her mind.

As was her way, she never went into any situation blind if she could help it. Before she had come to the Isle of Charron, she had researched the island, the casino, and the man who owned both. She had learned a great deal, but not all.

Nicholas Charron was a mysterious man. It was known that he was an American expatriate, but exactly what he had done from the time he left America to the time he bought the Isle of Charron was shrouded in mystery. However, over the last five years he had developed an island resort and casino like nothing Australia had seen before, especially on the Great Barrier Reef. They called his casino and hotel complex Charron's Glass Palace—like everything else on the island, his name was attached, whether he intended it to be or not. As a result, the Isle of Charron had gained an international reputation among jet setters and high rollers. They came to spend money, to have a good time, and if possible to see Nicholas Charron.

Speculation ran high, and extraordinary things were whispered about him. He had an aura that was as dark as the night, and to the thrill-seeking gamblers, his mystique was as big a draw as his casino.

But he never came down onto the casino floor, and only rarely did he invite anyone to his apartment at the top of the resort complex. Unless . . .

People talked and word spread. She hadn't been on the island more than a day, when an excited lady she had encountered on the beach had told her that sometimes Nicholas Charron would stand in his control room above the casino floor and scan the action below him to choose a woman for the night.

Sydney had watched women do things she knew were calculated to attract the attention of the dark man everyone talked about but very few ever saw. Somehow she had known the women wouldn't be successful. Somehow she had known it was *she* he watched.

She was being pursued by someone who couldn't be seen, only felt, but Sydney refused to give in to the agitation that ran through her veins with a singing excitement. She had to keep her mind on her purpose for being in the casino. Since she had been on the island, she had carefully studied the action of each of the games, and tonight she had chosen craps to observe. It was a fast-paced game, and the chances of winning large amounts of money seemed good. Wondering about the odds, she opened her purse and pulled out a small calculator.

Within the space of a few seconds two men stood on either side of her.

And watching from the control room, Nicholas Charron reached for the phone.

One man was big and muscular and had a face so grooved and pitted, it looked as if it had been pulled straight off the side of Ayers Rock. The other man, an Oriental, was short and wiry with flat black eyes that stared at her without expression.

It was the larger of the two men who spoke. "I'm sorry, miss, you'll have to come with us."

"Where exactly is it that you're taking me?" she asked as they halted before a set of black stainless steel doors.

"To Mr. Charron's apartment."

The doors swished open, and they stepped into a lift. The doors closed, sealing her and the strange men by her side off from the comfort and familiarity of the crowd in the casino.

Three floors above ground level, the lift glided to a stop, the doors opened, and Sydney was facing the silent sanctuary of the owner of the Isle of Charron. Slowly she began to walk forward.

She was truly lovely, Nicholas thought, watching her.

Exquisite. Instinct had told him that she wasn't like the women he usually summoned to him, and he had been proved right. When she had first looked up and seen his men on either side of her, his theory had been confirmed. Her expression had changed from composure to fear. For an instant she had looked so defenseless, that something like pain had twisted inside of him. To his mind, it hadn't seemed right that the first strong emotion he saw on her face should be fear. On a beautifully carved table a crystal swan swam on a mirror lake.

"Good evening."

She started at the deep voice. She hadn't even seen him, yet there he was! He was standing on a level above her, in front of a window, and for a moment she couldn't separate him from the night. They seemed as one.

As she had trained herself to do, she waited a beat before answering him. "Good evening."

Three long strides brought him down to her. "Thank you for coming."

"Did I have any choice?"

His mouth curved with humor. "Not really, but I won't apologize. I never apologize."

THIS FIERCE SPLENDOR

by Iris Johansen

It is 1870 and the Scottish beauty and scholar Elspeth MacGregor has traveled to Hell's Bluff in the Arizona Territory to hire Dominic Delaney to lead her to the magical lost city of Kantalan. Elspeth assumes her business with Dominic will be simple—but learns quickly that nothing is simple about this magnetic man-on-the-run who is the only person who knows the location of the fabulous city of dark mysteries and magnificent treasures. He refuses to guide her. He refuses even to speak with her again. But his nephew Patrick, a mischievous young man, is Elspeth's ally and has hatched a plan to create a confrontation between her and his uncle.

"Firecrackers?" Elspeth eyed with alarm the stack of slender sticks linked with long fuses. She had been curious about the large blanket-wrapped bundle since Patrick had picked it up from Sam Li's shack, but she had never imagined it contained anything as exotic as firecrackers. "What are we going to do with firecrackers?" she asked again.

Patrick was busy tying the fuses together. "You said you wanted to get Dom's attention and make a statement of your determination." He looked up and grinned at her. "This will make a very resounding statement, I guarantee."

"I'm sure it will," she said faintly. She glanced at the large whitewashed house across the street. "But I had a more sedate statement in mind."

"You want Dom jerked from his lair and forced to confront you in the fastest possible way." His nimble fingers moved to the second string of firecrackers. "This is the only way I could think for you to do it."

"The only way or the most interesting way?" she asked dryly. "I think you're planning on enjoying this."

"Sure, I always did like a good show."

Elspeth wished she could think of something else. She had an idea Patrick's plan had elements more explosive than the firecrackers. "Your uncle is going to be very angry."

"Yep."

"But he'd probably be angry at my coming here anyway."

"Uh-huh."

"And it's really his own fault for being so narrow-minded and uncooperative. This is a very important undertaking; it can add greatly to our fund of knowl—"

She was interrupted by his low chuckle. "I think you're trying to talk yourself into something."

She grinned back at him. "I think I've done it." She knelt beside him. "Let me help you."

"Very well. You take these two packets and run them from the front door down the steps and into the street. I'll take the rest inside and string them along the hall on the second floor and down the stairs to the front door."

"No."

He lifted his head. "What?"

"I said no. This is my responsibility. I'll be the one to set the firecrackers inside the house and light them. You're clearly trying to spare me the risk of being discovered."

"What I'm trying to do is spare you a sight that might shock the bejiggers out of you. I think you'd better wait outside until I call you."

"No." She took the larger stack of firecrackers from him. "Do I light each one as I put it in place?"

He sighed with resignation. "All you have to do is to light the long fuse on the first packet. Place that one at the end of the corridor on the second floor. The fuse will allow you enough time to trail the firecrackers down the stairs to the front hall."

His enthusiasm was contagious. A tiny flare of excitement began to smolder beneath Elspeth's apprehension. "Is the front door left unlocked?"

Patrick nodded. "Rina wouldn't think of discouraging business, be it day or night."

"Then I guess I won't have any problem." She hesitated, then squared her shoulders and started across the street.

"You might have one problem," Patrick called out.

Elspeth stopped and turned to face him with swift alarm. "What?"

"Matches." He took a box from his pocket and grinned. "Catch." He tossed the box across the few feet separating them. "It's hard to light a fuse without them."

Ten minutes later she was standing in the foyer laying the last of the strings of firecrackers on the bottom step. The house was still in half darkness.

She wished there was more light. She would have liked to have seen if the furnishings of a bordello were as exotic as she had imagined. Perhaps when the firecrackers went off she would be able to see more.

The front door opened quietly to reveal Patrick's thick hair outlined against a pearl-gray wedge of sky. "All set?"

"Yes," she whispered. "I lit the first fuse just as you told me. Shouldn't it have gone off by now?"

"Any second." He closed the door behind him.

"What do we do now?"

"We get out of the line of fire." He drew her to the corner of the foyer farthest from the staircase. "And then we wait."

They didn't have to wait long. Patrick had scarcely gotten the words out when there was an explosion!

"Here we go," Patrick murmured over the barrage of explosions. "How's this for a statement, Elspeth?"

The first explosion jerked Dominic from sleep. Gunfire. In the hall outside. He moved with the sure instinct that had guided him for the last ten years. By the time of the second explosion, he was on his feet reaching for his gunbelt. When the third explosion rocked the hall, he was at the door.

"Dominic," Rina said sleepily. She sat up and brushed a shining brown lock of hair from her cheek. "What the hell—" She broke off as another explosion jarred her fully awake. "No, Dom, don't go out there." She jumped out of bed, reaching hurriedly for her lacy peignoir.

Dominic wasn't listening. All his senses were strained toward the danger in the hall. God, he was tired of this. Tired of never going to sleep without worrying if he'd face gunfire when he woke. He yanked open the door, stepping quickly to the side to avoid a possible spate of gunshots. The explosions continued, but there were no bullets sailing through the air, impacting floors and woodwork. He cautiously looked around the doorframe. The hall was filled with smoke and the explosions weren't coming from a gun. He stared blankly at the string of explosives on the floor going off one after the other. "Firecrackers!"

"What?" Rina was beside him. "Who would do a thing like this?"

He didn't have to consider the possibilities for more than a minute. He had been in the Nugget when Patrick and his friends had ridden through the doors on horseback throwing firecrackers right and left. "For Patrick, every day is a day for celebration," he said dryly. "I imagine this was his way of bidding us a fond good-bye until next week. But, if I know my nephew, he wouldn't be able to resist staying and watching the fun." He was striding down the hall following the exploding string of firecrackers. "And when I catch up with him, I'm going to tie a string of firecrackers to *his* tail." The explosions had reached the head of the stairs and so had he. He called down into the dimness at the foot of the stairwell. "Patrick, I'm about to lift your scalp."

He thought he heard a shout of laughter amid the explosions sparking down the stairs. It didn't improve his temper. He started down but was forced to move slowly to keep behind the exploding firecrackers. "Did you consider the possibility you might have set the house on fire? Or that someone could have started shooting before they realized it was a tom-fool trick?"

"It wasn't Patrick's fault, Mr. Delaney." Elspeth moved out of the shadowed hallway to the foot of the stairs. She stood very straight, her eyes fixed on him as if mesmerized. "This was entirely my idea."

She could barely get the words past her dry throat. She had never seen a real live man naked, and Dominic Delaney was boldly and unashamedly naked. "I've come to ask you to reconsider."

The expression of stunned surprise on his face was superceded by a fierce look. "The hell you have." He started down the steps toward her, each word punctuated by the explosion of the firecrackers. "I don't like women who use their sex as a shield to invade a man's privacy and put him at a disadvantage. I don't like it one bit."

"You said you wouldn't see me. I had to do something to change the state of things."

In case you didn't hear me the first time, the answer is *no*." His blue-gray eyes glinted fiercely through the smoke. "But you knew it would be no, didn't you, Miss Elspeth MacGregor?"

"Yes, but it appeared to be the only way to get you to take my offer seriously."

"Dom, what's going on?" asked a lovely brown-haired woman clad in a blue lace peignoir from the top of the steps. Her gaze fell on Elspeth's prim, black-gowned figure at the bottom of the stairs. "Jesus, what's happened?"

"Nothing to concern you, Rina. Go on back to bed." Dominic Delaney's gaze never wavered from Elspeth. "I'll take care of this."

There were other faces peering over the banisters now, but Elspeth was scarcely aware of them. All her attention was focused on the naked man coming down the stairs toward her. She was exquisitely conscious of everything about him. The sleek ripple of the muscles of his thighs, the way his chest moved in and out with each breath. His strange eyes gazing at her with insolence and anger and something else.

The Delaneys, The Untamed Years:

GOLDEN FLAMES

by Kay Hooper

Victoria was waiting for him in the lobby of her hotel, and Falcon paused for a moment just inside the doors to gaze at her before she saw him. The black velvet cloak she wore hid a part of her gown from him, but he saw with a feeling of triumph that she had indeed worn red, as he'd asked her to do. The gown was obviously tulle, and the red was a deep, rich color which, along with the black cloak, set off her fair beauty strikingly. Her hair was up in an intricate style, made curiously fragile by a black satin ribbon woven in among the gleaming strands. She had fastened the cloak at her throat, which prevented him from seeing if the rubies dangling from her delicate ears were matched by a necklace, lending fire to her creamy breasts. Fortunately, his imagination where she was concerned was vivid.

He approached her on cat feet. "Beautiful. Just beautiful."

She looked up at him, startled by his silent approach, and a faint color swept up her cheeks. But there was something new in her eyes, something half shy and half excited, and he knew his seductive efforts had borne fruit. He offered his arm with a slight bow, and amusement rose in him when she accepted the arm, her sidelong glance showing a rueful appreciation of his gentlemanly manners.

The lady was no fool; plainly, she found his publicly donned courtesy quite definitely suspect.

"Why do I feel I'm being led into the lion's den?" she murmured as he guided her out to the waiting carriage.

Falcon laughed softly. "I can't imagine. Are you afraid of me, Victoria?"

She didn't answer until they were inside the closed carriage and moving. "Afraid of you?" She seemed to consider the matter, gazing at him in the shadowed interior. "I think it would be unwise of me to pretend you aren't a dangerous man."

"Not dangerous to you, surely," he said in a silky tone.

Her green eyes were serious. "Western men are a peculiar breed, a law unto themselves. Sometimes their gallant manners would make a European nobleman cringe in shame at his own lack, and at other times they're as rough and raw as the land that bred them. Dangerous to me? To any woman, I should think."

After a moment, he smiled. "I was born in Ireland."

"Were you? But you're a Western man nonetheless. A Texas Ranger, didn't you say?"

"Yes, for several years."

"And a Union soldier before that." Her tone was thoughtful. "And before that—a scout, perhaps? An Indian fighter?"

"Both," he confessed, oddly pleased by her perception.

"And the scar?"

He lifted a hand to finger the crescent mark on his cheekbone. "This? When I was a boy, my brothers and I often rode through Apache camps near our ranch, borrowing the Indian custom of counting coup."

"Trying to touch as many braves as possible? I've heard of it. Is that how you were hurt?"

He smiled. "In a way. My half-broke mustang took exception to a raid one night and threw me. I landed on a sharp stone. A battle scar, of sorts."

She smiled in return, thinking of a young boy cursing his temperamental mount.

"Did I tell you how beautiful you are?" he said suddenly, huskily.

Her smile faded slightly, leaving only the curve of delicate lips. "Yes. Yes, you did. Thank you."

Falcon reached out to touch her cheek gently, and then his hand dropped to toy with the fastening of her cloak. "Is this to keep out the cold? Or me?"

Her gloved fingers tightened around each other in her lap, and Victoria felt her breath grow short. "The dictates of fashion," she said finally.

He unfastened the cloak slowly, holding her eyes with his, very aware that her breath, like his, was shallow and quick. And some distant part of him marveled at these incredible feelings. She felt it too, this aching fire, and he was delighted by her swift response to him. "Fashion can go to hell," he muttered.

Victoria made no move to stop him, though she knew she should be ashamed of her wanton desire to have him see her, touch her, kiss her. What she felt was excitement.

He opened the cloak completely, pushing it back over her shoulders, and caught his breath at what he saw. The gown was cut low, baring her luscious breasts almost to the nipples, and against the creamy flesh a ruby necklace gleamed with dark fire. The lanterns hung outside the carriage sent a part of their light into the shadowed interior, playing over her exposed flesh with the loving glow of pale gold. Her breasts rose and fell quickly, each motion suggesting that the gown couldn't possibly hold the full mounds captive a moment longer.

"God, you're so beautiful," he said hoarsely, and his hands were on her bare shoulders, turning her toward him. He was inflamed even more by her instant, pliant response.

Victoria didn't even try to resist him. She had invited this, she realized dimly, invited this by agreeing to accompany him tonight, by wearing the provocative gown. And why couldn't she feel ashamed of that? Why did she feel only achingly, vibrantly alive and incredibly excited? Why did she want to feel his hands on her, his lips . . .

One of his hands slid down her back, finding the swell of her buttocks and pulling her as close as possible, even as his other arm surrounded her, crushing her upper body against him. He could feel the firm pillow of her bosom pressed to his chest, feel as well as hear her soft gasp, and an urgent sound escaped him just before his lips captured hers.

She was prepared for the shocking possession of his tongue this time—as well as she could be prepared for a sensation so devastating—and her body responded feverishly. Against his hard chest her breasts swelled and ached, and her arms slid up around his neck of their own volition. He was easing her back into the corner, and she could feel his arousal against her hip, bold and demanding.

When he released her lips at last she could only gasp, and her head fell back instinctively as he plundered the soft, vulnerable flesh of her throat. Her fingers twined in his thick, silky hair, and she wanted suddenly to remove her gloves so that she could feel his hair, his skin. And then his lips moved lower to brush hotly against her straining breasts, and she forgot everything except sheer pleasure.

"So sweet," he whispered thickly. Her low moan sorely tested his control. "Victoria . . ."

She had never known such pleasure existed, and the only coherent thought in her mind was the desire to feel more. She was hot, cold, shaking, her body a prisoner of the sensations sweeping over it with the relentless rhythm of an ocean's waves. The hot, wet caress of his tongue seared her skin, and his hand gently squeezed her breast until she thought she'd go out of her mind, until the stiffened nipple thrust free of confining silk and his mouth closed hotly around it.

All her senses were centered there, drawn by his pleasuring mouth, burning with a hunger she had never known. Something inside her, some dimly perceived barrier, melted in the heat of his caress, and she couldn't even find the breath to cry out her astonished delight.

She was hardly aware of his hand sliding down over her quivering belly, but a sudden touch at the vulnerable apex of her thighs jerked an instinctive, shocked protest from her lips. "No! Falcon, don't!"

"Shhh," he murmured against her skin, his hand rubbing gently through the layers of clothing while his mind vividly imagined the soft, damp warmth too much material hid from him. He wanted to draw her skirt up, find his way through the delicate feminine underthings until he could touch that heat, caress the womanly core of her. His entire body ached with the need to feel her naked and passionate against him. His tongue teased her nipple delicately with tiny, fiery, hungry licks. "Don't stop me, sweet. So sweet. You taste so good."

Victoria wanted to protest again, but the heat at her breast had sent a part of its fire lower, deeper into her body, and the hot clamoring inside her became a hollow, bittersweet need. "Falcon . . . you shouldn't . . . I can't . . ."

He lifted his head slowly, his darkened eyes intent on her flushed face. She looked thoroughly kissed, heartbreakingly beautiful in her innocent awareness. Her lips were red and swollen, her eyes sleepy with desire and dimly shocked. He slid his hand back up over her belly, cupping her breast gently and briefly before easing the silk upward until she was decently covered again. Then he surrounded her flushed face softly in one large hand and kissed her, vaguely surprised at the surge of tenderness he felt.

He brought them both upright, drawing the cloak back over her shoulders as she slowly lowered her arms, and fastening it again. And when she was sitting demurely, gazing at him with huge eyes, he leaned back into his own corner and sighed softly. "No one at the party will doubt that I want you," he murmured. "A man can never hide what a woman does to him."

Her eyes flicked downward to the straining evidence of his arousal, and then skittered hastily back to his face in confusion. Between the plantation of her childhood and Morgan's thriving ranch, she could hardly have avoided learning of the physical evidence of male sexuality, but his soft, bold reference to his body's response to her was both shocking and—in some part of herself she didn't want to acknowledge—exciting.

He chuckled softly. "Making love in a carriage is an awkward business," he offered. "If there had been a bed nearby, sweet, a loaded gun wouldn't have stopped me."

The Delaneys, The Untamed Years:

WILD SILVER

by Iris Johansen

Mikhail, Nicholas's servant and friend, threw open the door to the cabin and strode into the stateroom. Nicholas rose easily to his feet, his gaze on the bundle over the giant's shoulder. "Good Lord, Mikhail, did you have to use two blankets? She must be smothering."

"I should have used ten," Mikhail muttered as he strode across the room and dropped his burden on the bed. "And I should have let you come with me. I should have let an army come with me." He unwrapped the blankets with two quick jerks and Silver tumbled free, rolling over to the opposite side of the bed. Her wrists were tied behind her back and a handkerchief gagged her mouth, but her eyes blazed up at them as she continued to struggle to free herself. Mikhail tossed the blankets on the floor and reached over to pull the gag from Silver's mouth, quickly jerking his hand away as her strong, white teeth snapped at him. "She is a wild animal." There was a curious note of pride in his voice as he gazed down at Silver's face. "If I had not taken her by surprise, I do not think I would have been able to overpower her. She is a fine, strong warrior." He carefully brushed a strand of hair from Silver's eyes, his expression gentle. "It is all right now. No one is going to hurt you."

"But *I* will hurt you." Silver glared up at him fiercely, still struggling desperately against her bonds. "You can't do this!"

"It appears that he can, because he has." Nicholas strode forward to stand over her. Her long hair was lying in wild, silken disarray against the peach-colored velvet of the spread, and he felt a sudden thrust of desire tighten his groin. He had been sitting there, imagining how she would look lying on his bed, and the reality was even more erotic than his vision. "Though not without some effort."

"You!" Her light eyes glittered with rage as she began to curse him with venom and amazing proficiency.

He lifted a brow. "My, my, she's quite talented, isn't she, Mikhail? The last time I heard a vocabulary so explicit was from my groom at the estate on Crystal Island. Should we release her, do you think?"

"Only if you wish to relieve yourself of a few fistfuls of excess hair," Mikhail said dryly, gingerly touching his own tousled red mop. "Before I got her hands tied I was sure she would strip me bald. Best wait until you have talked reason to her."

"Reason?" Silver struggled into a sitting position. "There is no reason connected with this outrage. It's madness, as I'll soon show you."

"I'm sure you'll try." Nicholas smiled. "And it will be fascinating to watch your attempts. I may even be sorry to see you depart after you tell me where your uncle has disappeared to."

"You'll be sorrier to see me stay," Silver hissed.

A flicker of anger crossed Nicholas's handsome face. "I believe you're beginning to annoy me. So far you've cursed me, threatened me, and insulted me."

"Let me loose and I'll do more than that to you. I'll stick my knife in you, as I did your friend."

Nicholas stiffened. "Knife?" His gaze flew to Mikhail. "She *stabbed* you?" His attention had been so absorbed with the girl he had scarcely glanced at Mikhail. Now he saw that the Cossack's tunic was torn, and a rivulet of blood stained the whiteness of the left sleeve.

"A pinprick." Mikhail bent down, pulled a small dagger out of his boot, and tossed it to Nicholas. "Yet it might be wise to remember she is not without fangs."

"Like all vipers." Nicholas looked down at the dagger, his beautifully molded features hard as the marble of a tombstone. "She could have killed you. I should have gone myself, my friend."

A touch of anxiety clouded Mikhail's features. "A pinprick," he repeated. "She was only defending herself. The wound will be gone by tomorrow."

Bewilderment pierced Silver's seething fury. It was clear the big Russian was defending her from Nicholas Savron's anger. Why would he help the prince abduct her and then rush to her defense?

"Do you need a doctor?" Nicholas asked gently. "I'll have Robert dock again and send someone for help."

"The woman—"

"The woman is not worth one drop of your blood." Nicholas gave Silver a glance as cold as winter sleet. "I will deal with her later."

Mikhail shook his head. "I have no need for a doctor. She did not hurt me."

"Only because you—" Silver broke off as Mikhail shook his head warningly at her. "I *will* speak. Do you think I'm afraid of either of you?"

"You obviously have no need to fear Mikhail. It seems he's been foolish enough to take a liking to you," Nicholas said softly. "But you'd do well to be afraid of me. I value Mikhail, and I don't think I've ever been quite so angry with anyone in my entire life."

"Liking? He *abducted* me."

"On my orders. And he insisted on going alone, because he felt it would be safer for you."

"Or because you were too cowardly to go with him," Silver said contemptuously.

Mikhail inhaled sharply and took an impulsive step forward, as if to place himself between Silver and Nicholas. "Nicholas, she is only a woman. She did not—"

"Only a woman," Silver repeated indignantly. "A woman can do anything a man can do! She can do more! Why do—"

"*Shut up!*" Nicholas shouted, enunciating with great precision.

"I should not have taken the gag off her." Mikhail sighed morosely. "I should have known her tongue would be as sharp as her dagger."

"Go take care of your wound." Nicholas's gaze was narrowed on Silver's face. "I have a fancy to prove myself to the lady."

Mikhail gazed at him helplessly. Nicholas was dangerously infuriated, and it was evident that Silver Delaney was not about to try to placate him. "You gave your word."

Nicholas glanced at him incredulously. "Good Lord— she stabbed you and you're still defending her?"

Mikhail's jaw squared stubbornly. "You promised me."

Nicholas muttered something fierce and obscene beneath his breath. "And I'll keep my word, dammit."

Mikhail turned toward the door, and then glanced over his shoulder at Silver, a gentle smile lighting his craggy features. "I will be back soon. Do not be afraid."

Silver gazed at him. "I'm not afraid and I need no protection."

Mikhail slowly shook his head and shut the door quietly behind him.

Silver immediately turned to Nicholas and opened her mouth to speak.

Nicholas raised his hand. "Not one word, or I'll put the gag back on you."

She hesitated, and then pressed her lips together.

"Very wise. I'm holding on to my temper by a very precarious thread, Silver."

He sat down on the bed beside her, not touching her, but close enough so that she could feel the heat emanating from his body. The faint scent of musk, brandy, and tobacco drifted to her nostrils.

"I'm about to give you the rules that will govern your stay while you're on the *Rose*. Are you listening?"

She gazed up at him mutinously.

"I see you are." He smiled faintly. "First, let's discuss why you're here."

"You want Dominic."

"Exactly. I suppose I should give you the option of telling me where he is."

"Would you let me go if I did?"

"I'm afraid I'd be forced to do so. Do you wish to oblige?"

Silver drew a deep breath. Lord, she hated lies. Still, if it would give Dominic a little more time . . . "He and Elspeth went back to Killara, in the Arizona Territory."

Nicholas's expression hardened. "I see you're as prone to falsehood as the rest of your sex. Randall's investigators ascertained that your uncle was most definitely not at Killara. It's obvious that asking you for the truth will accomplish nothing, and I admit I'm a trifle disappointed. I thought you more honest than most."

A flush stung Silver's cheeks. "I'm honest with those I respect. You deserve only lies from me. I'll tell you nothing about Dominic."

"But when he finds you're gone from Mrs. Alford's nunnery, I'd say there's an excellent chance of him coming after you," he said softly. "I posted a letter to your former headmistress, telling her you'd decided to accompany me on a little pleasure cruise. If he's as loyal to you as you are to him, he should be waiting at the levee when we return to St. Louis."

"He won't even hear that I'm gone. There wouldn't be—" She stopped. "You'll be disappointed if you think you can use me to draw Dominic to you."

His gaze centered on her face. "You seem very certain." He shrugged. "No matter. Then you'll remain on the *Rose* until you tell me where he is."

"You can't keep me here."

"Oh, but I can. Shall I tell you how?" Nicholas's long, shapely hand reached out and smoothed her hair back from one temple, his touch as delicate as the brush of the wings of a butterfly. "There is no one to help you here. This boat belongs to me, and you'll find no one interested in any plea for aid. Mikhail and my friend Valentin are completely loyal to me. And the crew would lose very lucrative positions if they displeased me."

So she would be alone in her struggle. For a moment she felt a tiny *frisson* of apprehension. She dismissed it impatiently. Her struggles had always been faced alone, except when Rising Star had been there to support her. This was no different. "I don't need help. I'll still get away from you."

A flicker of admiration crossed his face. "No tears? No pleas? I can almost see why Mikhail has developed a fondness for you."

"I never cry." She met his gaze. "And you will never hear me plead."

"Oh, but I will." Passion flared in the darkness of his eyes. "And it will be my very great pleasure to grant those pleas."

ENTER
THE DELANEYS, THE UNTAMED YEARS
MISSISSIPPI QUEEN' RIVERBOAT CRUISE
SWEEPSTAKES
WIN
7 NIGHTS ABOARD THE LUXURIOUS
MISSISSIPPI QUEEN STEAMBOAT
including double occupancy accommodations,
meals and fabulous entertainment for two

She's elegant. Regal. Alive with music and moonlight. You'll find
a Jacuzzi, gym, sauna, movie theatre, gift shop, library, beauty
salon and multi-tiered sun deck aboard…plus a splendid dining
room and lounges, beveled mirrors, polished brass, a Grand
Saloon where big band sounds soothe your soul and set your feet
to dancing! For further information and/or reservations on the
Mississippi Queen and Delta Queen' Steamboats
CALL 1-800-458-6789!

Sweepstakes travel arrangements by
RELIABLE TRAVEL INTERNATIONAL, INC.

RELIABLE TRAVEL II INTERNATIONAL, INC.

Whether you're travelling for business, romance or adventure,
you're a winner with Reliable Travel International!
CALL TOLL FREE FOR INFORMATION AND RESERVATIONS
1-800-645-6504 Ext. 413

MISSISSIPPI QUEEN RIVERBOAT CRUISE SWEEPSTAKES
RULES AND ENTRY FORMS ALSO APPEAR IN THE
FOLLOWING BANTAM <u>LOVESWEPT</u> NOVELS:

THE GRAND FINALE	**MAN FROM HALF MOON BAY**
HOLD ON TIGHT	**OUTLAW DEREK**
***CONFLICT OF INTEREST**	***DIVINE DESIGN**
***WARM FUZZIES**	***BABY, BABY**
***FOR LOVE OF LACEY**	***HAWK O'TOOLE'S HOSTAGE**

and in

THE DELANEYS, THE UNTAMED YEARS:
COPPER FIRE; WILD SILVER; GOLDEN FLAMES

*On sale week of May 2, 1988   SW'10

OFFICIAL DELANEYS, THE UNTAMED YEARS
MISSISSIPPI QUEEN' RIVERBOAT CRUISE
SWEEPSTAKES RULES

1. NO PURCHASE NECESSARY. Enter by completing the Official Entry Form below (or print your name, address, date of birth and telephone number on a plain 3" x 5" card) and send to:

> Bantam Books
> Delaneys, THE UNTAMED YEARS Sweepstakes
> Dept. HBG
> 666 Fifth Avenue
> New York, NY 10103

2. One Grand Prize will be awarded. There will be no prize substitutions or cash equivalents permitted. Grand Prize is a 7-night riverboat cruise for two on the luxury steamboat, The Mississippi Queen. Double occupancy accommodations, meals and on-board entertainment included. Round trip airfare provided by Reliable Travel International, Inc. (Estimated retail value $5,500.00. Exact value depends on actual point of departure.)

3. All entries must be postmarked and received by Bantam Books no later than August 1, 1988. The winner, chosen by random drawing, will be announced and notified by November 30, 1988. Trip must be completed by December 31, 1989, and is subject to space availability determined by Delta Queen Steamboat Company, and airline space availability determined by Reliable Travel International. If the Grand Prize winner is under 21 years of age on August 1, 1988, he/she must be accompanied by a parent or guardian. Taxes on the prize are the sole responsibility of the winner. Odds of winning depend on the number of completed entries received. Enter as often as you wish, but each entry must be mailed separately. Bantam Books is not responsible for lost, misdirected or incomplete entries.

4. The sweepstakes is open to residents of the U.S. and Canada, except the Province of Quebec, and is void where prohibited by law. If the winner is a Canadian he/she will be required to correctly answer a skill question in order to receive the prize. All federal, state and local regulations apply. Employees of Reliable Travel International, The Delta Queen Steamboat Co., and Bantam, Doubleday, Dell Publishing Group, Inc., their subsidiary and affiliates, and their immediate families are ineligible to enter.

5. The winner may be required to submit an Affidavit of Eligibility and Promotional Release supplied by Bantam Books. The winner's name and likeness may be used for publicity purposes without additional compensation.

6. For an extra copy of the Official Rules and Entry Form, send a self-addressed stamped envelope (Washington and Vermont Residents need not affix postage) by June 15, 1988 to:

> Bantam Books
> Delaneys, THE UNTAMED YEARS Sweepstakes
> Dept. HBG
> 666 Fifth Avenue
> New York, NY 10103

- -

OFFICIAL ENTRY FORM
DELANEYS, THE UNTAMED YEARS
MISSISSIPPI QUEEN' RIVERBOAT CRUISE SWEEPSTAKES

Name _____

Address _____

City _____ State _____ Zip Code _____

SW'10

THE DELANEY DYNASTY

where it all began . . .

Six daringly original novels written by three of the most successful romance writers today — Kay Hooper, Iris Johansen and Fayrene Preston.

THE SHAMROCK TRINITY

Heirs to a great dynasty, the Delaney brothers were united by blood, united by devotion to their rugged land and to the women they loved.

RAFE, THE MAVERICK by Kay Hooper
YORK, THE RENEGADE by Iris Johansen
BURKE, THE KINGPIN by Fayrene Preston

THE DELANEYS OF KILAROO

Three dazzling sisters, heirs to a rich and savage land, determined to fight for their birthright, destined to find wild and wonderful love . . .

ADELAIDE, THE ENCHANTRESS by
  Kay Hooper
MATILDA, THE ADVENTURESS by
  Iris Johansen
SYDNEY, THE TEMPTRESS by
  Fayrene Preston

THE DELANEYS . . . men and women whose loves and passions are so glorious it takes many great romance novels by three bestselling authors to tell their tempestuous stories.

Ask your bookseller for these Bantam books or use the handy coupon on the last page of this sampler to order.